De

For   ing
and   nd
cele
diff
Than Words program honors three women each year
for their compassionate dedication to those who need
it most, and donates $15,000 to each of their chosen
causes.

Within these pages, you will find stories written by
Debbie Macomber, Brenda Novak and Meryl Sawyer.
These stories are beautiful tributes to the Harlequin
More Than Words award recipients who inspired them,
and we hope they will touch your heart and inspire the
real-life heroine in you.

Thank you for your support. All proceeds from the
sale of this book will be reinvested into the Harlequin
More Than Words program so we can support more
causes of concern to women. And you can help even
more by learning about and getting involved with the
charities highlighted by Harlequin More Than Words,
or even nominating a real-life heroine in *your* life for
a future award. Together we can make a difference!

Sincerely,

Donna Hayes
Publisher and CEO
Harlequin Enterprises Lt

DEBBIE MACOMBER

BRENDA NOVAK
MERYL SAWYER

More Than Words

STORIES OF THE HEART

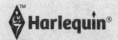

Harlequin®

TORONTO NEW YORK LONDON
AMSTERDAM PARIS SYDNEY HAMBURG
STOCKHOLM ATHENS TOKYO MILAN MADRID
PRAGUE WARSAW BUDAPEST AUCKLAND

Recycling programs
for this product may
not exist in your area.

ISBN-13: 978-0-373-83769-4

MORE THAN WORDS: STORIES OF THE HEART

Copyright © 2012 by Harlequin Books S.A.

Debbie Macomber is acknowledged as the author of *What Amanda Wants*
Brenda Novak is acknowledged as the author of *Small Packages*
Meryl Sawyer is acknowledged as the author of *Worth the Risk*

This edition published by arrangement with Harlequin Books S.A.

For questions and comments about the quality of this book please contact us at Customer_eCare@Harlequin.ca.

® and TM are trademarks of the publisher. Trademarks indicated with ® are registered in the United States Patent and Trademark Office, the Canadian Trade Marks Office and in other countries.

www.Harlequin.com

Printed in U.S.A.

CONTENTS

STORIES INSPIRED BY REAL-LIFE HEROINES

LAUREN SPIKER
—Teens Living With Cancer—

Lauren Spiker's daughter Melissa was a typical high school senior, preparing for her prom and graduation, excited about attending university to study nursing. And then Melissa was diagnosed with a rare bone marrow cancer. In June 2000, after two courageous years, Melissa lost her battle with the disease. She was nineteen years old. But before Melissa died, she asked a promise of her mother. "If you have learned anything from me through all of this, do something with it to make a difference—to make things better."

Lauren kept her promise, establishing Melissa's Living Legacy Teen Cancer Foundation, a foundation dedicated to helping teens with cancer meet their life challenges in productive, creative and satisfying ways. Committed to upholding and fostering the basic values of honesty, compassion, self-determination, courage and perseverance, Melissa's Living Legacy's mission is to provide resources and support that enhance the quality of life for teens with cancer throughout each stage of their disease, from diagnosis through treatment and remission and, if necessary, when facing death.

Motivated by the special needs of teens

Nearly 15,000 teens are in active treatment for cancer each year and the challenges confronting *all* teens are magnified in those with this disease. Teens with cancer face physical changes and/or disfigurement at a time when appearance is a paramount concern, loss of peer groups and acceptance when inclusion is a primary need, and reproductive challenges and sexual dilemmas at a time of emerging sexuality. They also must deal with unwanted dependence at a time of newfound independence and a loss of control when new boundaries are just being tested.

Though Melissa received excellent medical care, Lauren was struck by the limited focus on the unique issues faced by teens with cancer, as well as the absence of helpful resources. Information in books and on the internet was either filled with complicated medical jargon or too simplified and geared toward children. To combat this problem, in September 2002, the foundation launched the Teens Living with Cancer website (www.teenslivingwithcancer. org) in order to bridge this gap. Providing online resources to support teens, their families and friends, as well as ways to connect with others, the TLC site is now the most comprehensive web-based resource available for teens with cancer.

The website provides information about the various forms of adolescent cancer and describes treatments and their effects on the body in "teen-friendly" terms and based on the real-life experiences of teens with cancer. Teens Living with Cancer is also an online community offering a forum for teens struggling with the disease to meet online and share their experiences. It's an opportunity to connect, interact and encourage each other, bridging emotional gaps with an understanding the teens can't truly get from people who aren't living with cancer.

The website offers information and advice that is medically sound *and* nonjudgmental—answering important questions that teens may be hesitant to ask their parents or medical team. The goal is to empower young people to make the best decisions for themselves, both physically and emotionally. Teens want to have a voice in what happens with their care, but often feel they have no spokesperson. Teens Living with Cancer encourages them to be their own advocate.

Support for families and friends

Teens Living with Cancer also addresses issues relevant to the families and friends of teens living with the disease, providing information, as well as stories, from family members and friends of teenage cancer patients. So often, friends and loved ones want to be helpful but they aren't sure what to say or do. Through Teens Living with Cancer, family and friends find ways to provide help and understanding—even if they can't take away a friend or relative's suffering.

The Teens Living with Cancer website connects groups and individuals with ways to volunteer and participate in fundraising for the cause. Lauren especially encourages healthy teens who want to help others and works with groups of young people on fundraisers, giving them the chance to feel they are doing something concrete and productive to help their peers who are living with cancer. Lauren has recruited people in all walks of life to use their individual talents—from music to juggling to gardening—to come up with imaginative ways to participate.

Lauren also works closely with the medical community to involve them in new projects and help raise money for endeavors that will benefit hundreds of teens with cancer. Doctors and nurses are not immune from human emotions when treating teens with this disease. Each day, they face their teen patients with a warm smile on their faces and deep pain in their hearts. Lauren says that words cannot adequately express her gratitude for their efforts.

A commitment...for life

In addition to having a full-time job running her management training company, Lauren continues to devote countless hours as executive director of Melissa's Living Legacy, helping the foundation reach its goals. These include creating local peer support networks, where teens have access to age-appropriate programs and services, and the development of innovative, educational resources for health-care professionals.

With three grown sons, two stepdaughters and five grandchildren, Lauren tirelessly balances family and work with traveling on the foundation's behalf, speaking at conferences as an advocate for teens with cancer and heading charitable events that raise funds and awareness for the cause. The subject matter is an emotional one, and some of her speaking engagements are difficult, but Lauren never shrinks from the opportunity to help others dealing with cancer. She is committed to motivating teens with cancer to live life to the fullest, just as her daughter Melissa did— to have a sense of their own ability to influence their situations and lead meaningful, productive lives.

Lauren Spiker continues to be inspired by her daughter Melissa's extraordinary zest for life and by the promise Lauren made to her daughter—to make things better for teens with cancer. Today, Melissa's Living Legacy Teen Cancer Foundation is helping to support and celebrate the courageous journeys of thousands of other teenagers— just like Melissa.

DEBBIE MACOMBER
⚬—WHAT AMANDA WANTS—⚬

∽—DEBBIE MACOMBER—∾

is a number one *New York Times* and *USA TODAY* bestselling author. Among her recent books are *1225 Christmas Tree Lane*, *1105 Yakima Street*, *A Turn in the Road*, *Hannah's List* and *Debbie Macomber's Christmas Cookbook*. The story in this volume, *What Amanda Wants*, is connected to her popular Blossom Street books, which include *The Shop on Blossom Street*, *A Good Yarn* and *Twenty Wishes* among others. Debbie Macomber has become a leading voice in women's fiction worldwide and her work has appeared on every major bestseller list, including those of the *New York Times*, *USA TODAY*, *Publishers Weekly* and *Entertainment Weekly*. She is a multiple award winner, and won the 2005 Quill Award for Best Romance. Two of her MIRA Books Christmas titles have been made into Hallmark Channel Original Movies. There are more than 100 million copies of her books in print. For more information on Debbie and her books, visit her website, www.debbiemacomber.com.

CHAPTER
~ONE~

Amanda knew. She knew even before Dr. Fleishman stepped into the room with her chart in his hand. Before he spoke the words that would forever change her life. She knew.

The cancer was back.

She'd always realized that it might return, but she'd been cancer-free for almost eight years. An intellectual understanding of something wasn't the same as an emotional acceptance. Perhaps she'd grown complacent, convinced that after all this time she was cured. As a childhood-cancer survivor, perhaps she'd come to believe she was invincible.

The silence that followed his announcement reminded

her of the eerie lack of sound before a storm. Before the thunder and lightning and torrential rain.

"Amanda," Dr. Fleishman said, breaking into her thoughts.

He wanted her attention, but she couldn't give it to him. Instead, she continued to stare at the floor. She didn't look up. She couldn't. Not just then. It would take a few minutes for the news to settle, a few minutes before she could face him.

It was the same with her mother. Joan Jennings sat in the chair next to Amanda's and it seemed as if all the life had drained out of her. Suddenly, after that long, awkward silence, Amanda's mother started to weep.

"I'm so sorry," Dr. Fleishman said softly.

Amanda nodded. Needing to hold on to something, she reached for her mother's hand. "It'll be all right, Mom," she whispered. She didn't know where that encouragement came from because she didn't feel it. Her entire world was about to implode.

"I guess this means I won't be cheerleading at the pep rally, doesn't it?" She tried hard to make a joke of it. She failed miserably; she didn't even sound like herself.

"Not this year," Dr. Fleishman murmured in reply.

She honestly hadn't expected an answer. He seemed so calm about it, but why shouldn't he be? It wasn't *his* life that was taking a nosedive. Anyway, the cheerleading thing was minor. More importantly, the Junior/Senior Prom was in May. By then her hair would've fallen out and

Lance… She couldn't do that to him, couldn't embarrass him that way. The dress she loved, and had saved countless months for, would languish in her closet. Maybe she could be buried in it. Funny, the idea of dying didn't immediately upset her. She noticed then that her mother and Dr. Fleishman were carrying on a conversation.

Amanda sat there, half listening while they exchanged questions and answers. When he saw that he finally had Amanda's attention, Dr. Fleishman outlined a treatment schedule.

Amanda tried to take it all in but she couldn't. By the time they left the office, her mother had stopped crying. She clutched a wet tissue in her hand, and Amanda was afraid she'd dissolve into heart-wrenching sobs once again. Maybe in public.

"I don't want anyone to know," Amanda insisted as they walked toward the parking complex.

"We're going to do whatever it takes," her mother said with a grim set to her mouth. "I don't care what it costs. I don't care how much the insurance company fights us— I'll fight harder."

Her mother hadn't even heard her.

"You weren't listening to me," Amanda said. All her mother could think about was the money and how much these treatments were going to cost and struggling with the insurance company. Amanda wanted an iPod and her mother had claimed it wasn't in the budget. But chemo, radiation, a bone-marrow transplant would cost a whole lot more.

"What did you say?" her mother asked.

"When?"

"You said I wasn't listening. Tell me what you said."

"Annie," she whispered. "I'll tell Annie." Annie was one of her best friends, and Amanda wouldn't be able to keep this news from her. Besides, when she didn't show up for the pep rally rehearsal, Annie would know something was wrong. So would Laurie, another of her good friends.

"I blame this on that party job," her mother said angrily.

"What?" Amanda stared at her in shocked disbelief. She worked with Annie and her mother on their birthday party business. Almost every weekend, Bethanne organized a number of birthday parties for youngsters, and she paid both Annie and Amanda to help. At first Amanda had tagged along…just because. She soon discovered it was a lot of fun; she liked helping kids celebrate their birthdays in a creative way. Annie's mother was really good at this. The money was a bonus, and Amanda had used it to save up for her prom dress.

"Those kids exposed you to all their germs," her mother snapped. "Those birthday parties are breeding grounds for—"

"I didn't get cancer at a birthday party."

Amanda could see it already. Her mother was going to smother her. In a misguided effort to protect her from harm, Joan would make everything worse. It'd been bad enough when Amanda was eight and nine. She couldn't even *imagine* what her mother would be like now. Amanda figured she'd be lucky to step inside a movie theater again—the germs floating around in places like that. And if her mother had anything to say about it, she'd be banned from shopping, too. How ridiculous was that! Amanda sighed heavily. Even if she survived, she'd be doomed to her mother's heavy-handed protection for the rest of her life.

And that remark about the birthday parties! It was as though her mother would feel better if she had someone or something to blame. Amanda didn't understand why. It wouldn't make the cancer magically disappear. And it didn't benefit anyone, except maybe her mom. That kind of thinking would drive Amanda crazy.

Neither spoke on the ride home. The minute she got out of the car, Amanda went straight to her room and shut the door. Once inside the relative privacy of her bedroom, she placed headphones over her ears and immersed herself in music.

Someone—obviously her mother—knocked loudly on her door, but Amanda ignored it. She didn't know if Joan came in to check on her, because she kept her eyes closed.

For whatever reason, the cancer was back and Amanda would be the one dealing with it. This wasn't a trig problem she could pass off to Lance in study hall to solve for her. Her parents couldn't help her, either. She was alone, and that was the most frightening thing of all.

Ten minutes later, the phone rang. Even with the music turned up full blast, Amanda could hear it. She ignored that, too. When her mother came into her room, Amanda reluctantly removed the headphones. "What?" she demanded.

Her mother's eyes filled with tears. "That was Annie."

"I don't want to talk right now." She was seventeen and she was dying and if she didn't want to answer the phone she shouldn't have to.

"I called your father...."

Amanda closed her eyes again. She didn't want to hear it. "Mom, please, give me a few minutes by myself. Just a few minutes." She didn't know why her mother was doing this. A little time alone shouldn't be that much to ask.

"I can't," her mother sobbed. Joan sank onto the edge of the bed, covered her face with both hands and began to cry.

Amanda bit her lower lip and knelt on the carpet at her mother's feet. After a moment she laid her head in her mother's lap. It occurred to her then that this diagnosis wasn't only about her. Her cancer affected everyone in her life.

Slowly Amanda's arms went around her mother's waist and she straightened. Her mother clung to her, burying her face in Amanda's shoulder, still sobbing.

Surprisingly, Amanda shed no tears. The emotion was there, just beneath the surface, pounding, throbbing, pulsing. What shocked Amanda, what threw her completely off guard, was her mother's reaction. This was the second time she'd faced cancer, the second time for her *and* her parents. You'd think her mom would know how to cope. Or maybe it was the exact opposite; maybe knowing what to expect made it worse.

"I'm going to be fine," Amanda cooed softly.

"I know."

Amanda had been too young the first time to remember how her mother and father had dealt with everything. Certain memories were strong: the pain, throwing up, losing her hair—and her mother at her side. Other memories had faded. The one constant had been her mother's devotion. She'd desperately needed it then and Amanda knew she'd need it now.

"I'm...sorry," her mother whispered. "I didn't mean to do this. You need me—but I'm so frightened. I can't bear to see you go through this again."

Amanda gently kissed the top of her mother's head. "It's all right, Mom. It's all right."

"I should be the strong one."

"You are." In the months to come, Amanda would need to lean on her mother's strength. Her mother would be her advocate, her nurse, her coach and her friend.

CHAPTER
∽TWO∽

Dumbfounded, Annie Hamlin hung up the phone and gazed blankly at the wall, trying to assimilate Amanda's dreadful news. Surely this was all a horrible mistake. Amanda looked fine. Okay, she'd been a little tired lately, but then so was Annie. Everyone was these last few months before graduation.

Her mother walked into the kitchen, humming "Home on the Range." That meant Bethanne was getting ready for a Wild West Birthday Extravaganza. This particular party involved a cookout over a campfire, plus a bale of hay where Annie sat strumming a guitar and singing cattle-drive favorites. Little boys loved this theme because they got to wear cowboy hats and sheriff's badges, and the villain was quickly found out when the cake was sliced. Her mother dropped a black jellybean into the batter and who-ever got that slice was declared the bad guy.

Bethanne walked past her, paused and then glanced back. "What's wrong? You look like you've lost your best friend."

At those words involuntary tears welled in Annie's eyes. "Amanda just phoned. She had a doctor's appointment this afternoon."

"I remember. You were upset because she was supposed to go shopping with you."

Annie nodded, hardly able to believe she could've been angry with her friend over something so meaning-less. "Mom, she told me…" She blinked hard and tried again. Even saying the words caused her pain. "Amanda has cancer."

Her mother stared at her. "Cancer?" she repeated slowly.

"It's leukemia."

Her mother pulled out a chair and sat down at the table next to Annie. "How long has she known?"

"She just found out."

"I'm so sorry." Her mother frowned. "Has anyone in her family ever had cancer?"

"Yes." Annie swallowed. "Amanda has. Don't you re-member me telling you she had leukemia when she was in second grade?"

Her mother wrinkled her brow, suggesting that if Annie

had mentioned it, she'd forgotten. "Her poor mother," she said.

Annie wasn't sure what Amanda's mother had to do with it, but she didn't ask. "The cancer's back and according to the doctor, it's worse than before."

"Oh dear." Her mother's eyes met hers.

"You know what's really sad?" Annie whispered, glancing away from her mother. It was embarrassing to confess this, even to her own mother.

"What?" Bethanne asked.

Annie felt horrible. Her friend had cancer and might not survive and when Amanda had told her, all Annie could think about was herself. "My first thought—my very first thought—was that I'd have to find someone else to double with for prom night." She paused and waited for her mother to berate her. Bethanne didn't.

"It was…so unexpected," Annie continued, as the beginnings of this new reality settled in the pit of her stomach. "I didn't know what to say and neither did Amanda. Then she started to cry and asked if I thought she should tell Lance so he could ask someone else to the prom."

"What did you say?"

"I didn't say much of anything. I just muttered something and she seemed to think I said yes. But I didn't… If I were her I wouldn't know what to do, either. I feel awful, like I'm going to throw up." Annie almost wished her mother would chastise her for being so self-absorbed.

"Amanda's still in shock."

Annie knew that had to be true.

One of her dearest friends was desperately sick, and she had no idea how to help her.

"What'll happen now?" Bethanne murmured.

"I asked Amanda that." Well, it was one point in Annie's favor. "She said there'd be a series of chemotherapy sessions and she'd lose her hair and then she'd have to go through a bone-marrow transplant."

"There's a good donor in her family?"

"I hope so," Annie said, wishing she'd asked more intelligent questions. "The thing is, Amanda doesn't want anyone other than me to know."

"People will find out. That's unavoidable, don't you think?"

Annie agreed. News like this would spread in about five minutes once Amanda stopped attending classes. Everyone would want to know where she was and why. Annie couldn't understand Amanda's reasons for not telling her friends.

"She wanted me to lie to Lance for her."

Bethanne's eyes widened. "Did you say you would?"

"No way."

Her mother nodded approvingly. "Good."

Refusing Amanda had been difficult. Still, Annie didn't feel she could lie to Lance. He genuinely cared for Amanda and in Annie's opinion, Lance was entitled to the truth.

"She's afraid, you know," her mother said.

"Of cancer?" Annie asked and then answered her own question. "I would be, too."

Bethanne shook her head. "The cancer's scary enough. But I was talking about everything else."

"What do you mean?"

"Other people's reactions." Bethanne took a deep breath. "After your father moved out," she said, "I was afraid to leave the house."

"But why? You didn't do anything."

"I didn't want people to know Grant had left. For the first couple of months, I pretended he was away on an extended business trip. If anyone asked, I made up this elaborate story about Grant's heavy traveling schedule. I even invented a date when he was supposed to return."

This was all news to Annie.

"In my mind, I actually came to believe that within that time frame, your father would realize what he was doing and move back home. After two months, I was forced to admit that Grant meant what he said. He wanted out of the marriage."

Bethanne so rarely mentioned the divorce, Annie actually felt privileged that her mother had shared this with her.

"In some ways," Bethanne continued, "I think Amanda is afraid of people talking about her and pitying her, just like I was. It's difficult enough to accept devastating news, but then you have to handle everyone else's feelings about it, as well."

Annie frowned in puzzlement. Some of this made sense to her, but part of it didn't.

"When people hear bad news, their first reaction is usually shock and sadness. Sometimes curiosity. And sometimes they think they can fix it."

Then Annie understood. She hadn't even disconnected from her conversation with Amanda when she'd begun making plans. She'd get all their friends together and they'd make a huge get-well card and fill a basket with gifts and… It was an automatic response. Looking for an easy fix. She was still trying to figure out how to deal with this shock.

"Other people aren't as kind," her mother said. "They want to find a way to blame you. One friend suggested…" She paused. "Never mind, that isn't important now. My point is that once the news is out, Amanda will be confronted with everyone's reactions—family, friends, teachers—not just her own."

Annie had a renewed respect for her mother's insight. "That's deep."

Bethanne laughed softly. "Are you making fun of me?"

"No," Annie said. "I meant it. You're so right, Mom. About people's reactions. All I could think about when Amanda phoned was what her cancer would mean to our friendship."

"That's perfectly understandable." Her mother stood and checked her watch. "If you need to talk more about this, let me know."

"I will. Thanks, Mom."

Her mother went to open the kitchen cupboard. After shuffling several things around, she asked, "Do you remember if I used the last of the liquid smoke?"

"No, you didn't." Annie's mind was back on Amanda and how she could best be a friend to her. Not a fixer or a comforter. Not a weeper or a gawker. Just a friend.

"Just a minute," Bethanne said, whirling around. "You know who you should talk to?" Before Annie could answer, she said, "Lydia Hoffman."

"The lady who owns the knitting shop—A Good Yarn?"

Her mother nodded enthusiastically. "Lydia had cancer as a teenager, too."

Annie vaguely remembered her mother mentioning that.

"She's been through this herself. Twice, in fact. She was only sixteen when she was first diagnosed."

"Did she have leukemia, too?"

"Brain tumor."

"And she survived…" Knowing that her mother's friend had come through this encouraged Annie.

"Yes, and she didn't have an easy time of it, either. She's never said much about it to me. Margaret's the one who let certain details slip."

"Who's Margaret?"

"Oh, sorry, her sister. She works at the shop, too."

Annie thought she might've seen her once.

"Lydia's just the person who could help you be Amanda's friend."

"I'll call her, Mom. Thanks."

She might have faltered when she'd first heard the news about Amanda's cancer, but Annie was determined that wouldn't happen again.

CHAPTER
THREE

LYDIA HOFFMAN GOETZ

I've known Annie Hamlin for over a year and I've never seen her looking this serious. Or this sad. She phoned me earlier in the afternoon and asked if she could come and visit after school. The request surprised me. Annie is the daughter of one of my customers and friends, Bethanne. I've often chatted with Annie but always on a casual basis.

She arrived at the store just before five. I needed to finish up with a couple of customers, so Annie waited for me. She strolled through the shop, studying the hand-knit socks and sweaters on display, and leafed through a pattern book. After I rang up the last sale of the day, I locked the front door and turned over the sign to read Closed. I was now free to talk to my friend's daughter.

"How about a cup of tea?" I said.

"Sure." Annie followed me into my small office. There really wasn't room for us to chat comfortably, so once I'd made the tea I carried two cups out to the table where I teach my knitting classes. I'd met Annie's mother in a sock-knitting class. Bethanne was an emotional wreck at the time, her self-esteem in the gutter after her divorce. Annie had experienced her share of emotional trauma, too. I was proud of the turnaround in both their lives.

"What can I do for you?" I asked.

Annie set her cup carefully back in the saucer. "Mom suggested I talk to you about my friend Amanda. She's one of my best friends and, Lydia..." Her voice shook, and she paused long enough to regain her composure. "Amanda just learned she has cancer."

So that was what had upset Annie so much. It also explained why she'd come to me. I'm a two-time cancer survivor. When I went into remission after the second bout, I opened A Good Yarn. You see, this store is an affirmation for me—an affirmation of life.

"The thing is," Annie went on, "Amanda had cancer when she was eight."

"So this is her second time facing the beast."

Annie nodded expectantly. I wished I knew what to say. "How can I help?" I asked.

"Amanda didn't want to tell anyone, not even me. One

reason she did was because we were supposed to double-date on prom night."

"She can't go now?"

"She didn't seem to think so. This hit her out of no-where."

That I understood. I'd been sixteen when the first brain tumor was discovered and in my early twenties the second time around. The second diagnosis was the hardest to accept; it blindsided me and my family. I think that's partly because I was sure I'd triumphed over cancer, and it seemed so *unfair* to go through it again. To this day, I believe it was my second bout with cancer that killed my father. The death certificate says it was a heart attack. Medically that's accurate, but I'm positive the underlying cause was dealing with my cancer. I could well understand Amanda's shock and horror at learning the disease had returned.

"Did she tell you what kind of cancer she has?"

"She had a technical name that I couldn't repeat if I tried. She explained it's a rare form of leukemia." Her gaze held mine. "She's acting all weird. Like I said, Amanda doesn't want anyone to know—not even Lance, and he's her boyfriend."

"Give her some time to adjust to the news," I advised.

"That's what Mom said I should do, and I'm trying." Annie didn't seem satisfied with that, however. "She's reeling from this. I want to be a good friend." Annie leaned toward me as if I had secrets to share. "I want to say the right things. I don't want to…to be insensitive, but I don't want to act like I pity her, either. Do you know what I mean?"

I nodded. "Amanda's fortunate to have you for a friend," I said, searching for suggestions that would help Annie feel she was contributing in an appropriate way. "It might not seem like she wants her friends around just now, but in a little while that'll change. She's going to need you."

"I haven't said a word to anyone at school."

I realized it must've been hard on Annie to keep this to herself.

"Lance is pestering me to tell him what's up. I told him he should talk to Amanda."

"Has she been to classes?"

Annie shook her head. "Her mom's homeschooling her for the rest of the year. She did say she wants to graduate with our class, but she doesn't know if that'll be possible now."

I knew that keeping Annie's friend away from school protected her from any unnecessary exposure while her immune system was compromised. At the same time, I was aware that Amanda was now isolated from everything familiar. The same thing had happened to me. I couldn't attend classes, either. My friends had stuck around for a while. But later, as my treatment wore on, they lost interest. There wasn't much entertainment in a cancer ward. It was awkward, too, because my life in the hospital was so completely unlike their carefree times.

When I was a teenager I was first put in a pediatric ward, along with the little kids. I didn't appreciate visits from clowns who thought their antics would amuse me; I felt humiliated when my friends showed up to find some ridiculous-looking character at my bedside, blowing up a balloon for me. Nor did I appreciate the Sesame Street drawings on the wall. I was a teenager, and everyone treated me like I was a three-year-old.

"Amanda said she won't go to the dance but I know that deep down she really wants to."

"Of course she does." I understood that, too. "When I first found out I had cancer, I'd just turned sixteen." I'd gone in a for a routine eye exam and that was when it all began. Soon afterward, the brain tumor was discovered. I paused to sip my tea. "As crazy as it sounds, one of the first things I did after I was diagnosed—" I hesitated to tell Annie this because it embarrassed me "—I...I cut up my driver's license."

"Why?"

Even after all these years I couldn't exactly say. "I don't know. I guess it was because I felt that every good thing in my life was about to be destroyed, so why not that, too? It doesn't make any sense, I know. I can't explain what came over me. I took a pair of scissors and cut my brand-new license into tiny pieces."

"Did you... Do you drive now?"

"Yes." I smiled. "I realize it was rather melodramatic of me. I wish I could explain it better."

Annie grew thoughtful. "I think I understand. Amanda's rejecting the things that used to matter to her. She's pushing all her friends away from her, too."

"So did I, at first. I tried to close everyone out." I took another sip of tea. "That didn't last long, though. I got lonely and bored, and I missed my friends."

"Lance needs to know. He's driving me crazy."

My smile was sad as I recalled my relationship difficulties. "It's up to Amanda to tell him. She'll do that when she's ready."

"Can you give me any other advice?"

Annie was so sincere that I reached across the table and gripped her hand. "Amanda needs you more than ever now. Be her friend."

"That's what I want to do, but I'm still not sure I know how."

"She's going through a hard time emotionally. It might sound like a cliché—but just be there for her. In time, she'll want to discuss uncomfortable subjects. Don't let that frighten you. Hear her out."

"Do you mean she'll want to discuss...dying?"

"Probably." I watched Annie and was pleased that she didn't flinch. When you're dealing with cancer, the threat of death is a constant presence. In the beginning I ignored it. Later, the sicker I became, the more at ease I got to be with it. Death became a very real companion and the fear and mystery of it vanished.

"Okay," Annie said. "I won't let talk of death upset me."

"Good. She might mention her treatment and how sick she feels. Don't let that gross you out, okay?"

"All right." Annie finished her tea.

"Don't wait to hear from her, either. Take responsibility for maintaining the friendship."

Annie nodded. "Thank you, Lydia."

"You're welcome. If there's anything more I can do, please give me a call."

We both stood at the same time and then Annie did something unexpected. She hugged me. I hugged her back and wished her friend the very best.

Amanda watched her mother as she slipped away from the darkened bedroom doorway. In the silent stillness of dawn, Amanda could hear her weeping. She hated this, hated the way her mother reacted to the slightest sigh or moan. It was just as she'd expected. Her mother was suffocating her. Twice before, Amanda had awakened in the middle of the night to find Joan standing inside the bedroom, watching her. She hated feeling smothered, but most of all she hated causing her mother so much grief.

This morning, Amanda would begin what Dr. Fleishman had termed aggressive chemotherapy, followed by total body radiation. Although she'd only been eight when cancer struck the first time, Amanda remembered the hellish side effects of those treatments. The nausea had been the worst—until she'd suffered brain seizures. Back then,

Amanda had been mostly out of it. She remembered how sick she'd felt and asking God to let her die.

She was older now, more experienced in life, and she knew the horrors she faced. Her parents did, too, and her older brother, as well. Joe hadn't said much. He was at Washington State University in Pullman and had called her as soon as he heard the news. Like her friend Annie, Amanda's brother had been at a loss as to what to say. He wanted to help, but didn't know how. She sensed he was grateful to be away at school and frankly she didn't blame him. If their situations were reversed, Amanda figured she'd feel the same way. Finally, after several awkward minutes, he managed to croak out that if she needed anything, all she had to do was ask.

What she needed was a life. A real life. Her biggest fear wasn't the treatment, which she already knew wasn't going to be any picnic. No, top on her priority list was graduating with her friends. It wasn't so much to ask, was it? Graduation was six weeks away. Six weeks wasn't that long. She'd wear a wig for the ceremony. Apparently there were some really good ones.

At six her mother came into her bedroom to wake her. "Rise and shine," Joan said, wearing a bright smile.

Amanda saw through her facade immediately. This false cheer was hard to swallow. "Mom," she said, sitting up in bed. She patted the space next to her. "I have something I want to tell you and Dad."

"Leon," her mother shouted over her shoulder. "Amanda wants to talk to us."

Her father stepped into the bedroom, dressed and ready to leave for his job at Boeing as a control systems analyst. "What is it, pumpkin?"

Amanda smiled. She was close to her father; her mother, too, only it was different with her dad. They were more alike, and they had a similar sense of humor.

She released a pent-up sigh. "I don't want to sound like a drama queen, but you need to know I've reached an important decision."

Both her parents stared at her. There wasn't any reason to keep them in suspense. "I know I might die. Cancer is serious, and I'm going through it for the second time. Dr. Fleishman didn't say it, but he didn't have to—I could see it in his eyes."

"Now, pumpkin, don't talk like that. You're going to lick this."

"Dad," she said, meeting his gaze without flinching. "You were the one who said 'prepare for the worst and hope for the best.' That's all I'm doing."

Her mother's eyes filled with tears. "I want you to think about living, not dying."

"I am. I will."

Her mother sobbed again.

"Mom," Amanda shouted, losing patience with her. "Stop crying! I can't stand seeing you cry all the time. Get a grip. I've got enough on my plate without having to worry about you." She sounded harsher than she meant to, but it had to be said.

"I'm sorry." Her mother's voice quavered.

Amanda's father placed a protective arm around his wife's shoulders. "There's no need to snap at your mother, pumpkin. She loves you. We both do."

"I know, I know."

"You w-wanted to say something?" her mother asked, her resolve clear.

Amanda nodded. "Let's try this again." She took a deep breath. "I know I could die and I want you to know I'm fine with that."

Her mother crumpled emotionally and couldn't suppress a protesting sob. "You're giving up, aren't you?"

"No way." This was the really important part. "The thing is, I'm willing to do everything necessary to get well. I know it isn't going to be easy. I accept that from this point forward, my life will change. It sucks, but I don't have many options. I'll fight the disease with everything in me."

"But?" her father pressed. He knew there was one coming.

Amanda let her love for them show in her eyes. "But I won't fight death."

Tears rolled down her mother's pale cheeks and she started to shake her head; if Amanda wasn't going to fight death, she seemed to say, then she'd do it for her. Somehow, some way, regardless of the cost, Joan Jennings would hold back the Grim Reaper.

"I was thinking about it this morning lying in bed," Amanda explained, eager to share this new insight with her parents. "It was because of something Annie said." She had her parents' attention. "When I told her about the cancer, she didn't know what to say at first. The next day she phoned back, and the two of us talked for a long time."

"Annie's a good friend," her mother whispered.

Amanda agreed. She hadn't realized how good a friend until now. It felt good to discuss what was happening to her with someone her own age. "Annie said she was afraid for me, afraid I might die."

Her mother covered her mouth as if to hide her fear. But it was unmistakable. Her eyes were ablaze with it. Amanda wanted to cry out that she needed her mother to be strong, that she'd have to lean on her, especially during the chemo. It would take everything she had to get through this, and she didn't have the strength to support anyone else.

"What was it Annie said that you found so enlightening?" her father asked.

Amanda loved the way he always got right to the point. "When she talked about how I might die, it occurred to me that eventually everyone dies. I will. So will you, Mom. You, too, Dad. Just like Grandpa did. I remember his funeral. I was really little when he died. What was I, six or seven?"

"Six," her mother said.

All Amanda remembered was that she'd barely started second grade when her wonderful grandfather died of a heart attack. Everyone had been sad and crying and upset. There were lots of people at the service. "When we went to the funeral home and saw Grandpa resting so peacefully, I thought dying mustn't be so bad, especially if you weren't afraid. And I'm not." She meant that. Death wasn't an alien darkness one struggled against. She no longer considered death the end of everything; it was a new beginning. When you saw it that way, the meaning of death changed. She couldn't explain that to her parents—it would freak them out.

For the first time since entering her bedroom, her father smiled. "When did you get to be so smart?" he asked.

Although Amanda shrugged, she was pleased by her dad's praise. "I didn't know I was."

"You're going to make it," her mother insisted.

"If that's what God wills." Amanda didn't explain her feelings about God to her parents, either. She wasn't sure they'd understand. For now, it was enough that they know and accept her feelings about the cancer. Although her illness affected them, too, it was hers and hers alone, and she was the one who'd have to deal with it.

Her father glanced at his watch. "I have to get to work."

"It's all right, Dad. Go. I've said everything I have to say."

He leaned forward and kissed Amanda's cheek before leaving the room. Her mother walked out with him.

By herself again, Amanda threw aside the comforter and sat on the edge of her bed. It was about to start. This morning her mother would take her to the oncology center, and by noon she'd be heaving her guts out. Annie had promised to stop by after school. Amanda would look forward to that—the one bright spot in what was going to be a hell of a day.

CHAPTER
∞FOUR∞

Everyone at school knew. After a month of chemotherapy, Amanda had ceased to care. It was all she could do to function on a day-to-day basis. She'd lost weight, weight she could ill-afford to lose, and much of her hair. A few dark strands stubbornly remained, but they'd disappear soon. Annie's mother had knit her a really cute hat out of lime-green and orange yarn that she wore almost constantly.

What had once seemed important, joining her high school class for graduation, no longer concerned her. Amanda didn't possess the energy to stand for even brief periods of time. The chemo had been worse than she'd expected, and the doctors were now giving her morphine, which helped with the pain. Because of her weakened condition, she'd been hospitalized shortly after prom night.

Fortunately, she had a private room, even if it *was* on the pediatric floor. That way she and Annie could visit. Laurie would come by later, too. Her friends always closed the door, and Amanda didn't have to worry about a roommate.

Propped up against pillows, Amanda looked over at the clock on the wall and realized school was out for the day. Annie had been her only really faithful friend. She came at least three times a week, and often four and five times. Annie was her link with her other friends, with school activities and the world she'd once known. Laurie didn't visit as often, but at least she stopped by every week or so, which was more than most of her other friends did.

Someone tapped lightly at the door. Amanda rolled her head to one side and smiled when she saw Lance. He'd brought a single long-stemmed red rose and a card. It'd been ten days since his last visit.

"Hi," she said and wished he'd let her know he was coming. Amanda would've put on makeup and her knit hat. She hated that he was seeing her almost completely bald. On his last visit, she'd had a respectable amount of hair left. She self-consciously placed her hand on her bald head.

"Hi, yourself." Lance cautiously stepped farther into the room. "How are you?"

Amanda didn't understand why anyone would ask a

cancer patient that question. She was irritated because it should be fairly obvious that she felt like crap. She looked like crap, too, and everyone pretended not to notice.

He didn't meet her eyes but gazed past her to the window. It was a lovely day and the sun was shining. This was the first time Amanda had noticed.

"I'm okay. How about you?" she said, deciding to fall into a meaningless exchange of pleasantries.

Lance set the rose and envelope on the nightstand and approached the other side of her bed, facing the hallway. "I'm sorry I haven't been by lately."

"You're busy. I understand." Amanda was willing to offer him excuses. It was hard not to stare at him—he just looked so good. She'd had the biggest crush on Lance for two years. It'd taken him almost eighteen of those twenty-four months to even notice her. He played defensive back for the football team. He was tall and dark-haired, with strong features and an endearing smile. He didn't kiss her or reach for her hand the way he had on his last visit.

He shuffled his feet and slid the tips of his fingers into the back pockets of his jeans, as if he wasn't sure what to do with his hands.

"How is everyone?" she asked, wanting him to talk because carrying a conversation drained her of the little energy she still had.

"Okay."

This wasn't working. "Something on your mind?" Amanda asked. She knew what was coming, could feel it, and in fact she'd sensed it the instant she saw him standing in the doorway.

"You've been out of school a whole month now."

Like he needed to tell her how long she'd been sick! Yeah, well, he had it wrong. She'd been puking up her guts, literally pulling out her hair, for exactly thirty-two days, fifteen hours and ten minutes.

"Everyone's been real worried."

That was a joke, too. Her first week in the hospital she'd had visitors every day. Her bedroom had been crowded with friends until her mother had to usher everyone out. The second week, a few had stopped by and five or six had phoned. At the end of the third week, there were only Annie, Laurie and Lance. Her so-called boyfriend had made a couple of token visits; he never stayed long. The funny part was, she didn't expect him to.

"Tell everyone I'm thinking of them."

"Jake and Kristen came up to see you, right?" He seemed grateful to have a question to ask.

Amanda knew they hadn't. "I must've been asleep."

"Yeah," he said, animated now. "That's what it was. They came and you were sleeping. More people would come but everyone's busy with graduation and all." He frowned as if he'd said something he wasn't supposed to say. "You aren't upset about not attending the ceremony, are you? I mean, you'll have your diploma and everything, so it doesn't really matter."

In spite of what she'd told herself, it mattered a lot. This was one more thing to add to the list of what cancer had stolen from her.

"Thank Jake and Kristen for me." She ignored his question and did her best to keep the sarcasm out of her voice.

Lance stared down at the floor. "I will."

Suddenly she was overwhelmingly tired. Her eyes closed and she struggled not to drift off. Amanda always welcomed sleep. It was an escape.

"Have you listened to the new U2 CD?" Lance asked.

Amanda shook her head.

"Ellie and I——" He stopped abruptly in midsentence, faltered a moment and tried again. "I bought it the day it came out," he finished lamely.

Apparently Amanda wasn't supposed to be aware of his slip. At first she'd pretended not to hear. Only she had, and she knew. This small revelation didn't surprise her. She opened her eyes.

"I like Ellie," Amanda murmured. Her voice was weak now, partly due to her exhaustion and partly to the lump forming in her throat. Amanda did like Ellie Logan; she'd never believed Ellie would sink so low as to steal her boyfriend.

Lance shrugged, guilt written plain as a warning label across his face. "She's okay."

His effort to conceal his betrayal failed miserably. Amanda knew she had every right to scratch his eyes out. Her first thought was that she wanted him to hurt the same way she did, but a moment later, she decided she didn't care anymore. She didn't have the energy.

The best thing to do was make this breakup as easy for him as possible. "Lance, would you like your ring back?" He'd bought her a sterling silver promise ring at Christmastime. She'd worn it every day since.

Now the question was out in the open, and she waited for him to respond. She didn't want to delay this any longer than necessary. He'd already hung around two weeks more than she'd figured he would.

"I...I said I'd be there for you, remember?" His husky voice was low and timorous.

Amanda did. Annie had convinced her to tell Lance she had cancer. He'd been terribly sympathetic and concerned, and to his credit, he'd spent prom night with her at the house. Her mother had cooked a wonderful meal just for her and Lance. Afterward her parents had left them alone to dance in the dimly lit living room. The evening had been sweet and romantic. For as long as she lived, Amanda would treasure that one night with Lance.

"I can't walk out on you now." His protest sounded weak. A self-deception.

He wanted out so bad she could feel it. Amanda wasn't sure which of them he was trying to convince.

"I'm not a good bet, Lance."

"Don't say that!" he barked angrily.

"Don't say what—that I could die?" She relaxed against the pillow, closed her eyes again and smiled. "The thing is, there's a very good likelihood I might. Did I tell you there's only a twenty-percent survival rate with the form of cancer I have? In other words, there's an eighty-percent chance I'll kick the bucket. Deal with it, Lance. I have."

He backed away from her as if she'd scorched him with a live wire. "Don't talk like that—like you've given up."

"Lance, listen," she said, mustering her strength to rise up and lean on one elbow. "It's all right about you and Ellie. I understand. I want you to know I don't hold any ill will toward either of you."

"I...I can't walk out on you when you need me most."

Amanda did her best to comfort him. "You aren't. So don't worry, okay?"

"I am worried."

"Lance, please." She didn't have the energy to argue anymore. Her head fell back to the pillow as she slipped the ring from her finger and handed it to him.

It was a long time before he reached for it. "I feel like I'm letting you down."

She didn't answer; she couldn't.

"I wrote you a letter," he said. He sounded perfectly miserable now. "I explained everything about how it happened with Ellie and me."

She nodded, letting him know she'd read it later. Right now, she wasn't in the mood.

"Are you going to cry?" he asked. "I couldn't stand it if you started to cry. I don't know what I'd do."

Despite herself, Amanda nearly burst into peals of

laughter. Her lips trembled and it took all her restraint to keep a straight face. "No, Lance, I'm not going to cry."

"We didn't mean to hurt you."

"I know... I'm very tired. I don't mean to be rude, but I think you should leave now."

The look on his face was almost grateful as he moved away from her bed. "Annie's kept me updated.... She's been a really good friend, hasn't she?"

"Compared to you, you mean?" It wasn't fair to say that, but Amanda couldn't help it.

"Yeah," he said and he seemed genuinely regretful. "I thought I could handle this, you know? I couldn't. I'm sorry, Amanda, sorrier than you'll ever know."

"It's all right, Lance. Don't worry," she said again.

He left, and Amanda suspected Ellie was sitting in the waiting room, anxious for him to return.

Amanda slept then, and when she woke, she found Annie by her bedside, knitting.

"So you're awake," her friend said as she put down her knitting needles and yarn.

"What are you making?" Maybe she'd learn herself one day. Knitting appealed to her. When the chemo was finished, perhaps...

Annie glanced at her knitting bag on the floor. "Leg warmers."

"Cool."

She smiled and picked up the needles again. "They're for you."

"Really?" This was an unexpected surprise.

"Yeah. You might need something extra to keep your legs warm."

Annie completed a row in silence, then noticed the red rose and unopened envelope. She stood so they could talk at eye level. "Lance was here?"

Amanda's pleasure slowly faded. "He stopped by right after school. Did you know about him and Ellie?"

Annie's shoulders rose with her sigh and she nodded. "Are you upset?"

"Should I be?"

"No," was her adamant response. "He isn't worth the energy."

That had been Amanda's thought, too. "It's funny, you know?"

"What is?"

Amanda hesitated and wondered if she dared mention this. It might freak Annie out, and friends were in short supply these days. "I knew the minute he walked in the door. Do you think people who are close to dying develop ESP? I mean, I literally knew when Lance showed up with the flower and the card that he'd come to break up with me."

Annie's eyes widened but she didn't comment right away. "I suppose it's possible. When my mother's aunt Paula died, she saw angels. To this day, my mother believes that, and so do I. So if you've developed a sixth sense or whatever they call it, then it's a gift. Accept it."

Annie's response assured her she could share even her most unconventional feelings with her friend. It felt good to know that. Although Amanda wasn't so sure she wanted this so-called gift.

"You didn't answer my question," Annie said. "Are you upset? Because you don't seem to be, and that kind of surprises me."

Amanda shrugged. "I thought I should be, but I wasn't. Not really. The thing is, Lance and I don't have that much in common anymore. I'm wondering if I'll live long enough to spend Christmas with my parents, and his biggest concern is which college to choose." She grinned then, because she did feel bad about what she'd said to Lance.

"What's so funny?"

"You won't believe what I told him. I made up some gruesome statistic about only having a twenty-percent chance of surviving."

Annie's eyes grew huge. "You *wanted* him to think you were dying?"

Amanda laughed out loud. It was wonderful, truly wonderful, to find humor in this situation. "It was all I could do not to place my hand over my heart and call out to St. Peter to take my soul."

Annie had the giggles now, too. "You're kidding."

"I'm not," Amanda said. "I guess I should feel a lot worse about losing the love of my life. Oh, well. To quote my uncle Mortie, 'C'est la vie.' Ellie's welcome to him."

"Are you holding out on me?" Annie asked, hands on her hips. "Have you met someone else?"

"Holding out on you? Where am I going to meet any guys?" She was certainly in no condition to attract one.

"Doctors," Annie said. "I've seen dozens of really cute residents on every floor. This is a teaching hospital, you know."

Amanda arched her brows—or what was left of them—and decided her friend was right. Hey, if she attracted a handsome resident, there might be a medical discount in it for her mom and dad.

CHAPTER
~FIVE~

LYDIA HOFFMAN GOETZ

It was a couple of weeks since Annie had told me about her friend Amanda, and I hadn't been able to stop thinking about her. I was going into my junior year in high school when I was diagnosed with cancer. I remember it so well; it feels like only yesterday that I sat in Dr. Wilson's office that first time. Now it was happening to another girl, not unlike me. I'd asked Bethanne about Amanda's progress several times and she'd filled me in, but I still couldn't stop wondering about this young girl.

"You're looking thoughtful," Margaret said as I sat knitting furiously, which is something I do whenever I'm troubled. My sister works for me, and during the last couple of years we've grown close—closer than we've ever been. I blame my cancer for the disjointed relationship we had. It's a disease that ravages more than your body; it ravages relationships, families and lives.

Margaret seemed to think I wanted those brain tumors because of all the attention I got from being sick. I found the idea so offensive and ridiculous that I dismissed it entirely. What I didn't realize until this past year was that while I hated being sick, there were—in more ways than I'm comfortable admitting—certain advantages to being coddled by those I loved. I got used to being looked after and having decisions made for me. Not until I lost my father did I take my first bold step out into the real world.

I'd assumed that Margaret was jealous and if she were to examine her feelings, she'd discover that I'm at least partially right. But I guess it doesn't matter anymore. Over the last two years we've learned valuable lessons from each other. We remain about as different as two sisters can be, but since I opened the yarn shop, our differences are less important than our similarities. We don't act or think alike, and yet the bond we share is stronger now than ever.

"I did mention Annie's friend, didn't I?" I asked, looking up from my knitting. The store would open in a few minutes.

"You did," Margaret returned in that gruff way of hers. "She's the reason you've been spending so much time on the internet, isn't she?"

My sister has the uncanny ability to predict what I'm

going to do in certain situations. I nodded. "I keep thinking about her."

"You can't save her, you know."

"Now, Margaret…"

"I know you," my sister cut in sternly. "You've got a soft heart and you've decided there's something you might be able to do for her. Think, Lydia," she ordered, frowning now. "Think of all the responsibilities you already have and then ask yourself just how much energy can you afford to give anyone else."

I knew she was right, but I couldn't get Amanda out of my mind because I understood exactly what she was going through.

"I suppose you want to go to the hospital to visit her yourself." Apparently Margaret wasn't finished yet.

I had thought about doing exactly that, but Annie hadn't told me where she was and besides, I didn't want to interfere. Amanda didn't know me, and I wasn't sure how she'd feel about getting a visit from a stranger. There might be restrictions on visitors, too, depending on what stage of treatment she was entering. My main purpose would be to tell her about a link I'd found on the internet that might help her and her family. Still, I felt uneasy about involving myself in someone else's business.

"I remember what it was like," I reminded my sister as I set aside my knitting. Now that I owned the shop, I had less and less time for my personal projects. I walked over to the front door and switched the sign to Open.

"You have a husband and a son," Margaret said unnecessarily.

It was during moments like this that I had to bite my tongue. She was only being protective, but I find her meddling a bit annoying. I know she does it because she cares about me, so I do my best to let such comments slide. She was right about my responsibilities, of course. I'd recently married Brad Goetz and I was now stepmother to nine-year-old Cody. His dog, Chase, and my cat, Whiskers, were cohabiting for the first time, too. We were learning to be one cohesive family. We'd had only a few minor dissensions, and all in all, things were going well.

"Did you say anything about this girl to Brad?" Margaret asked, continuing with her interrogation.

Thankfully I had, otherwise Margaret would have leaped on that like Whiskers on his catnip mouse. "Yes. In fact, Brad was the one who helped me find the website."

Margaret looked puzzled. "Which website is that?"

I was about to answer when the door opened and in walked my first customer of the day. The woman wasn't familiar, otherwise I would've greeted her by name.

"Hello," I said as I walked toward her. "I'm Lydia Goetz. Welcome to A Good Yarn."

"Thank you." She stood there awkwardly, just a few steps past the door, as if she wasn't sure she'd come to the right place. "My name is Joan Jennings."

"Do you knit, Joan?" I asked.

She shook her head. "I've never even been inside a yarn store.... It's a bit intimidating."

"Oh, please don't let it be. How can I help you? Are you interested in taking a beginners' knitting class—because we're about to start one and we'd love to have you."

She shook her head again. "I...I don't think so, but thanks."

I backed away, not wanting to hover as she slowly ventured forward. She stopped at a display of pattern books and reached for an *Easy Knitting* magazine. I went behind the counter and turned the page on my day-by-day knitting calendar. Each day featured a new pattern. The one for today's date was a lacy bookmark with a heart design in the middle.

Joan returned the magazine to the rack, then wandered over to the shelf where I displayed the worsted weight yarn. She ran her fingertips over a skein. "It's very soft, isn't it?"

I nodded, realizing that Margaret was in our small office making a pot of coffee.

"I assumed a knitted sweater would be that scratchy wool most people find so irritating."

"Oh, not at all," I was quick to assure her.

Joan glanced down at the floor and then back up at me. "Actually, your name was given to me by a friend, Bethanne Hamlin."

"Bethanne," I repeated enthusiastically. "She's one of my dearest friends."

"That's what she said." Joan approached the counter, biting her lower lip. "Her daughter, Annie, is a good friend of my daughter's."

"Annie's a sweetheart."

"She's been wonderful with Amanda," Joan said, and her voice shook with emotion.

"You're Amanda's mother?" I asked, astonished that this woman had walked into my shop at the very moment her daughter had weighed so heavily on my mind. I didn't remember whether Annie had given me Amanda's surname and, even if she had, I'm not sure I would've made the connection. "How is Amanda?" I asked, almost fearing what Joan was about to tell me.

She shrugged as if it was hard to explain. "She's doing about as well as can be expected. The physicians are optimistic, but they're in and out of her room. They don't spend the time with her that I do. They don't see how sick she is and how she struggles each and every day." Tears glistened in Joan's eyes. "I'm the one at Amanda's bedside, the one who sees what it's really like for her. She hides it from everyone else, even her friends."

"I remember," I said and gently placed my hand over hers. It was my father who'd sat at my bedside and, in some ways, I think the emotional agony he endured watching over me was more painful than the physical ordeal I went through myself.

"Bethanne said you had cancer as a teenager." Joan lifted her gaze until it met mine.

"I did. The first time at sixteen and then later at twenty-four."

"Twice?"

I nodded.

"This is Amanda's second bout, too. She's been in remission for so long we'd all believed—we'd all hoped—that the cancer was completely gone. I blame myself.... If I'd been paying better attention, if I hadn't been so wrapped up in my own life, then I might have recognized the signs. I should've—"

"That's not true." I didn't mean to be rude by cutting her off. But I'd heard my parents discussing this very topic, looking for blame when there was none to be found. It was a frustrating, pointless exercise.

I motioned for Joan to sit down. The door opened again and the bell chimed. Margaret had obviously overheard part of our conversation because she stepped out from the office and hurried over to assist the customer.

"Would you care for some coffee?" I asked.

Joan hesitated. "I don't want to take you away from your store."

"It'll be fine. My sister, Margaret, is here." I could tell she wanted to chat; at the same time, I was grateful because I had information to impart. "How do you like your coffee?"

"Black, please."

I went into the office and filled two mugs, then carried

them to the table at the back of the store. Joan had already taken a seat, and I sat across from her.

"I can't tell you how much I appreciate this. When Bethanne said she knew a cancer survivor, I felt the strongest urge to talk to you. I don't know why or what you could possibly tell me, but something or rather Someone urged me to seek you out." She lowered her head as though a bit embarrassed. "I've been doing a lot of talking to God lately."

"I did, too, and I know my parents also prayed a great deal when I was sick. Believe it or not, I consider that closeness to God one of the benefits of cancer. It shoves everything else aside and forces us to focus on our priorities."

Joan held my gaze an extra-long moment. "Priorities," she murmured. "Cancer sets those straight, all right."

"Tell me more about how Amanda's doing."

She nodded and then released a deep sigh. "Medically, she's on schedule, according to the physicians. We won't know anything, really, until after the bone-marrow transplant."

"You have a donor?"

Again Joan nodded. "Her brother is a match, thank God."

I wasn't all that familiar with leukemia, although I was better informed than some registered nurses when it came to malignant brain tumors. I knew more than I'd ever wanted to about those. However, I lacked knowledge of other cancers.

"How's she doing emotionally?"

The dark circles beneath Joan's eyes seemed more pronounced. "Her boyfriend broke up with her last month."

"How did she handle it?" I remembered how I'd felt. I'd gone through several stages when Roger and I broke up. I started off angry and then I'd wrapped myself in self-pity and wept for days on end. It was a long while before I could look at the relationship with any perspective. In retrospect I realized that, although it had been difficult at the time, ultimately it was for the best.

Amanda's mother managed a half smile, her first since entering the shop. "I'm surprised by how well Amanda took it. I thought, you know, that she'd be really upset. She seemed to like him so much. He gave up prom night to be with her." Joan shrugged as if she couldn't understand her daughter's reaction even now.

"Amanda has more important things on her mind," I said.

A weary sadness came over Joan. "Amanda didn't attend her graduation, either, and I know she wanted to. From the minute she heard the cancer had returned, she said she had every intention of graduating with her class, but when the time came she was just too weak."

I could almost feel Joan's disappointment for her daughter.

"My husband and I were going to take her in a wheelchair so she could at least be with her friends, but Amanda said no, she'd rather not." Joan's eyes moistened and she bit her lower lip hard enough to make me wince.

"Just before you dropped by, I was talking to my sister about Amanda."

"You were?"

I smiled. "Annie came to see me a few weeks ago, when she found out about Amanda's illness, and we had a long talk. There are plenty of support groups that offer emotional encouragement for parents. I hope you and your husband have been able to avail yourselves of those, because it's important for your marriage and your own emotional health."

"We have."

"Good." I hadn't taken a sip of coffee yet and paused to do so. "Have you heard of Melissa's Living Legacy Foundation?" I asked next.

Joan shook her head.

"I discovered this site on the internet and I think it would be worth looking at—for both you and Amanda. Melissa Sengbusch was a teenage girl who died of cancer in 2000. Her mother founded the organization to help other teenagers experiencing the same things her daughter did. I was deeply impressed when I read Melissa's story. She lived an inspiring life and her mother's working hard to give other teenagers hope. Teenagers with cancer have special needs."

"I didn't know such an organization existed. You're

right. Teenagers are different. My husband and I were just discussing this the other day—how we can let Amanda be Amanda, especially while she's in the hospital. She feels she's too old to be on the pediatric ward, but we don't feel right having her in the adult ward, either."

"This is one of the very issues the website addresses. Promise me you'll check it out."

"I will. Oh, Lydia, I feel so much better just talking to you."

Margaret approached the table then. I knew she'd been listening in on the conversation, but it didn't bother me.

"Are there other children?" she asked.

Joan reached for a tissue and dabbed her eyes. "We have a son, too."

"How's he dealing with all this?"

"Joe's been great. He said he'd be willing to do whatever he could to help his sister, and he has."

Margaret crossed her arms. "Try to be aware of his needs, too. Make sure they don't get ignored. It's easy to let it happen, you know. He might not feel comfortable coming to you when you're already burdened with everything Amanda's going through."

Joan looked at me and then back at Margaret. "I'll do my best to see that doesn't happen," she said quietly.

The bell chimed and another customer entered the shop.

Margaret seemed relieved to have an excuse to abandon us.

The bell chimed again and Joan stood. "I've taken enough of your time. I'm so grateful to you, Lydia. And I'll check out that website you mentioned right away."

I watched as Joan left and hoped she followed through on that. After logging onto Melissa's Living Legacy, I knew there was something else I could do. This was important, and I was sure that once I told Brad and Margaret, they'd both agree.

CHAPTER
~SIX~

The regimen of chemotherapy was finished now. It'd been so hellish, Amanda sometimes thought the cure was worse than the disease. She'd lost weight and all her hair, but she'd slowly begun to regain her strength. The hospital was preparing her for the second stage of this healing process.

Funny, when she was eight years old and had cancer she'd never really thought she would die. She knew she was sick and that her mother cried a lot, but the possibility of dying hadn't even entered her mind. It did now. People died every day. People her age. She could be one of them.

When the cancer came back, it'd been a shock—to everyone. The difference this time was that Amanda knew what she faced. Although she was only a kid before, she'd learned a lot more about the disease than she'd realized. This second bout was more serious than the first, and chemo and radiation weren't enough. The treatment was more intense, lengthier, scarier.

Closing her eyes, Amanda tried to think positive thoughts. She'd made that big announcement to her parents early on, about fighting the cancer but not fighting death. She'd meant every word and she *was* fighting, harder than she'd dreamed possible. What she hadn't recognized at the time was how badly she wanted to live. Even though her friends had dwindled down to relatively few, and Lance, her bastard boyfriend, had walked out on her. Okay, she'd given him permission, but what other choice did she have? Her feelings toward him weren't nearly as gracious these days. If he'd had the slightest idea of what love was about, he wouldn't have taken up with Ellie. Instead, he'd be with her, lending her his strength, encouraging her, loving her. But he was gone, like so many others.

Annie claimed Lance wasn't worth the emotion. Not that she had much emotion to spare. Isolated as she was, Amanda had come to know herself well. She wanted to leave this hospital one day in the future and live a relatively normal life.

What was normal, anyway? Amanda no longer had any idea. She'd taken so much for granted. Until a few months ago, she'd been normal, lived a normal life, but she hadn't appreciated it. Someone with cancer took very little for granted.

Here it was, the middle of summer and the sun was shining and she was stuck in a hospital room by herself. Her steroid treatments had started and soon her face would swell up, become moon-shaped, grotesque. The thought of anyone seeing her with her features all distorted appalled her. This was so much worse than she'd expected. She hadn't known until she saw the others. They looked gross.

There was another problem. Amanda's parents were almost constantly at her side. If Amanda so much as hinted that she wanted a milkshake or a book or the latest CD, her mother or father made it happen. That cloying attention drove her to distraction. Amanda had sent her mother out of the room this afternoon, pleading with her to go home and make dinner. She also called her father and asked him not to visit her that evening, claiming exhaustion. She wanted her parents to have a normal night together. Her dad usually arrived at the hospital after work and spent a few hours; Amanda couldn't remember the last time her parents had actually left her before eight or nine in the evening. They liked to be available, they said, to make sure she ate everything in order to keep up her strength.

Now that her mother had gone home, the peace was wonderful, but at the same time, Amanda felt terribly, terribly alone. She wanted Annie. And although she'd never openly admit it, she wanted Lance back, too. She hated the thought of him with Ellie. They'd been the perfect couple,

Amanda and Lance. Everyone had said so; and now everyone had forgotten her.

A nurse entered the room. It was Wendy, her favorite, who didn't seem that much older than Amanda. Wendy was old in cancer years, though; she'd seen it all before. Amanda figured that was why Wendy so often knew what she was feeling.

"Hello, Amanda," Wendy said as she approached her bed and checked the IV tube. It was hooked to a monitoring machine—this was something new since her last visit at age eight. Three bags hung from the contraption, and each was connected to a digital monitor. She wasn't sure what all those numbers meant, nor did she care.

"Hi," she mumbled back, turning her head so she wouldn't have to see what Wendy was planning to subject her to next.

"Hey, what's that glum face all about?"

"Want to trade places?" Amanda asked sarcastically.

Wendy didn't respond immediately. "Not today."

"That's what I thought."

Wendy moved to the other side of the bed. "Do you want to talk about it?" she asked in a gentle, concerned way.

Amanda clenched her teeth and shook her head.

"It might help."

"No, thanks."

Wendy hesitated. "I saw Annie get off the elevator a few minutes ago."

Amanda's mood instantly brightened, but then she re-membered Annie's last visit. It'd been humiliating. Bad enough that she'd finally caught on to the fact that Annie and her parents coordinated their visits. Annie only came by when Amanda's mother wasn't there. Even worse, though, was the incident with the CD Annie had brought.

"Do you know how mortified I was the other day?" she asked the nurse. "My friend's visiting me, and then some old biddy comes rushing into the room and tells me I've got to turn down the music? I felt like I was back in grade school."

"I'm sorry, Amanda, but you're not the only patient on this ward."

"The music wasn't that loud," Amanda protested. "I suppose if I'd been listening to Frank Sinatra, it would've been perfectly fine."

"Well, there *are* a number of older patients here." Wendy patted her hand. "Anyway, you told me you didn't like being on the pediatric ward."

"I didn't. I'm not a kid who appreciates being serenaded by a troop of Boy Scouts. I know they meant well, and the other kids really enjoyed it, but I'm almost eighteen years old—an adult."

"Which is why we moved you to the adult ward," Wendy reminded her.

"I know." Amanda had asked, pleaded actually, to be transferred shortly after the clown had come to her room. He'd done some stupid tricks, and then, to add insult to injury, he'd twisted pink and purple balloons into the shape of a French poodle in her honor. She was supposed to wear that idiotic thing on her bald head. *Very* funny.

Wendy seemed to have trouble holding back a smile. "As I recall, you described that nice clown as a form of cruel and unusual punishment, and you asked what you'd done to deserve it."

Amanda almost smiled herself. "You're right, I did."

"So we transferred you. It might not seem like it, but we really do want you to feel as comfortable and relaxed as possible."

Amanda felt bad about her grumpy mood. "I know."

"Chin up," Wendy said, encouraging her with a warm smile. "It's practically over and then you'll be home with your family and friends. All of this will be behind you."

Amanda nodded, although she understood it wasn't that simple. From this point onward, everything would be different. Any hope of living a completely normal life was forever gone. The long-term effects of the chemotherapy were depressing, and there'd be drugs to take for the rest of her life. She couldn't allow herself to think about it, otherwise she'd want to give up, and she was determined to fight this disease and win.

No sooner had Wendy left the room than Annie walked in. Amanda had never had a friend as good as Annie. Two years ago they'd barely known each other, even though they were in the same year. That was the period Annie referred to as the Dark Years, shortly after her parents' divorce. Annie had been furious with her father and tried to destroy everything that was positive in her life. She'd dropped out of the swim team and started hanging with a questionable group at school.

Something happened over that summer, Amanda was never sure exactly what. When Annie returned for their junior year, she was almost back to her old self. She'd become friends with a new girl in school named Courtney, who was in the senior class. Amanda didn't remember her last name. She recalled that Courtney and Annie's older brother had been an item. They'd both graduated since and gone to different schools. She should ask Annie if they were still involved.

Then in the last trimester of their junior year, Amanda and Annie were in earth sciences together and were also chosen to be part of the yearbook staff.

They'd met after school a few times and Amanda had volunteered to help Annie and her mother with the party business. That had been a lot of fun. All through senior year, they'd remained friends. Even now...

Amanda closed her eyes again, mentally readying herself for this next confrontation. She didn't want to do it, but she just couldn't let anyone—well, other than her parents—see her once she started to look like a...a gargoyle or something during the next stage of treatment. And that included Annie. She heard her friend enter the room and considered pretending she was asleep. She couldn't do that, though.

When she opened her eyes, Annie had made herself comfortable in the bedside chair, flipping through a magazine. She smiled and stood the moment she saw that Amanda was awake.

"How's it going?" she asked. She was wearing a bright pink summer dress with big white flowers and matching pink sandals.

Amanda stared past her. "All right, I guess. Why do people always ask that?" she demanded. "How do you *think* it's going? I'm in the hospital. I'm about to have a bone-marrow transplant and get stuck in an isolation chamber for God knows how long."

Annie raised her eyebrows. "My, my, aren't we in a testy mood this afternoon."

"Out in the sunshine, were you?"

Annie nodded. "I was working a birthday party with Mom. It was a ten-year-old girl and she wanted a Bratz theme."

Amanda knew the teenage dolls were popular with the younger set. Annie's mother had at least a dozen inventive party themes; Amanda's favorite was the Alice in Wonderland tea party.

"I had sixteen ten-year-olds screaming in my ear all afternoon, so don't you start," Annie joked.

With an effort, Amanda sent her friend a weak smile. "Listen, I've been thinking that you're probably getting really busy, with work and all."

"It's been like that for a while," Annie said. "No big deal."

Amanda briefly looked away. "You should have a life."

"I do."

Annie wasn't making this easy. "When's the last time you went out with friends?"

"Saturday night. Why?"

"Because."

Annie's eyes narrowed as if she'd suddenly caught Amanda's drift. "Are you trying to get rid of me?"

Finally. "Not exactly," Amanda said, being careful not to hurt her friend's feelings.

"What is that supposed to mean?"

"It means," Amanda elaborated, "that things are changing for me."

"In what way?"

"Steroids."

Annie stared at Amanda, her gaze blank. She made a circular motion with her hand. "And?"

"You don't know?" Amanda hated having to spell it out. "My face is going to swell up to gigantic proportions. In a little while, a few days, I don't know how long, I'm going to look like a freak."

"I see. And that's supposed to frighten me off?"

"No," Amanda cried. "Why are you making this so hard?"

Annie seemed utterly baffled.

"Don't you understand?" She was struggling not to cry.

"I don't want you to see me like that…. I don't want *anyone* to see me. It's going to be horrible and then later…later I'll be in isolation."

"I've already talked to the nurse about that," Annie said. "I can still visit but you'll be behind this glass and—"

"It'll be like visiting someone in prison."

"No, it won't," Annie insisted. "I'll be coming to see my dearest and best friend. You've been through so much already," she said. "You're the bravest person I've ever known."

"Don't say that," Amanda pleaded, her voice quaking. She was afraid she really would break into tears.

"I mean it. You can make a big fuss, say whatever you want, but it isn't going to make any difference to me. You're my friend, and I'm not leaving. I need you."

"No, you don't."

Annie shook her head. "Don't argue with me. I want you to be in my wedding and I plan on being in yours. You're a friend for life, so just accept it."

Amanda covered her face with both hands. "Go away."

"Sorry, did you say something? Because I can't hear you." Annie sank down in the chair next to Amanda's bed and reached for the magazine, which she opened and resumed reading. It was one of the teen magazines, filled with the latest celebrity gossip they loved to read.

Amanda ignored her, although she was dying to get her hands on this issue.

"Oh, my goodness, you won't believe it," Annie gasped.

She uncrossed her legs and leaned forward as if in shock. "Madonna's pregnant again—with Britney Spears's baby."

"What?" Amanda's jaw dropped open.

Annie waved her index finger. "Gotcha."

Amanda wanted to be mad, but she laughed instead. "That was ridiculous."

"It got your attention, didn't it?"

Amanda had to admit it did.

Annie's eyes sobered as she put down the magazine. "Amanda, I'm serious. It doesn't matter to me what you look like when the steroids kick in. I'm not that kind of friend and you aren't, either. If I was the one going through this, you'd be here for me."

Amanda sighed. "I don't know," she whispered, being as honest as she could.

"What do you mean?"

"Just what I said," she returned, her voice gaining strength. "I thought Heather and Jenna were my friends, too, but they're gone. Lance is gone. You and Laurie are the only ones who even make the effort to come and see me anymore."

"We're your true friends," Annie said.

"I just wonder if I'd be as good to you as you've been to me."

"You would," Annie said without a hint of doubt. "Besides, the worst is over." She got up and hopped onto the edge of Amanda's bed. "It's going to be clear sailing from here on out."

"Well, I don't know…" But now that Amanda had completed her chemotherapy, she'd begun to feel a tiny, new sense of hope. "I don't really think it could get much worse than it's already been."

"It won't." Annie sounded so positive, Amanda could almost believe her.

CHAPTER
SEVEN

LYDIA HOFFMAN GOETZ

I'd spent so many hours in front of the computer Sunday evening that my vision had started to blur. I felt Brad's hand on my shoulder. Covering it with my own, I looked up at him.

"What time is it?" I asked. My husband tended to be the night owl, not me. He often stayed up to watch the news and Jay Leno. I tried to join him but was usually too tired.

"Almost eleven-thirty," he said and yawned. "I've got work in the morning. Are you ready for bed?"

I was and I wasn't. I'd logged onto the computer right after Cody had gone to bed around nine, and those two and a half hours had passed in the blink of an eye. "I've been on discussion boards," I explained, twisting around in order to talk to him. "Oh, Brad, I just felt I had to give these teens some hope." I'd typed so fast my hands ached and my fingers could barely keep up with my thoughts. Many of the teens I'd met on the boards were in a state of despair. I heard the fear and anxiety in their messages.

"Where are these discussion boards?" he asked.

"On that website I mentioned—teenslivingwithcancer. org. It's part of Melissa's Living Legacy. She's the teenage girl I told you about who died a few years back. Melissa asked her mother to help other teenagers who were going through cancer. She wanted to make a difference, and she left this request with her mother, who took on the task and did a magnificent job. Because of Melissa, a lot of kids now have a voice. They're able to connect with one another and become their own support group."

"You're really passionate about this, aren't you?" Brad said, and he gave me the sweetest smile, as if he knew something I didn't.

"What?" I asked, not knowing what he meant.

"You," he said, his face alive with love. "I wish I had a mirror so I could show you to yourself. Your eyes are bright and intense, and I think, my dear wife, that you've just stumbled on something that's going to change your life."

I hadn't realized it until just that moment, but Brad was right. "I want to be a positive influence for these teens. I was one of them. I understand what they're enduring. I've suffered the same way they're suffering now, and I can give them hope. I can encourage them."

Brad leaned toward me. "Then do it." He yawned a second time, hiding his mouth. "Ready for bed?" he asked again.

I nodded and shut down the computer, but my mind was racing, with ideas and memories and hopes. "All these years," I mumbled, unaware I'd spoken aloud.

"All these years what?" Brad slipped his arm around my waist as I stood up and we headed toward our bedroom.

I hesitated as I considered my reply, and he stopped, too. I was slightly uncomfortable with this confession. "I used to hate telling anyone I had cancer. I didn't want people to know unless it was absolutely necessary."

Brad's soft laugh followed my painful admission. "Tell me about it! I remember when you told me that first time. Your body language said *warning, danger, stay away,* I've had cancer, so beware—don't get too close."

"It did not!" I said, laughing at my husband's exaggeration.

The smile left his eyes. "Lydia, you did. It was as if you assumed that because you'd had cancer—twice—you weren't entitled to a real life. You pushed me away with both hands. Lucky for you, I don't take rejection personally. I wanted to get to know you and eventually I wore you down."

I was grateful for that. Still, what he'd said gave me pause. Because of my medical history, I'd lived a sheltered life. No one could blame me for being cautious; if you've fallen through the ice not once but twice, you don't step onto a frozen lake without trepidation. That was how it was for me. I was cautious, afraid...and then my father died.

Without Dad standing guard over me, I felt unsteady. But I knew I had to step out of my small, protected world and live, really live. As I've often said, opening my yarn store was an affirmation of life. I wanted to stand on the street corner and shout, "I'm alive! Come and look at me. I'm a normal person with dreams and aspirations." That's what A Good Yarn was all about. Brad's words confused me.

"I wasn't *ashamed* of my cancer," I insisted after a moment. "All I ever wanted was to be normal." The teens I'd met that evening felt the same way. I read that again and again on the discussion boards. These kids were describing exactly what I'd felt when I was their age. To be different, to have this disease, set us apart. Like me, they were overwhelmed by the consequences of their illness.

Many of them were wise beyond their years. The things they'd written had deeply touched me, and I knew I wanted to help. I *needed* to help. Like Melissa, I, too, wanted to make a difference.

Wearing my nightgown, I sat down on the side of the bed and tried to explain. "After each remission, especially the second, I made an effort to put the cancer out of my mind entirely," I said to Brad. "I longed to pretend it had never happened, although that wasn't easy. I told myself I'd move forward with my life and not look back."

"And you feel differently now?" Brad asked as he climbed into bed.

"Now...now I understand how wrong that thinking was. I feel I have something to offer and that I'd miss out on a wonderful blessing if I ignored it."

I climbed under the sheets, too, and nestled against my husband. When Brad had turned off the light, he wrapped his arm around me. "You're making progress in stepping out of your comfort zone—although I guess it was more of a *discomfort* zone. You married me, didn't you?" He kissed my temple and then settled back in bed.

With my head on his shoulder, I closed my eyes and smiled, awash with contentment. Brad was a very special man, who loved me despite my fears and flaws. I realized while we were dating that it was my fears that held back the relationship. I'd given up counting the number of times Brad wanted to talk about marriage. I was the one who'd balked, continually putting him off.

Oh, there'd been a brief period when his ex-wife had re-entered the picture and I thought I'd lost him. Thankfully, nothing had come of it. That period had been difficult for both of us because Brad loved me and I loved him—so much that it frightened me. When I believed I was on the verge of losing him, I'd experienced a whole new kind of fear. It was as if life was about to cheat me again.

In that time of emotional turmoil, I made a mistake. When I was faced with the challenge presented by his ex-wife, I'd walked away. With the clarity of hindsight, I knew I should have fought for my husband and son. Without a doubt, I would now.

In a few minutes, Brad's breathing evened out and I could tell he'd fallen into a fast and peaceful sleep. Although I was physically tired, my mind remained wide-awake, popping with ideas. I'd occasionally wondered about visiting oncology centers and teaching knitting. It was while receiving lengthy chemo treatments myself that I'd first learned to knit. I began to think about that again.

A new world of possibilities had opened up to me since Annie had talked about her friend. I don't think anything happens by accident. Some greater power had sent Annie to me that day. The timing was right; I was at a point in my life where I could make a difference to these kids, and I was determined to do so.

In the morning, when the alarm rang at seven, I groaned, reluctant to get out of bed. Brad threw aside the covers and went to the kitchen to start the coffee. A few minutes later, Chase, my stepson's dog, skidded enthusiastically into our room. At Brad and Cody's urging, Chase hopped onto the bed next to me. My two men found it downright funny when Chase decided to lick my face. Apparently even the dog couldn't stand the sight of me lazing away in bed. There are advantages and disadvantages to living in an all-male household. One of the disadvantages is the way they find amusement in the most unlikely situations. I've concluded that there's something unremittingly juvenile about most male humor.

"Are you ready to get up yet, or do I need to get Whiskers, too?" Brad asked, hands on his hips.

"Very funny." I shoved Chase away and rolled onto my back. It helped that the sun was shining; when the sun's out in the Pacific Northwest, there's no place lovelier on earth.

"I'm up, I'm up," I muttered.

"I've got camp today," Cody reminded me. This was a compromise for our son, who felt, at age ten, that he was way too old to go to day care during the summer months. Brad and I had found a day camp that offered a variety of activities we knew Cody would enjoy. Although it was early August, Cody was still excited about going off to camp every morning. If this continued, heading back to school in a few weeks would be a major disappointment.

"What are your plans for the day?" Brad asked as he brought me a cup of coffee and set it on my nightstand.

Oh, how my men spoil me. There might be disadvantages in being the only woman in a household of men but there are significant advantages, too. I sat up in bed, reached for the cup and leaned against the headboard. I sipped my coffee, listening to the classical music playing softly on the clock radio, luxuriating in my morning ritual. Because my yarn store is open on Saturdays, I close on Sundays and Mondays. "I'm going into the shop. I have a lot of paperwork to catch up on this morning," I said.

"I'll probably have a delivery to make on Blossom Street around midmorning," Brad said. He was already dressed for work. We took turns dropping Cody off at camp, and it was my turn.

"Come in for a coffee," I invited. While we were dating, Brad often stopped by for coffee. I'd go into the office to pour him a cup and he'd follow me—to steal a kiss. Marriage hadn't changed his habit of visiting me at work, and I was glad.

"This afternoon I thought I'd walk over to the hospital," I said, watching for his reaction.

"Which hospital?" Brad asked.

"The one where Annie's friend is having her treatments."

Brad grinned as if he'd known what I planned to say.

The instant Cody heard the word *hospital,* he flew into the room. "Mom's going to the hospital?"

"To ask if I can volunteer and to visit a friend," I said. Amanda wasn't a friend yet, but she soon would be. I knew she'd undergone the bone-marrow transplant; Bethanne had told me. I also knew that Annie had taken my advice and stayed in close contact with Amanda. She and another girl were the only two who'd stood by Amanda's side throughout the whole ordeal. I was proud of Annie, and Bethanne was, too. This was exactly what Melissa's Living Legacy meant—teens helping other teens.

Brad didn't seem surprised by my decision to volunteer. I could see from the look in his eyes that he approved.

"You aren't going to have a baby?" Cody asked. His face fell with disappointment.

"Cody," Brad chastised and the two of us exchanged a mournful glance.

This was one sad effect of my cancer—and the treatments that had cured me. *Saved* me. There would be no babies for Brad and me. Brad and I had discussed adopting, but because we were still newlyweds, the agency wanted to be sure the relationship was stable before they considered us as candidates. I'm in my thirties now, and so is Brad. If they do decide to let us have a child, it won't be for several years.

Infertility was just one more factor these teenage girls faced. And many of the boys, too. It wasn't anything they needed to concern themselves with yet. I know they're thinking about it, though. I can't really speak for the boys, but I can imagine their emotions about this. I am, of course, familiar with what a girl would feel. It's disquieting to any woman, no matter what her age, to know she might never have the choice to be a mother.

I'd only recently learned I was infertile. All along, I'd suspected the chemotherapy had destroyed my chances of having a family. It was another thing cancer had stolen from me, and I'd taken the news hard. I'm just grateful to have a wonderful husband who comforted me. He suggested adoption, and we're going to pursue it. But if we're not successful, I won't let it ruin my life.

We'd put the matter in God's hands and were prepared to accept His decision.

"What are you volunteering for at the hospital?" Cody asked. "I know what that word means," he added proudly.

I smiled at him. "I'm hoping to help teenagers who have cancer."

"But what can you do?" He frowned a little, as if this worried him.

Brad kissed me on the cheek, rubbed the top of his son's head and said, "Gotta go."

"Bye, Dad." Cody sounded a bit distracted.

"Bye, Cody."

Our eyes met, and my husband whispered, "See you later, Beautiful." He gave me a little wave and left the bedroom. I heard him walking down the hall.

Cody returned his attention to me. "But how are you going to help teenagers?" he asked.

"I'm working on that," I told him. "I want to encourage them and be there for them." I'd emailed Melissa's Living Legacy Foundation to find out exactly what I could do. I'd explained that I understood the problems of being a teenager with cancer because I'd been one. Perhaps I could help educate health care professionals, too.

Cody gave me a quirky look. "I know why my dad loves you so much," he said, his face thoughtful.

"Why is that?" I asked.

"Because you have a really big heart."

I hugged my stepson. "That's so I can love *you* so much," I told him.

CHAPTER
⚛—EIGHT—⚛

If Amanda never saw the inside of a hospital again, she'd be happy for the rest of her life. In a day, two at the most, she'd be officially discharged and could go home. Home was her family and her friends. Home was where she had her own room and her own things that she could touch and feel and hold and treasure. Home was located in the land of normal.

If she died—if the cancer got her despite all the chemo and the steroids and the bone-marrow transplant—Amanda wanted her family to understand that she refused to die here in this sterile environment. It was her highest and most important goal. She wanted to leave this hospital and never come back. It didn't matter how cute the doctors were. Not a single one of them was worth stepping foot inside this place again.

The nurses and other staff were great. Amanda's feelings weren't personal. It was the disease itself that had driven her to think this way. She would always associate the hospital with cancer, and it was an association she desperately wanted to break.

No matter what was happening to her blood, she told herself she was better. She prayed with everything in her that her body would accept Joe's bone marrow. So far it looked promising. She knew that simply from what she saw on the physicians' faces as they read her charts.

As for feeling stronger and having more energy, Amanda *thought* she did but she wasn't sure. Funny how easily your brain could fool you. She'd been fooled before. She was trying not to set herself up for disappointment, so she didn't demand answers from any of the doctors. She left that to her parents. She didn't ask them questions, either; she was afraid they'd only tell her what she wanted to hear.

Annie would be coming later in the day and although it was only midmorning, Amanda was already looking forward to seeing her. She owed Annie so much; Annie had taught her what it meant to be a friend. On her last visit they'd had a blast. Through her mother's party business, Annie had gotten wigs in every color and style. There must have been twenty of them. Together they'd tried them all on and laughed themselves silly.

Amanda had found it difficult to keep the wigs on her head. Being bald was a real detriment there. The wig would slip to one side and then forward until it reached the bridge of her nose. They'd laugh and laugh and giggle some more. Amanda had lost count of the number of times the nurses had come into the room and asked them to keep the noise down. They'd honestly tried, but to no avail.

Amanda had forgotten how good it felt to laugh. Someone wise—she thought it was a man called Norman Cousins—had written a book about the healing properties of laughter. After Annie's visit, she believed that. For the first time since she'd been admitted, she'd slept through the entire night. Laughing had worn her out. It'd been a delicious feeling and so…she'd almost come to hate this word…so normal.

A quiet knock sounded at her door and Amanda turned to discover a petite woman with shoulder-length dark hair and brown eyes standing just inside her doorway. She didn't recognize her but felt that perhaps she should.

"Are you Amanda Jennings?" the other woman asked.

Amanda nodded. "Should I know you?"

The other woman's smile drew her into a warm embrace. "There's no reason you should. My name is Lydia Goetz."

The name wasn't familiar to Amanda.

"I own a yarn store in Blossom Street."

"Oh, yes," Amanda breathed, as everything clicked into place. "My friend Annie went to talk to you because you had cancer as a teenager, too." Amanda gestured for her to come into the room.

"You look good."

Amanda dismissed the compliment and rested one hand on her bald head. "I look better with hair."

Lydia agreed with a slight smile. "Most of us do. I was referring to the color in your cheeks."

Amanda avoided mirrors whenever she could. The wig session with Annie had been the one exception to that. As soon as she'd started taking the steroids and the swelling had begun, Amanda decided it was better for her own peace of mind to remain as uninformed as possible about her appearance.

"At least you didn't ask how I'm feeling," Amanda said, then made a face. "Sorry, that's a pet peeve of mine."

"Don't you *hate* that?" Lydia cried. "You'd think people would get a clue. You're in the hospital and you're afraid you've already got one foot in the grave and someone bebops into your room like it's a garden party and asks you a stupid question like that."

This was exactly how Amanda felt and she was delighted to have her sentiments echoed by someone else. Someone who'd been there.... "They did that to you, too?"

"Oh, yes." Lydia set down her purse and knitting bag. "Even worse is when a friend sits at your bedside and complains because she's broken a fingernail."

Amanda rolled her eyes. "People can be *so* insensitive."

"They mean well," Lydia reminded her, "it's just that

they don't have any idea. A broken fingernail isn't a disaster. It isn't going to tear your life apart."

Amanda nodded. "Cancer does that."

"Yes, it does. It tore mine apart twice."

"Twice." Amanda paid close attention now.

"Yup, I'm a two-time winner," Lydia said, "and so are you."

Amanda wasn't so sure about that, but... "How old are you?" she asked.

"Thirty-four."

"Wow."

Lydia was smiling. "Is that old?"

"In cancer years, you bet." Amanda had gotten curious and done a little research one day, using some medical periodicals from the hospital library. What she'd learned depressed her. "The first time I had cancer I was eight."

"That's young."

Far too young, Amanda agreed, but she'd known children who'd had it much younger. "I remember the names of some of the other kids I was in the hospital with. I used to get together with a couple of the girls for our birthdays and stuff, and then we stopped meeting. I recently found out why." A lump formed in her throat and she swallowed hard. "They both died, and my mother never told me."

"I'm sorry," Lydia whispered gently. Tears gathered in her eyes.

"Why them and not me?" It was a question that had gone repeatedly through her mind.

Lydia shook her head. "I can't answer that any more than you can."

"I'm probably going to die, too." She might as well accept the truth of that now. The likelihood of surviving another five years wasn't good.

To Amanda's surprise, Lydia nodded. "There's about a one-hundred percent chance that you're right. The thing is, we all die."

"You know what I mean."

"I do," Lydia said, "but what makes you assume it'll be anytime soon?"

"I'm looking at my odds compared to other people with this kind of cancer, and I can see that—"

"Looking at your odds is a bad idea," Lydia said, cutting her off. "It'll drive you nuts. If so and so had cancer twice by age eighteen, then died at twenty-two, I should live another sixteen months, and so on and so on. I've played that game and, trust me, it goes nowhere. Take my advice and don't do it."

"You did that, too?" No matter how many times she tried to avoid it, she found herself making those comparisons. Amanda had thought she was the only one. No one needed to tell her it was a stupid thing to do, but she couldn't stop. Whenever she came across statistics or heard about someone else's survival, she automatically started calculating her chances of having a *normal* life after this—there was that word again. *Normal.* For someone with cancer, nothing was ever normal again.

Lydia's sigh was deep enough to raise her shoulders. "Everyone does. I forced myself to stop, and look at me—I'm thirty-four. Furthermore, I have my own business."

"You're married, too." Amanda had noticed the ring.

"Married with children," Lydia boasted proudly. "Or rather, child."

This was beyond anything Amanda had hoped for. "You had a baby?"

"I have a stepson who's as much a part of me as if I'd given birth to him. I'm his mother. Yes, he has a biological mother, but she's rarely around." She paused. "Cody knows how much I love him."

Amanda hadn't dared to dream she could ever have that much. Still, she wasn't completely convinced. After two bouts with cancer, the future didn't seem that promising. It remained cloudy. Dark. Uncertain.

"I don't know if I'll make it to thirty-four," she said and meant it. This wasn't a ploy so Lydia would quickly dismiss the notion. This was the naked-as-her-bald-head truth.

"Who knows?" Lydia asked without a qualm. "We might both make it to eighty. Or older."

That would be a miracle of biblical magnitude, as far as Amanda was concerned.

"On the other hand, I could get run over by a taxi on my way out the door. Life doesn't have any guarantees. If you're looking for one, then shop at Sears. For me, it's a day at a time. Yes, the cancer might come back. I had a scare a couple of years ago when another tumor was detected."

"What happened?" Amanda whispered.

"It was benign."

"What if it hadn't been?"

Lydia didn't hesitate. "Then I'd be dead now." Surprisingly, she smiled. "But I would've gone knowing I'd done something I'd always wanted to do, which was to open a yarn store. I'd fallen in love, too."

"You knew your husband then?"

"We'd met and dated a few times, and I loved him, really loved him. These feelings were a lot more intense than anything I'd experienced with anyone else."

Amanda didn't want to ask this question, but she needed to know. "If...if the tumors had been cancerous would he...this man you loved and married, would he have stayed with you?"

Lydia's face relaxed into a soft smile. "His name is Brad, and yes, I believe he would have." The smile went away. "I take it your boyfriend broke up with you?"

Amanda stared down at her hands and nodded. Her feelings toward Lance were mixed. She'd been hurt and disappointed by him. It was crazy; the last thing she wanted was for Lance to see her like this, bloated and bald, yet she wished he'd come back. She missed him and loved him. Half the time she referred to him as the bastard and the other half she dreamed he'd return to her and beg her forgiveness.

"There's someone out there who's going to love you, Amanda."

She started to argue, but Lydia stopped her.

"I speak from experience on this one. I lost two loves-of-my-life and was convinced it would never happen for me."

Amanda would believe it when it happened for her; until then she was reserving judgment. Despite enjoying Lydia's visit, she yawned, drained of energy.

"I never did tell you the reason I came," Lydia said. "Let me do that, and then I'll go."

Amanda nodded sleepily.

"I talked to the hospital staff and described Melissa's Living Legacy Foundation. I think your mom told you about it?" When Amanda nodded again, Lydia continued. "I'm going to help raise money so the hospital can provide teenagers who can't afford them with laptops. That way they can log onto the message boards. Communication will help."

"You mean I'd be able to link up with other teenagers who have cancer and talk to them about…anything?"

"Absolutely."

Amanda was thrilled. "That would be great!"

"The head of oncology thought so, too." Lydia beamed.

"Wow!" Lydia had already been hard at work. "Yeah," she added, "my mom did tell me about Melissa. I was planning to check it out when I got home. But it'd be even better if kids could do it while they're still in the hospital."

Lydia agreed. "At some point in the future I'm going to be talking with staff here about the special needs of adolescents with cancer. My hope is that they'll set aside an area for teenagers to meet their friends and chat, play music, whatever."

"You mean taking us out of the pediatric ward *and* the adult ward?" That would be perfect.

"I might need a bit of help convincing the powers-that-be that this is necessary. This is where you come in."

Amanda didn't need to think about it. "I'll do whatever I can, and I know a few other kids who'll volunteer, too."

"Wonderful." Lydia looked really pleased. "Rest now, and I'll be in touch. We'll talk more later."

"Okay. Only..." She hesitated, not sure how to ask. "Why are you doing this? I mean, it's really cool and everything, but why now? You're not a teenager anymore."

"Far from it," Lydia said readily. "Why am I doing this?" she repeated. Her eyes grew serious. "I'm doing it to help a mother keep a promise to her daughter. A very special daughter and an equally special mother."

That was a good enough reason for Amanda. She wanted to be part of it, too.

CHAPTER
∾ NINE ∾

Amanda and Annie walked along the Seattle water-front. It was only two weeks since Amanda had been released from the hospital, and her energy level was still low. Annie knew that and they strolled at a leisurely pace.

"I can't tell you how good the sunshine feels," Amanda said, pausing to gaze up at the sky. "Let's sit for a while," she suggested.

"Sure." Sensitive to her friend's needs, Annie was immediately prepared to stop.

They found a bench and sat facing the dark green waters of Elliott Bay in Puget Sound. The breeze off the water had a briny scent, and the sky was as blue as Annie had ever seen it. A white-and-green Washington State ferry glided toward the end of the pier; there was a long line of vehicles waiting to board for the next sailing.

"Tell me when you're feeling tired," Annie said urgently.

Amanda smiled, and again turned her face skyward, letting the sun bathe her in warmth and light. Annie closed her eyes and did the same thing. Amanda wore the hat Bethanne had knit for her, and it nearly slipped from her head.

Annie knew that beneath the lime-green hat, Amanda's hair resembled peach fuzz. It was already apparent that when it did grow back, it would be in tight curls. That was kind of funny, since Amanda's hair had always been straight as a broomstick. Apparently one of the side effects of chemotherapy was that when hair returned, it was often completely different from the way it had been before.

"Want to go to a movie?" Annie asked.

Amanda took a long time to consider that suggestion. "I hope you won't mind if I say no. I feel like I've been in a dark place for so long, I want to soak up as much of this fresh air and sunshine as I possibly can."

Annie didn't mind at all. The only reason she'd suggested it was that sitting in a theatre wouldn't drain her friend's energy. "I want to do whatever you want," Annie assured her. This was one of Amanda's first times out, and Annie was trying not to overtax her.

"I don't need to *do* anything," Amanda explained.

"That's okay, too."

"Is it?" Amanda asked. "I mean, before I was always the one who wanted to go and see and do. I thrived on being in the middle of the action. I don't feel like that anymore."

"I'm comfortable doing absolutely nothing, if you are."

"It's what I want for now."

Annie didn't fully understand this change of attitude in her friend. Amanda was different. She'd noticed that before her release from the hospital. She wasn't sure exactly why, but the friend who'd been admitted to the cancer ward wasn't the same girl who sat next to her now. Amanda had changed, and Annie guessed that in the process of being her friend, she had, too.

"The things that used to seem important don't anymore," Amanda admitted with a thoughtful frown.

"Give me an example."

"Well, Lance. I mean, okay, yeah, he broke up with me. It hurt at the time—it still kind of hurts—but my mother called it a blessing in disguise, and she was right. Naturally, I didn't see that, but now I understand what she said. Before I discovered the leukemia was back, it was just so important to have a boy in my life. It...sort of defined me. I wasn't just Amanda, I was Amanda-and-Lance. And that's wrong."

Annie knew a lot of girls felt the same way. Having a boyfriend was ultra-important, as if their identity was linked to their ability to attract someone of the opposite sex. She wasn't like that herself, although she dated lots of guys.

"Lance disappointed me," Amanda said, "yet at the same time, I didn't blame him."

Annie wasn't so willing to forgive Lance—or his new girlfriend. "I was even more upset with Ellie." By graduation, Annie could hardly keep from glaring at the other girl. She found it impossible to believe that Ellie could live with herself after what she'd done. Ellie was supposed to have been Amanda's friend. One of her best.

Amanda shook her head. "I didn't mean to get side-tracked by rehashing all the he-done-me-wrong stuff, because breaking up with Lance isn't the point." She paused as if to consider what she'd discovered about herself in the process of the breakup.

When she spoke again, her voice had gained conviction. "I'm content being who I am, cancer and all. I don't need validation from the opposite sex, and for me that's personal growth."

Annie nodded vigorously. "I know what you mean."

"I know you do," Amanda told her softly.

There was a long blast from the ferry, and a line of bicyclists boarded the vessel, pedalling onto the long ramp.

"Do you remember the summer between our sophomore and junior years?" Annie asked her. "That was a year after my dad left us and moved in with his girlfriend."

"Of course I remember."

It had been hellish for Annie and her mother. "I was furious with my father, and I blamed my mother for being such a wimp. I thought she should've done something to get him back—anything. All I wanted was my life the way it used to be." Annie didn't care if her parents still loved each other or not. She just wanted her mother and father in one place, because even if they didn't love each other, they at least loved her.

"It was a hard time for you," Amanda sympathized.

"For my entire family. The only one who seemed exempt from all the grief was my dad. He bought himself a new Cadillac and took trips to Vegas with *her*. What's funny is that now Mom, Andrew and I are the ones who are doing well." She grinned. "Hey, did I tell you my brother might get to play first string quarterback at Washington State University this fall?"

"That's fabulous!" Amanda sounded genuinely pleased.

Annie couldn't resist bragging about her brother. "He's doing great." She smiled again. "He's still in touch with Courtney. You remember her, don't you?" She didn't wait for a response. "They're really close, even though Court's in Chicago."

Last year Annie and her mother had attended every home game and cheered for Andrew. Her dad was probably somewhere in the stadium, too, Annie assumed, although she didn't know where and neither did Andrew, who had limited contact with his father.

"My mom's business has really become a success," she added.

"I think her party business was such a clever idea," Amanda said.

"It was." Annie frowned darkly. "When my dad left, he assumed Mom would get some minimum-wage job and live a dull existence without him. Dad was the center of her world, and his leaving hit her hard. She might never have regrouped if it wasn't for her Blossom Street friends."

"I really admire her."

"Mom found her niche and I'm going to tell you something that won't be announced publicly for another week." Annie had been dying to let someone know.

"About your mom?" Amanda asked.

"It's just so exciting I can hardly keep still. Mom is starting a party franchise. So many other people wanted to copy her ideas that she saw an attorney and set everything in motion. Some good friends Mom met through her knitting group are helping her with the finances, and it feels like things are really going to take off. The lawyer figures that within the next five to ten years, Mom's party franchise will be all over the country. Is that exciting or what?"

"That's wonderful!" Amanda squealed. "Just *wonderful*."

Smiling, Annie shrugged. "I shouldn't brag about my mom, but I can't help it."

"And your dad? What's your relationship with him these days?"

That was more difficult to explain. "Okay, I guess. Dad got passed over for a big promotion at his company and that set him off, so he quit and went to work for another company. The new job didn't turn out to be everything he thought it would. He isn't happy, and I don't think he and *Tiff* are getting along."

"Tiff's the woman he left your mother for, right?"

"Yeah, and it wouldn't surprise me if they ended up getting divorced, too. It's sad, you know. I think Dad had all these expectations when he left. He was going to start his life over with this younger woman and leave all his responsibilities behind." Annie gazed at the ferry, which was just pulling out. "I have this feeling he was trying to stay young, if you know what I mean."

Amanda nodded. "Do you and Andrew see him?"

"On occasion. I was supposed to spend every other weekend with him until I turned eighteen. I didn't. Tiff and I never saw eye to eye—although a lot of that was my fault. I gave her plenty of reason to dislike me. That was because I blamed her for stealing my father. My dad seems to think Mom turned Andrew and me against him. She didn't. What he doesn't get is that *he* was the one who turned against us." Annie sighed. "I don't mean to talk about my own family so much."

"No, I'm glad you did. It helps me understand why we're such good friends."

"It does?"

"We're honest with each other. We can say all kinds of things, whatever we feel, and know it's okay." Amanda threw her a quick grin. "Even before the cancer, I admired you." She looked away suddenly, as though embarrassed to be admitting this. "You just seemed to have it all together."

"Oh, hardly," Annie muttered.

"No, I mean it. You didn't let stuff bother you like I did. You just sort of let it go. I understand that now, and I think in some ways I've reached the same place."

"Really?" Annie said, nearly blushing at her friend's praise.

"Yes. You're content with yourself. It's more than just being content with who you are. There's an inner peace about you. I think it comes when you've had to walk through a hard stretch of your life. For you it was when your parents split. It must've seemed like a betrayal, so you reacted with anger. You lashed out." Amanda turned away. "When I heard I had cancer again, I did, too. But my anger didn't last long. It couldn't, because I was immediately thrust into the medical world and they took over my life. I had no choice but to submit."

"You're not the same person you were six months ago."

"You're right. I don't want to be, either. Even if I could change the last six months, I wouldn't. It wasn't easy, and yet I feel as if what I've learned about myself, my family and my friends——" she glanced significantly at Annie "——my very *good* friends, made all that suffering worth it."

By unspoken agreement they stood and began walking again, enjoying the lovely afternoon. Soon the October rains would arrive and this afternoon's azure skies would turn gray.

"I was upset with my mother when I was first diagnosed," Amanda continued. "All she seemed to do was weep, and I hated that. In the middle of the night I'd find her standing in my doorway, crying and crying."

"She hated to see you go through this."

"I know," Amanda whispered. "I feel differently about my mom now, and my dad, too. Mom fought for me. She stood up to that insurance company and demanded I get the treatment I needed. Dad had to work in order to support the family, but he came to see me almost every day, no matter how late he'd worked. It was Mom who took on the insurance people and the doctors and everyone else. Nobody did a thing to me until she understood why it was necessary, the pros and cons of the procedure, long-term effects—everything. She was a medical warrior for me. Mom wasn't the emotional wreck I assumed she was in those first few weeks. She's been my advocate, and I needed her."

"Our moms are incredible," Annie said. She'd seen her own mother in an entirely different light since that summer she'd mentioned to Amanda. Her respect for Bethanne had grown a hundredfold.

"As for friends," Amanda told her, "I know who my true friends are. They're the ones who stuck by me through all of this." She paused for a moment. "Ruth phoned me not long ago when she heard I'd been released from the hospital. She wanted to chat, and I was glad to hear from her. Sure, I was disappointed that she'd wandered away when things got really tough for me, but I was willing to overlook that."

Again Annie wasn't so sure she'd be as willing and applauded Amanda for her forgiveness.

"Then Ruth started in about getting charged too much for a skirt she bought and went on and on about this buck ninety-nine she overpaid." Amanda shook her head as if astounded even now, repeating the story.

Annie knew Ruth and it sounded just like her.

"I don't have the patience for that anymore. My mom says I have a low threshold for unimportant concerns." She laughed as she said it.

Annie smiled.

"You're my friend, Annie, a true friend. I don't know if I can ever find the words to thank you for being there for me."

"You're my friend, too," Annie told her, and it was the truth. As Amanda had said, they could tell each other anything. She didn't have a sister, but she felt Amanda was the sister of her heart.

"You introduced me to Lydia, too," Amanda reminded her.

"Lydia's the one who advised me how best to be your friend."

"She's just so impressive with everything she's doing," Amanda said. "I don't think the hospital knew what hit them. Lydia's energy has turned that entire place upside down."

Annie couldn't keep from laughing. "She's a ball of fire, all right."

"A woman with a mission." Amanda glanced at her shyly. "I'm going to be working with her, you know."

Annie was exceptionally proud of that. "My mom told me."

"We're going to make a difference."

Annie breathed in the fresh warmth of the day. "I believe you already have."

CHAPTER
~TEN~

One year later

"Hello," Amanda said as she stepped into the hospital room. "I'm Amanda."

The sickly pale teenager who stared back at her with blank eyes didn't immediately acknowledge her. After a moment, he said, "So?"

Amanda moved closer to his bedside. "So a year ago I was in this same room. I had leukemia."

Her announcement was followed by stark silence. "I've got it now. Do I have you to thank?"

It was a weak attempt at humor, and Amanda rewarded him with a warm smile. "You can thank me later."

"Thank you?" He wasn't amused by her response and

then, as if he'd suddenly understood, he added, "Oh, you're one of those Pollyanna types who want to play the glad game. Well, if you're here to tell me everything'll be better in a few weeks, then you should leave now. I don't want to hear it."

"I don't have much in common with Pollyanna," Amanda told him, "although I saw the Disney movie when I was a kid. As for everything getting better in a few weeks, it might not." She wasn't going to lie to him.

"In other words, I could be dead."

She nodded. "You could. I was one of the lucky ones. The survival rate gets better every year with medical advancements, but there aren't any guarantees."

"Yeah, right," he said with a snicker.

Amanda set the laptop computer on his nightstand and removed it from the case.

"What's that for?"

"Tell me your name first."

"Derek."

"Hi, Derek."

He offered her what could best be termed a half smile. "Hi—what was your name again?"

"Amanda."

"What's the computer for? If you think I want to catch up on homework, think again."

Homework had been the last thing on her mind while she was hospitalized, too. She shook her head, wanting to reassure him that wasn't the reason for her visit. "I'm here to help you get through this."

"Why do you care?"

"Because I've been where you are. I know what chemotherapy is like and what it means to feel the way you're feeling right now. I hated it, and I hated the whole world. Nothing seemed fair, and I wanted to know why this was happening to me. I can help."

Derek didn't bat an eyelash; of course, he didn't have any to bat, but Amanda understood that, too. "The laptop is so you can connect with teenslivingwithcancer.org. It's a website where you can chat with other kids going through this at the same time as you."

His eyes remained focused straight ahead and, for a moment, it seemed he hadn't heard her. "Why won't the pain stop?" he asked instead. "It just won't go away, and I don't think I can handle it anymore."

"It's like that for everyone in the beginning," Amanda told him gently.

"My ears hurt, my teeth, my head. I can't stand this. It's unbearable."

"Yes, it is. I cried and screamed, but it didn't make any difference. I couldn't stop begging for someone to take the pain away. That's the main reason I ended up in the hospital. They had to give me morphine."

"Me, too," Derek confessed, sounding embarrassed, as if he considered himself weak for not tolerating the pain without drugs.

"You've had how many days of chemo?" she asked.

"Four."

Amanda reached for his hand. She remembered how hard it was; no one who hadn't experienced it could appreciate the pain.

"So you're in remission." When she nodded he said, "I still don't get why you're here. Once I'm out of this place, I'm gone."

"I used to feel the same way," she explained, "but I'm here because of Melissa."

He stared back at her, frowning, and Amanda smiled. "You'll read about her once you get online. Like us, she was a teenager with cancer. She wanted to help other teenagers with cancer, and she has in a big way."

"She died?"

"But I'm still kicking."

"You gonna live to see thirty?"

"Maybe." She laughed. "As a good friend of mine says, if you want a guarantee, shop at Sears."

"Interesting company you keep."

"The best." She gave his hand a small squeeze. "I'll be back later to see how you're doing. Once you're through with the chemo, everything else will seem like a party."

He frowned again. "This is the worst of it?"

"It was for me."

She turned to leave, but Derek called her back. "Hey, Amanda," he said, his voice shaky but with more energy than before. "Thanks for coming."

"Be kind to this room."

He gave her a thumbs-up, and she returned the gesture.

At the end of the hallway, Lydia was waiting for her. She stood and smiled as Amanda approached. "Did you give out all the laptops?"

"I did. I think that connection with other teens will help." She thought about Derek, and her heart went out to him because she knew so well what he was enduring. He wasn't in good shape, but she hoped he'd be better once he went on the message boards.

"I know it'll help," Lydia agreed. "I spoke with the nursing staff at the oncology center here, and they want me to give a presentation at a series of hospitals in the area."

"That's wonderful, Lydia!"

"I'd like you to join me."

"Me?" The invitation flustered Amanda. She was happy to visit other teenagers and talk to them about Melissa's Living Legacy Foundation. Speaking in front of a bunch of physicians and nurses and hospital staff was a different story altogether.

"Yes, you," Lydia reiterated. "You have a lot to offer."

"But..."

"Remember how you mentioned Wendy, your favorite nurse? Why was she your favorite?"

"Because she understood that I wanted to watch videos other than *Barney* or *Blue's Clues*."

"Right. She let you be a teenager."

"Yes," Amanda said. "Yes." She hadn't considered it in

those terms but Lydia was exactly right. Wendy didn't treat Amanda like she was six years old, but she didn't expect her to behave like an adult, either.

"Other medical professionals need to know how to treat the teens on their wards. No one can explain how to do it better than someone who's been in that position."

Still Amanda hesitated. She'd never stood up before a group of adults, and the prospect was intimidating. She thought about Lydia who'd done so much for her. And she thought about Melissa.

"It's what Melissa would have wanted, isn't it?" Amanda asked.

"I think it is," Lydia said quietly.

Melissa Sengbusch had died five years earlier and although Amanda and Melissa had never met, the other girl had made a powerful impression on her and on so many other teenagers. Amanda would like to think that, had she lived, the two of them would've been good friends.

They had a lot in common. They'd both been teenagers with cancer. Both of them understood the struggles and the pain. Both were determined to live life to the fullest, no matter how long or short that life might be.

Amanda met Lydia's eyes. "Okay," she said, taking in a deep breath. "I'll do it." She wanted to honor Melissa and her Living Legacy Foundation. She could help others just the way Melissa would have wanted. It was what Amanda wanted, too.

* * * * *

TERA LEIGH

For award-winning artist and author Tera Leigh, life is all about living one's passion. Tera's passion is creativity—and following her passion led her to found the Memory Box Artist Program. Through the program, Tera has mobilized a community of women to put their passion and deep sympathy into creating hand-decorated boxes to hold cherished mementos for mothers grieving the death of an infant. The boxes are a way for mothers to acknowledge the baby's brief life and always keep their child close.

The Memory Box Artist Program began with Tera's decision to pursue her own passion for creativity. Tera had been writing and painting most of her adult life, but her energy was focused on her career as an attorney. Tera was an excellent attorney. She'd followed in her father's footsteps, but it wasn't her dream. Painting was—and inspiring creativity in others. In 1995, feeling a need to connect with other painters, Tera began a website for decorative artists. It was a fortuitous first step in unexpected ways. The same day she launched her website, she met her future husband online. They married five months later. And it was through her website that Tera first heard about the need for Memory Boxes.

About this time, one of Tera's closest friends died of cancer at the age of forty-two. This loss brought home to Tera how precious and fleeting life can be. So she decided to follow her dreams. She left her job as an attorney, and she and her husband concentrated on living a life that would make them happy and fulfilled—emotionally and spiritually. Tera realized life wasn't about making money. It was about giving back. "At the end of your life, it's all you have," says Tera. "What you did is all that matters—how you lived your life."

Creating Memory Boxes touched Tera on a personal level, too. Because of a medical condition, it's unlikely she and her husband will ever be able to have a child together. Tera understands about the loss of a child—for her, the children she might never have. Tera's mom, Marie Gemmil, who has been instrumental in the program since it began, had lost a baby—the child between Tera and her brother. Her mom says there isn't a day that goes by when she doesn't think of that baby.

Few of us know what to say or how to help when a mother is grieving the loss of her infant, even though we all feel compassion. Mothers want desperately to talk about the child they've lost. Instead we may say "It's for the best" or "You'll have another one." Tera herself had said those very words to a dear friend who'd lost a child two years before she started the Memory Box program. After that, she was determined to help other women in the way she had not been able to help her grieving friend. A Memory Box holds precious memories—the child's birth and death certificates, footprints, wristband, crib card and other treasured mementos of a tiny life. The boxes become a bridge to allow the mother to discuss the child by beginning with "look what a woman made for me to hold my baby's things."

Tera launched the Memory Box Artist program in June 1998 with the help of her mother and a neonatal nurse, with twenty boxes going to three hospitals. Tera's mom painted the basecoat on the boxes and Tera did the decorating. Other artists and hospitals quickly came into the program. To this date, volunteer artists have donated more than 113,000 boxes to hospitals around the world for use in neonatal infant bereavement, late-term miscarriage or stillbirth. But the ongoing need for more boxes is a key motivator for all involved in the program, as more than two million infants are stillborn every year worldwide.

Loss of a child is difficult for families, and also for the hospital staff who must cope with these tragic deaths. They, too, mourn the loss of a baby. There is a definite need for a compassionate, nonclinical form of support, and doctors and nurses are grateful for the opportunity to offer grieving mothers the caring touch of a Memory Box. One nurse told Tera about a mother who wanted to take home mementos of her stillborn baby and the only thing the nurse could find to carry them in was a biohazard trash bag. It is Tera's goal, her dream, that one day, no bereaved mother will ever leave the hospital without a Memory Box in hand.

The artists themselves also benefit from the Memory Box program. One of Tera's purposes in starting the program was to give women a way to use their creativity to make a difference. Most volunteers will tell you that their creative work brings them joy. Using their talent to help others provides a double blessing. And many of the women who've lost a child themselves and received a box contribute art to the program, which becomes a form of therapy. Others have lost a child in the past and were unable to acknowledge and grieve the death fully until volunteering for the Memory Box Artist Program. Tera points out that the boxes don't have to be works of art to make a difference. The love and caring behind them is what matters.

MEMORY BOX ARTIST PROGRAM

The Memory Box Artist Program stands for everything Tera believes in. Living life with creativity and passion gives meaning and purpose to our lives, and in turn can enrich and touch the lives of others. Tera believes we are all creative beings…and all of us can make a difference.

In January of 2009, the Memory Box Artist Program was transferred to the Tole Friends Association, a registered Utah nonprofit corporation. It is, therefore, now known as the Tole Friends Memory Box Program.

BRENDA NOVAK
~SMALL PACKAGES~

ᕽ—BRENDA NOVAK—ᕽ

It was a shocking experience that jump-started Brenda Novak's career as a bestselling author—she caught her day-care provider drugging her children with cough syrup to get them to sleep all day. That was when Brenda decided she needed to quit her job as a loan officer and help make a living from home.

"When I first got the idea to become a novelist, it took me five years to teach myself the craft and finish my first book," Brenda says. But she sold that book, and the rest is history. Her novels have made the *New York Times, USA TODAY* and Borders/Waldenbooks bestseller lists and won many awards, including two RITA® Award nominations, a Book Buyer's Best, a Book Seller's Best and a National Reader's Choice Award.

Brenda and her husband, Ted, live in Sacramento and are the proud parents of five children—three girls and two boys. When she's not spending time with her family or writing, Brenda is usually working on her annual fundraiser for diabetes research—an online auction held on her website, www.brendanovak.com, every May. Brenda has raised over $1 million to date.

∞ PROLOGUE ∞

Yuba City, California

This was his dad. At least that was what his mom had just told him. Two seconds ago, Rosie Ferello had brought their old Buick to a screeching halt, jammed her finger out the open window and said, "There he is, Harrison. You happy now? You've hounded me all your life to meet your pa. Well, that rotten son of a bitch is your daddy."

His daddy... A man he couldn't remember...

Harrison scrambled out of the backseat to see a pair of work boots sticking out from beneath an old Chevy pickup sitting on blocks in the driveway across the street. He'd longed for this day, but the shabby house and tall weeds in the yard worried him a little. The place wasn't any nicer than where he and his mom lived....

Hesitating near the back bumper of the Buick, Harrison bit his fingernails into the quick while waiting to see what his father might do.

The stranger beneath the truck slid out and sat up on a wheeled dolly. His gaze locked with Harrison's, then traveled to the car and Rosie. When recognition dawned, he stood up so fast the dolly rolled down the drive and crashed into the gutter.

Rosie stuck her head out and waved Harrison forward. "Go on," she said. His mother was trying to punish him for stealing that candy bar from the Quick Stop a couple of hours ago. He'd known she'd be angry about it. He'd done it to *make* her angry. He was angry, too. *Most* days. He just couldn't explain why....

When Harrison didn't move, she frowned and lit a cigarette. "You've always had so much to say about your beloved daddy. Well—" the smoke curled from between her lips as she exhaled "—there he is. Let's see what you think of him now."

Obviously he wasn't expected to think much.

Forcing his hands to his sides, Harrison dried his fingertips on his jeans and drew a deep breath. It was June and blistering hot so late in the afternoon, but Harrison couldn't quit shaking inside.

He cast a hesitant glance in his mother's direction. The

rumbling engine reminded him that she could drive off any second. He was afraid she would. She threatened to give him to his father every time Harrison caused her any trouble—and Harrison caused her plenty of trouble.

"This is your big chance," she said. "Don't stand there all day."

For the better part of Harrison's nine years, he'd pictured his father to be like his best friend Jimmy's stepdad. Henry Spits wore glasses and suits, and smiled vaguely as he talked on the cell phone. But Harrison's dad didn't look anything like Mr. Spits. Dressed in a pair of grease-covered jeans and a Budweiser T-shirt that barely stretched over his round belly, Duane Ferello was one of the biggest men Harrison had ever seen. He had hair the same toffee-color as Harrison's, thick dark whiskers, and eyes that seemed as cold as a rainy day in January. He smoked, too. Harrison could see a pack of cigarettes rolled up in his sleeve.

"What're you after now, Rosie?" his father called out, squinting at her.

Harrison's heart beat faster as he waited for his mother's response.

Cigarette dangling from her mouth, she ran a hand through the dark roots of her hair and rolled her eyes. "God, it's been eight years since we broke up. Is that all you can say to me, Duane?"

His father grabbed a towel off the top of the red toolbox at his feet and leaned against the truck, making a show of wiping his hands. "What'd you expect? That maybe I'd write you a check?" He spit on the lawn. "Well, you can forget about that. You're not gettin' any more than the state's already takin' out of what I earn."

"You're only givin' me a hundred and fifty bucks a month," Rosie retorted. "Is that the best you can do?"

"I just told you, it's all you're gonna get."

Harrison's mother made a noise of disgust. "I didn't drive out to this dump to get another few bucks from a tight-ass like you. I didn't come for me at all." She hitched her thumb at Harrison. "There's someone here who wants to meet you."

Harrison knew he should speak, show his father that he wasn't as dumb as he probably looked, hovering there on the side of the road. But he couldn't think of a single thing to say. As soon as his father's attention swung back his way, he could've sworn someone had punched him in the chest and knocked the wind out of him.

"What're you starin' at, huh, boy?"

The gruffness of his father's tone did little to invite an answer, but Harrison had waited too long for this moment to let fear get the better of him. Maybe if he showed his dad that he wasn't as small and unimportant as he appeared, Duane would be happier to meet him. Hooking his thumbs in his pockets, he lifted his chin, adopting the tough-guy attitude he'd learned from the older boys in his neighborhood. "So you're my dad?"

SMALL PACKAGES

His father tossed the towel onto the toolbox. "That depends on what you mean by 'dad.' You're not gonna get another dime out of me, neither."

Harrison hadn't seen Duane since his parents split eight years ago, since he was only a baby.... "I'm not asking for money," he said.

But his father didn't beckon him closer. He didn't tell him he seemed like a fine boy or ask if he played sports. Duane pinched his neck and muttered, "Yeah, right. You think I'm dumb enough to believe it ain't gonna come down to that eventually?"

Suddenly Harrison's stomach hurt. His whole life he'd believed it was Rosie's fault his father never came around. She smoked too much, yelled too much, slept in too late. She bragged about naming him after Harrison Ford, as if that connected them to someone important. She didn't behave like the other mothers. But now he knew she wasn't entirely to blame. His father didn't want him, pure and simple. Probably never had.

A lump the size of a baseball rose in his throat. Hunching into himself, he hurried to get back in the car. He wouldn't let his father see him cry. He wouldn't let *anyone* see him cry.

But he couldn't blink the tears away quickly enough to fool his mother. Craning her head around, she took one look at him and cursed under her breath. Then she got out and called his father every cussword Harrison had ever heard—even more. She told Duane Ferello he was a boil on the butt of humanity and didn't deserve to know his own son. She told him that she and Harrison had never needed him and that they didn't need him now.

When she finished, she got in the car and peeled away, leaving behind only the echo of her words and some flying dust and gravel.

The hot wind from the open window rushed against Harrison's wet cheeks as the miles passed. He sat silently, waiting for his mother to say, "I hope you learned your lesson back there." He was in trouble often enough that she always wanted him to learn a lesson. But today she didn't say anything. She kept glancing at him in the rearview mirror, sniffling as she drove, and strangely enough, Harrison felt as though he *had* learned something. Even if she wasn't perfect, his mother was all he had. And it was time to make some big changes, because he was never going to look himself in the mirror and see a man like his father staring back at him.

CHAPTER
~ONE~

Sacramento, California
Twenty years later...

What was taking so long?

Harrison Ferello glanced nervously at his watch, then loosened his tie and continued to pace the length of the room. He'd been waiting almost thirteen hours. Surely Lynnette's mother would come out and tell him—

"Are you waiting for a baby to be born, too?"

Harrison looked over at the stout woman with gray hair who sat in the corner. She smiled kindly, but he didn't want her or anyone else to draw him into a conversation right now. He had too much on his mind, too many decisions to make. Still, he couldn't ignore her. Forcing a pleasant smile, he nodded.

Her grin widened. "I figured that had to be the case, the way you're worrying a hole in the carpet. Who's having the baby? Your sister?"

"Excuse me?" he said, resisting a scowl.

She waved toward the corridor leading to Labor and Delivery. "If you were the father, you'd be inside. So I thought maybe you're expecting a new niece or nephew. Am I right?"

Harrison struggled to come up with an appropriate label for his relationship with Lynnette. After their breakup almost eight months ago, they weren't even friends. They'd scarcely talked to each other since she moved away.

"No," he said abruptly. Any other response would only raise more questions.

"Oh." The woman's smile faded. "My daughter-in-law is having her second child," she said, obviously trying to smooth over the awkwardness. "She's having a girl."

"You must be very excited."

"I'm crocheting this blanket for her." She dug a large half-finished square of pink yarn from her purse.

"That's nice."

Shoving a hand through his hair, he went back to pacing, but after another hour, anxiety got the better of him.

"Does it always take this long?" he asked the woman, who was now crocheting quietly.

She pulled off her half-glasses and studied him. "This is your child, isn't it?"

Harrison nodded. What could he say? There wasn't even supposed to be a pregnancy, but Lynnette had lied to him.

"Your first?"

"Yes."

"How long have you been waiting?"

"Thirteen and a half hours."

"That's not unusual," the woman told him. "First babies generally take longer."

He knew that from working in the emergency room this past year, of course, but talking seemed to help. "Thanks."

"Do you know if you're having a boy or a girl?"

"Twins," he said. "Twin boys."

Her eyebrows shot up. "Twins! How wonderful."

Harrison couldn't agree, at least not yet. He was still reeling from the news. When he'd met his father at nine years old, he'd decided he was going to make something of himself. And he'd fought damn hard to do it. He'd avidly avoided anything that could threaten his goal. But he hadn't bargained on meeting a woman like Lynnette....

"I hope you'll have some help," the woman said. "My cousin has twins, and I can tell you, they're a handful."

Help? Lynnette's mother suffered from severe bipolar disorder, her sister, who had an infant of her own, was going through a divorce. Harrison's own mother had recently remarried and moved to Las Vegas. Rosie would be floored to hear that she was about to become a grandmother—almost as shocked as he'd been to learn he would soon be a father.

He opened his mouth to respond, when a nurse appeared and glanced around the waiting room.

"Dr. Ferello?" she said when their eyes met.

"Yes?"

Her expression was somber. "Could I speak with you for a moment, please?"

"Of course." The back of Harrison's neck prickled as he walked over to her. "Is there a problem?" he asked.

She drew him into the corridor.

"I'm Charlene Matheson, the nurse who's been caring for Ms. Donovan. I'm afraid I have bad news."

Lynnette was young and healthy, and the babies were nearly full-term. What could be wrong?

Harrison cleared his throat. "Tell me what's happened."

"There were...complications during delivery. Ms. Donovan's blood pressure skyrocketed and..." Charlene Matheson clamped her hands together in front of her and squeezed until her knuckles turned white. "There wasn't anything we could do. It happened too fast."

He couldn't quite comprehend what she was trying to tell him. "*What* happened too fast?"

"Ms. Donovan had a massive stroke, Dr. Ferello. She died a few minutes ago."

Harrison's heartbeat vibrated through his whole body, radiating outward from his chest to his arms and legs. "Wasn't there any warning?" he asked.

The nurse gently placed a hand on his arm. "Dr. Spring can explain in a few minutes. He's with Ms. Donovan's mother and sister now, or he would've come out to speak with you himself."

Numbly Harrison's brain registered that the woman who'd been so alive when he'd brought her to the hospital that morning was now dead.

Soothing words spilled from the nurse's mouth, something about the hospital offering grief counseling.

"Dr. Spring said he's never seen this happen before," the nurse was saying when he tuned in again. "I'm sorry. I know this has to be a terrible blow."

Harrison nodded. He didn't know what else to do.

"And the babies?" he managed to say. "Did they...did they die, too?"

Her eyes filled with sympathy. "The second baby died moments after he was born. He had spina bifida and several other problems."

Guilt immediately assaulted Harrison. He'd been so consumed with how the pregnancy was going to affect *his* life.... And now both Lynnette and one of the babies were gone. "And the first baby?"

"He's only five pounds and in an incubator, but we have every reason to believe he'll survive."

One out of three… "So what now?" he asked, almost to himself.

"I'm afraid I can't answer that for you. You'll have to speak with Ms. Donovan's family and make plans from there."

"Right," he said. They had to make plans. For two funerals and a new baby. *Lots* of plans. But Harrison didn't know where to begin unraveling such an emotional mess. He'd imagined himself playing a supporting role. Taking the children whenever he could. Paying as much child support as possible. But now…

"Will you be okay?" the nurse asked.

He rubbed the stubble on his chin, vaguely aware of the raspy sound. This had to be a nightmare. Any minute, he'd jerk awake and realize he'd dreamed all this, even the pregnancy. But the clock on the wall kept ticking. The automatic doors in the lobby *whooshed* open and shut. And the nurse stood before him, waiting expectantly…

Finally he hauled in a deep breath. "I'll be fine," he said, because he knew she couldn't stand there with him all day. "Just fine."

She smiled with a degree of relief. "Give me a few minutes, and I'll take you to the nursery to meet your son."

Harrison stared after her as she hurried away. She'd said she would take him to meet his son… *His son!* God, what was he going to do? He hadn't known he'd be having children until three weeks ago.

Now it wasn't children at all but one son.

And it was only the two of them.

Noelle Kane hurried through the hospital toward Labor and Delivery, carrying the Memory Box she'd created under one arm. "What did you say?" she asked, pressing her cell phone tighter to her ear.

Her friend Theresa raised her voice. "I said we'll miss the movie if you don't get here soon. Where are you?"

She tried to shut out the antiseptic smell, hushed voices and white walls of the hospital because they triggered such painful memories, and checked the time on her watch. She should've told Theresa and Eve she'd be late. She would have, except she'd never dreamed traffic would be so bad—and deep down she'd sort of liked knowing they were at the theater not far away and would be standing outside waiting for her when she finished this difficult errand.

"Listen, you two go on without me. We'll have to hook up afterwards."

"But you're the one who wanted to see this picture," Theresa protested. "You've been talking about it for weeks."

A nurse walked by pushing a pregnant woman in a wheelchair, and Noelle couldn't help watching them enviously until they disappeared around the corner. "I know, but—" she blew out a sigh "—I got a message from Charlene Matheson."

"Charlene Who?"

Noelle opened her mouth to answer but Theresa remembered before she could explain.

"Wait a second. That's the nurse from the hospital, right? Noelle, you're not still making Memory Boxes, are you?"

"Of course I am."

"I thought you said you'd quit."

"No, I just quit telling you about them."

"Because you knew what I'd say."

"Because I disagree with you. When I…" The familiar tightness in her chest made it difficult to get the words out. "When I lost Austin, people didn't know what to say to me, so most people said nothing at all. Those who tried to offer some comfort blundered through it with hurtful remarks like, 'You can have another one.'"

"I know, and I'm terribly sorry, but—"

"My baby came and went so fast that it felt as though he didn't matter to anyone but me."

"You're purposely misunderstanding me, and you know it. The Memory Box Artist Program is wonderful. I'm only concerned that—"

"There's nothing wrong with me participating in it," Noelle broke in again.

"There's nothing wrong with constantly poking and prodding at a painful wound? With never allowing your heart to heal?"

"That's not what I'm doing."

"Yes, it is. You're torturing yourself."

Noelle recognized some truth in what her friend said, but she deserved every poke and prod. Theresa just didn't know it and would probably be stunned to learn the real reason Noelle had lost her baby. Not that Noelle planned on telling her—or anyone else, for that matter. "Quit being so melodramatic. I'm simply trying—" *to atone* "—to help others, okay?"

Theresa made an impatient noise. "Then help AIDS patients or the families of cancer victims. Raise money for the Stanford Home for Children. But stay away from the hospital. Going there has got to be hell on you."

"I *want* to do this," Noelle said.

"Then at least let me deliver the boxes."

When she reached the labor and delivery area, Noelle hesitated outside, gathering the emotional strength to walk through those double doors. She would hand her gift to Charlene Matheson, who would in turn give it to the grieving parents of the lost infant. Then Noelle would leave immediately—before she fell back into the depression from which she'd barely escaped six months ago.

"We'll have to talk about it later," she said. "If you don't want to watch the whole movie without me, get some seats and I'll be there as soon as possible."

Without waiting for a response, she pushed the end button and slipped through the doors.

She couldn't see Charlene Matheson, but another nurse she recognized, Fiona Farley, sat at the nurses' station.

Focusing strictly on Fiona, Noelle hurried forward. *This won't take long, only a minute....*

"Noelle!" Fiona smiled the moment she glanced up. "Charlene mentioned you were coming, and I'm so glad. Someone has stored the Memory Boxes you brought us last month in such a safe place that we can't find them, and we're dealing with a really sad situation."

"I heard." Noelle set the silver papier-mâché box she carried down on the counter. She'd put her whole heart into painting the serene lake and pine trees on the lid and sides. "At least now the poor mother will have the prettiest box I could create to store the baby's personal effects in."

Fiona blinked at her. "The *mother?* Didn't Charlene tell you?"

"I got a message on my machine saying you needed another box, that's it."

"So you don't know that the mother died, too. Only one baby survived. There were twins."

"Oh, no!"

"It's been rough," Fiona said. "Especially on the father.

He wasn't married to the babies' mother, but he seems pretty affected. He's been walking around here looking shell-shocked."

Noelle's palms began to sweat. Theresa was right. She shouldn't have come. These situations upset her too much. "I'm so sorry."

"Me, too."

Noelle turned the Memory Box in a circle. "So this is for the father?"

"Yes. Charlene said he was here all night, standing near the nursery window, staring inside."

The memories, and the pain that went with them, rolled over Noelle like a suffocating blanket. She needed to go, right away. She needed to get out....

"Well, good luck." She forced herself to think of Theresa and Eve waiting for her at the movie theater. The sadness of this tragedy would lift as soon as she left the hospital and let the routine of life swallow her again.

Intending to do exactly that, she said goodbye to Fiona and headed out. But as she passed the hall leading to the nursery, Noelle couldn't help lingering. She knew it was a bad idea, but she had to stop by and see the baby that had survived.

CHAPTER
~TWO~

Harrison propped one hand against the glass of the nursery window and rubbed his burning eyes with the other. He hadn't gotten any sleep in the past forty-eight hours. After the first nine months of his residency, he was used to living on willpower and adrenaline, but the stress of his current dilemma seemed to have zapped his usual resiliency. He'd gone home this morning and tried to rest for a few hours, only to lie awake and stare at the ceiling, wondering what to do. He owed more than $120,000 in student loans, was working nearly eighty hours a week at the UC Davis Medical Center, earning barely $30,000 a year, and he had another twenty-seven months before he could practice medicine on his own.

Even then, his career would demand the better part of his time and focus for several years. If he kept the child, how would he care for it?

Maybe the baby wasn't even his.... He planned to get a paternity test, just to be sure, but deep down he had little real doubt. Lynnette had been absolutely unwavering when she promised him she'd slept with no one else in over a year. Considering how single-minded she'd been where he was concerned, how hopeful that they'd marry, she was probably telling the truth.

But even if the baby *was* his, he should let the child be adopted by parents who were eager and excited to have a newborn, right? Harrison's own mother, when he finally broke down and called her before returning to the hospital a few hours ago, had said as much. *What does it matter whether he's your son or not? You're not ready to be a father. Give him to someone who wants him.*

Unfortunately he couldn't really rely on her opinion. Rosie didn't have much of a track record for making good decisions. She'd messed up her life over and over again, usually because she was attracted to the wrong kind of man. And she didn't understand how he felt about his father. Harrison could easily imagine Duane walking away from the hospital without a backward glance, which was partly why he couldn't do it himself.

He smiled vaguely at the nurse who waved at him from inside the nursery and shoved off the glass. He should go.

He wasn't doing himself or anyone else any good standing here, stewing. But...

Jamming his hands in his pockets, he continued to watch his tiny, dark-headed baby sleep, so oblivious to the tides of fate. So innocent. So dependent...

Dependent on Harrison to make a decision as to what his future would hold. And soon.

The nursery door cracked open and the nurse poked her head out. "It's time for your baby to eat. Do you want to give him his bottle?"

Harrison knew he shouldn't say yes. He'd held his son once, earlier, and the weight of that small body in his arms had only added to the desperation he felt to find a solution they could both live with. But he couldn't refuse to feed him. This poor child—*his* child—didn't even have a mother.

"Sure." He blanked his mind while he waited, but like before, a flood of emotion welled up inside him as the nurse placed his son in his arms.

"Have you picked out a name for him yet?" she asked, passing him the bottle.

The moment the rubber nipple brushed his cheek, the baby turned his head and opened his mouth. "No, not yet."

"There are books with lists and lists of names, if you're having trouble thinking of one."

Harrison didn't want to look through any books. Until he made up his mind about the role he wanted to play in this child's life, he sure as hell knew better than to name him. "Thanks," he said, so she wouldn't press him further.

"Let me know what you come up with so we can fill out the birth certificate." With that, she disappeared into the nursery.

Harrison knew she'd return for the baby in just a few minutes, and was grateful for the time alone. But the solitude didn't last long. A tall slender woman with olive-colored skin approached the nursery. She was wearing a pair of snug-fitting jeans and a red sweater, and was so intent on staring beyond the glass at the new babies that she didn't seem to notice him sitting in the small alcove to her right.

Spotting her, the nurse waved and hurried to the door. "Hi, Noelle. Good to see you."

"Good to see you, too, Lana."

The woman named Noelle was so attractive, Harrison normally would've figured out a way to meet her. She wasn't wearing a ring. But in the process of one day, *this* day, dating had fallen completely off his list of priorities.

"Did you already find Charlene?" the nurse asked her. "I know she was asking if you'd been in."

"I didn't see Charlene, but Fiona was at the nurses' station."

"Great. So, what brings you by the nursery?"

"I wanted to see the baby boy who lost his mother and brother. Is he in there?"

Harrison sat up straighter, wondering how word of his predicament had spread to this elegant stranger.

The nurse immediately dropped her voice and jerked her head subtly in Harrison's direction. "He's with his father, over there."

Noelle turned and blushed to the roots of her shiny dark hair. "I'm so sorry," she said. "I didn't notice you. And I...I wanted to..."

"What?" he prompted curiously when she hesitated.

"I wanted to offer my silent support to the baby, I guess. But since you're here, I'll tell you how terrible I feel about what's happened. I know you're dealing with a very difficult situation. If there's anything I can do—"

"Do I know you?" he asked, confused. This woman had almond-shaped green eyes and a touch of the exotic in her face and bearing. Harrison felt pretty certain he would have remembered her if—

"No, we've never met."

"She helps us out here at the hospital," the nurse interjected.

"So you're in the medical profession?"

"No." Noelle hitched her purse higher on her shoulder and slid the fingers of one hand into the pocket of her jeans. "I'm an artist."

He didn't get the connection. "Are you also a grief counselor?"

"Definitely not. I—"

"Noelle heads up some of our community projects," the nurse explained. "We're all very grateful to her."

So how did that apply to him? He was about to ask, but the baby started to cry and Noelle didn't give him the chance. She'd been rummaging through her purse while the nurse talked. Now she stuck a card under his nose.

"I'd like to leave this with you just in case…in case you ever feel the need to talk. I may not be a counselor, but I've been where you're at now. I know it's not easy." As soon as he accepted her card, she left.

Harrison finally got the baby to take the bottle again and stared after her before turning questioning eyes on the nurse.

"I'm sorry if Noelle put you on the spot," she said gently. "But she really is a very caring person. If you ever need someone to talk to, I'd give her a call."

After leaving the hospital, Noelle sat in her car for several minutes, watching drop after drop of rain splatter on her windshield. She knew her friends were waiting for her, that it was rude not to hurry to the theater. But she couldn't seem to make herself put the key in the ignition. She didn't want to be around anyone tonight. She was too busy feeling sorry for the father and baby she'd seen in the nursery—and wondering why the heck she'd given the man her card. There really wasn't anything she could do for him.

Her cell phone rang. She stared down at the caller ID, saw that it was Theresa, and was tempted to ignore the call. She didn't want to talk right now. But Theresa wouldn't give up. The ringing stopped, only to start up again a few seconds later.

Finally Noelle answered.

"Where are you?" Theresa whispered. "You've missed half the show."

"I just got in the car. I'm coming."

"How'd it go?"

Noelle once again pictured the father she'd seen in the nursery. He'd looked rumpled and dazed, but if possible, he was even more handsome than her ex-husband. Steven was a bit shorter and stockier, perhaps—it was difficult to tell, because the man in the hospital had never stood up—but they both had very short blond hair, blue eyes and a confident air that worked a lot like gravity, constantly drawing hapless souls closer.

Hapless souls like her....

"Fine."

"Truly?"

"Truly," she said, and decided to forget about the man in the hospital. She'd just met him. What were the chances he'd ever really call her?

CHAPTER
~THREE~

Harrison sat in his spare bedroom, which he used as an office, and stared at the Memory Box the nurses at the hospital had cautiously presented to him. A card bearing the foot impression of the twin who'd died, the baby's photograph, a slip of paper with his birth statistics, and Lynnette's hospital bracelet were arranged neatly inside. Those items were all that remained to signify that his other child had even existed.

Harrison could see that, in a normal situation, the nurses' gesture would bring significant comfort to bereft parents. But he didn't know how to feel—about the baby who had died or the baby who had lived. His need to cut free from anything that might hold him back from the life he'd planned was waging war with his sense of duty, and he doubted he'd be the same person when it was all over, no matter which side prevailed. To make matters worse, he didn't have time to get his head together. The pediatrician had indicated that the baby who'd lived would be released from the hospital in a few days. A decision had to be made.

With a frustrated groan, he set the Memory Box on his desk and picked up his pocket planner. Lynnette's funeral was the day after tomorrow. They'd have a small service for Tyler Brent—who'd been named by Lynnette's sister—at the same time. It was tough to face Lynnette's mother. She was taking her daughter's death hard and seemed to blame him, but he wanted to attend the funeral. If only he could make arrangements at the Medical Center. They were having trouble covering his shifts.

Glancing at the Memory Box again, he remembered Nurse Matheson telling him that Noelle Kane, the woman he'd met in the nursery, had painted it. She was also the one who'd planted the thought that talking through his dilemma might help him arrive at a resolution. But he couldn't think of anyone close enough to call. His best friend Jimmy, who'd more or less stuck by him growing up even though their lives had taken very different paths, was in jail for getting into a bar fight and nearly beating a man to death. Most of the other people he knew were professional associates, except for the guys on his softball team.

Occasionally they went out for a beer after the game, but he doubted any of them would appreciate hearing from him at three in the morning.

He remembered the card Noelle had handed him and began to dig through his pockets. *I've been where you're at.* Obviously she didn't completely understand his situation, but the empathy in her eyes, along with the nurse's recommendation, seemed hopeful. And why not talk to a stranger? Noelle Kane didn't have any expectations where he was concerned. She would be less prone to make value judgments and had no reason to sway him one way or the other.

Finding her card jammed into his billfold, he stared at her personal information. Judging by the address, she lived twenty minutes away from him in Sacramento's Fabulous Forties, a neighborhood to the east of downtown that was made up of unique old homes. It was an expensive area, but it wasn't ostentatious. He could easily picture the woman he'd met living there. That section of town generally appealed to artists and other creative types.

Fleetingly he wondered if Noelle had a husband or boyfriend who might object to his call. But she hadn't been wearing a ring, and calling *had* been her suggestion....

With a sigh, he dialed the number in the bottom right-hand corner.

Three rings went unanswered. He almost hung up.

Surely when she'd said he could call, she'd never imagined he'd do it in the middle of the night—

"Hello?"

He winced at the muffled sound of her voice. He'd awakened her all right. "Noelle?"

"Yes?"

"This is Harrison Ferello."

A confused silence settled over the line.

"The guy you met at the hospital nursery tonight," he clarified.

"Oh!" He heard some rustling, and when she continued, she spoke more clearly. "Are you okay, Harrison?"

Despite the fact that he'd called her for help, he almost gave her the habitual, "I'm fine." Because his mother hadn't been capable of holding down a job or keeping a roof over their heads for more than a few months at a time, he'd grown up very fast. To admit weakness or need felt awkward, unmanly. But he reminded himself that he didn't know this woman, that he'd likely never see her again, and forced out the truth. "No."

Another pause. "What's going on?"

"Are you married?" he blurted out.

"Why do you ask?"

Wariness had entered her voice, making him realize she might think he was coming on to her. "My call could be… unwelcome, especially so late," he explained. "If you're with someone, I'll let you go, maybe call back at a decent hour." *Or maybe not...*

She seemed to relax. "We don't always need others according to a convenient schedule."

He wasn't very well-versed at needing anyone, anytime. He liked companionship, but dependence, especially any kind of *emotional* dependence, scared the hell out of him. "Still, I don't want to cause a problem for you——"

"You're not causing a problem. I'm not with anyone. I'm divorced."

"Do you have children?"

"No, but let's talk about you," she said firmly.

He'd called to talk about him, but now that he had her on the line, he didn't know where to start. "To be honest, I'm not sure what I expect you to do."

"Maybe you just need someone to listen. If you're like I was, you're drowning in grief and despair and there doesn't seem to be anything to stop the pain."

"I'm not sure what I'm feeling." He carried the cordless phone from his office to the living room. "Confusion. Anger. Resentment. Take your pick." He slouched onto the couch and stared at the television he'd left on earlier.

"Who or what are you angry at?" she asked. "God? Fate?"

"Lynnette." He blinked when he said that, surprised by his own admission. How could he be angry with Lynnette?

She'd left him in the lurch, but at least *he* was still around. Sadly, she'd lost her life.

"Who's Lynnette?"

"She's the woman who died in the hospital yesterday." He knew he must sound callous, stating it so baldly. But he was so overwhelmed by everything that had happened, he couldn't face Lynnette's death right now, not in addition to the decisions about the baby.

Somehow, Noelle didn't seem put off. "A lot of people are angry when their loved ones pass away. It's part of the grieving process."

He laughed bitterly as understanding dawned. She thought he was upset with Lynnette for *leaving* him. She thought he was the brokenhearted husband or lover. "I'm afraid my feelings aren't that noble."

Her response came slowly. "They're not?"

"No." Leaning his head on the couch, he closed his eyes and rubbed his temples. "I'm angry at her for—" he struggled to be specific "—for ever loving me, I guess. I never really wanted her to, especially after the first few weeks."

"Does that mean you didn't return her feelings?"

"I might have loved her a little. I don't know. Things got crazy pretty fast."

"Do you want to explain that?"

Harrison generally wasn't one to share the details of his relationships. He was busy and driven and knew he didn't focus on them as much as he should. But tonight, talking seemed to shove *the big decision*, the decision that would affect him and his child for the rest of their lives, into the background, bringing him temporary relief. "She became so...obsessive," he explained.

"In what way?"

"In every way. She hated it when I spent time with anyone else, resented the hours I studied or worked. She even tried to get me to give up softball so we could be together more often."

"Did you?"

Somehow Noelle Kane was beginning to seem less like a real person than a voice coming out of thin air to help him spill the torturous thoughts bottled up inside his head. "For a while. I wanted to make her happy. But enough was never enough. I decided I needed to create some space between us. Not long after that, I caught her following me around, checking up on me."

"Did she have reason to distrust you?"

"None." He propped his feet up on the coffee table and muted the television because the low hum he'd found comforting before now seemed too loud. "Anyway, it got to the point where I didn't want to see her at all. She'd pout if I couldn't come over. Or if we did get together, she'd beg me to stay longer, even though I had to work or get my laundry done or whatever. Pretty soon she started hinting that she wanted to get married."

"To be honest, it doesn't sound as though she was very stable."

"She seemed normal to everyone else."

"*That* doesn't mean anything."

He detected a note of bitterness in her voice but didn't give it much thought. Now that he was finally opening up, the words inside him seemed to be battling each other in their hurry to get out. "I tried to be as honest and up-front as possible. She knew I wasn't in the market for a wife, that I've never wanted kids."

"You don't want a family?"

"No."

"Why not?"

He was probably afraid he'd fail as badly as his father. "I don't know."

"Then, what *do* you want?" she asked.

He could tell his sentiment toward marriage and children hadn't endeared him to her, but he'd already committed himself to being ruthlessly honest. "I want to devote myself to medicine."

"You're a doctor?"

"Yes, but I'm in the first year of a three-year residency."

"What's your specialty?"

"Emergency Medicine."

"My ex-husband is the administrator at Wilheim General so I know how difficult it is to get into the medical profession."

That was a whole other subject. Med school had been beyond grueling, and his internship wasn't much easier. But he didn't have any complaints. He'd known from the beginning that his career path wouldn't be an easy one. Dealing with Lynnette had been a bigger challenge because the relationship had so quickly become one-sided. "I'd be fine if developing my career was all I had to worry about. But this…" He shook his head.

"I'm sure you wish you'd broken up with her long ago."

"I *did* break up with her," he said. "It's been eight months since we were together. After we quit seeing each other, she gave up her job at the sandwich shop where I met her and moved forty minutes away. I thought our relationship was over. Then, out of the blue, she contacted me."

"When?"

He leaned over to reach the remote and started flipping aimlessly through stations as a way to siphon off some of his nervous energy. "Three weeks ago. She called and asked me to meet her for lunch. And that's when I learned about the twins."

"You're kidding."

"No."

"Why didn't she contact you sooner?"

The outrage in that question validated his own reaction and goaded him to continue. "That's what I wanted to know. She said she was afraid I'd try to talk her into having an abortion."

"So, was the pregnancy an accident, or…"

He rested his elbows on his knees, tossed the remote away and forgot about the television as he stared down at the carpet. "I don't know. She claimed it was, but I can't imagine how that could be true. She told me she had polycystic ovarian syndrome and probably couldn't get pregnant. She was on the pill to regulate her periods, and I *still* used a condom." Fleetingly he realized this was a rather personal conversation to be having with a woman he'd barely met, especially such a beautiful woman. But he didn't care. He was in so far over his head that he couldn't consider anything except how to get out of the mess he was in.

"It wouldn't be the first time a girl got pregnant on purpose," she said.

Harrison was almost positive Lynnette had been hoping he'd break down and marry her, but now that she was gone, he wanted to give her the benefit of the doubt. "I guess it doesn't matter anymore. Knowing isn't going to help me."

"But do you think she was capable of that kind of deception?"

He picked up the ball and glove on his coffee table. "She was making me pretty uncomfortable there at the end," he admitted. "Right after I broke off with her, she paged me at the hospital. When I called her back, she started sobbing and saying she'd rather die than live without me."

"So that's what you meant by crazy. Well, I wish I could say I'm surprised, but it actually makes sense in a twisted way. You were backing off, she was feeling desperate. And you were so careful to use protection when you had sex, it probably gave her the impression that a baby was the one thing that could hold you."

If so, his concern with preventing pregnancy had actually *caused* his current predicament.

There was more rustling on the other end of the phone, and Harrison imagined Noelle trying to get comfortable in bed. "I'm sorry for interrupting your sleep," he said, suddenly aware that she was a living, breathing human being and not the disembodied voice he'd imagined earlier. "I should let you go."

"No, I'm okay."

He hesitated. He was reluctant to take advantage of her, but he had to admit that talking to her made a difference.

"What I can't figure out is why she waited so long to make you aware of the pregnancy," she went on. "If she meant to get pregnant but was afraid you'd push for an abortion, I'd expect her to call you somewhere in the fourth or fifth month, not right before the babies were due."

He tossed the ball into his mitt with a satisfying *thwump*. "When I never called after she moved away, she knew I was serious about the breakup and said she'd decided to keep the news from me indefinitely. But her conscience finally got the better of her."

Noelle's response was a small but honest, "Wow."

Growing agitated again, Harrison stood up. *Thwump.* The impact of the ball felt good as it hit the pocket of his glove. "And now there's a newborn lying in the hospital who…" He didn't know what ending to put on that sentence. Who had no mother. Who deserved a real chance in life. Who was tiny and perfect and yet—

"Who what?" she prompted.

Harrison could hear the wind driving rain against his living room window. The rest of the leaves on the trees would probably be in the parking lot by morning. It had been a wet November. "Who has no one but me," he finished.

Silence reigned for several seconds. He forgot about tossing the ball while he waited for her response.

"And from what you've told me, you don't want him," she said at last.

Scowling, he stretched his neck muscles and tried to explain. "It's not that simple. I don't have anything to give a baby. And I'm not sure I'd be the best person to raise him, even if I did. I was an only child. We moved around a lot. I was never around younger kids." Considering his relationship with Rosie and how they'd taken care of each other almost like equals, he felt as though he'd never really *been* a kid.

"Do you have anyone who might be able to help you?"

"No."

"Then why not put the baby up for adoption?" she asked. "Surely you've thought of that."

"I've thought of it, sure. But..." *Thwump*. The ball hit the glove again. "I can't be certain he'd go to a good home," he said, although he knew there had to be people, couples, who were far better equipped for a baby than he was.

"You could try to find a family with whom you feel comfortable," Noelle responded. "Depending on the type of adoption you choose, you might even be able to maintain a relationship with him."

He couldn't imagine passing his son off to complete strangers. Shirking his duty was something Duane would do, wasn't it? What Duane *did* do?

Somehow the important decisions in Harrison's life always came back to his father. Duane seemed to be standing in the corner of Harrison's apartment, glaring at him, taunting him. *You think you're different, boy? Better? Look at you. You're scrambling to get out of this one, huh?*

"How involved could I be?" he asked.

"That would depend, but there's got to be options."

"I'll have to do some research." As if he had the time... *Thwump*.

"Or…"

Her tone held the promise of a resolution. "Or?" he repeated hopefully, trying to banish Duane from his mind.

"I don't know if you'd ever consider this, but…I'd be happy to take him."

Harrison froze with the ball in his hand. "*Take* him? What do you mean by that?"

She sounded more than a little hesitant when she answered. "I haven't considered all the ramifications yet, but…I'd love to have a baby. *This* baby."

Her? He'd met Noelle only once. And yet he knew several important facts about her already, all of which seemed to recommend her. She was about his age, not too young or too old, obviously kind, definitely intelligent, and she came highly recommended by the nursing staff at the hospital.

"Are you talking day care or adoption or…what?"

"Not day care."

"Then adoption?"

"Yes," she said, almost defiantly. "I'm talking adoption. My heart. My home."

He froze, surprised that he wasn't more relieved to have someone ready to step in for him. "That sounds pretty permanent."

"If I'm going to care for him, I should have legal rights, don't you think?"

"But you're single. If I give him up, why not make sure he goes to a couple or maybe even a family?"

"Because you won't find anyone who will take better care of him than me. And I'll be flexible about letting you be part of his life."

"How big a part would you let me play?"

"How big a part do you *want* to play?"

He pinched the bridge of his nose, trying to answer the one question he'd found unanswerable so far.

"You say you don't want children, but at the same time, you seem reluctant to give him up," she said when he didn't respond right away.

Because he was torn. Before he'd left the hospital tonight, he'd decided his son looked like pictures of his mother's father, who'd died when Harrison was barely five. Ever since that moment, his baby hadn't been a nameless entity to him anymore. His baby had suddenly become Jeremy Ferello.

"Why don't we sleep on the idea and talk about it some more tomorrow," he said. "In person. Can we get together?"

"Of course. Is tomorrow afternoon okay?"

The day before the funeral. "Fine. Where?"

"We could meet here at my place."

Closing his eyes, he tried to envision handing his baby over to this woman. Could he do it? He wasn't sure, but he had to do something.

"Sounds good," he said. Then he set up a time, jotted down directions and hung up.

Noelle sat on the edge of the bed and dropped her head in her hands. Had she lost her mind? What had she been thinking? Basically she'd just offered to raise someone else's child. The son of a man she scarcely knew. And she'd promised Harrison he could be part of his son's life, which meant he'd be part of *her* life.

"I'll never learn," she groaned, and fell back on the bed. Harrison was handsome and seemed intelligent, successful. But Steven had been handsome and intelligent, too. Marrying him had been like biting into a creamy, delicious-looking truffle, only to get a mouthful of salt. She wasn't likely to forget the experience, or be tricked by another smooth-talking man.

Smooth-talking... Harrison definitely knew how to handle himself with a woman. She'd sensed that immediately.

She glanced at the phone. She should call him back and tell him she'd changed her mind. Except she wasn't sure she *had* changed her mind. She wanted a baby. She wanted a second chance to be a good mother, to protect the innocent. Nothing meant more to her than that.

And deep down, she doubted Harrison Ferello would stick around very long, anyway.

CHAPTER
~FOUR~

"Tell me you're not really going to do this," Theresa said, trailing Noelle into the house.

They'd been together all morning, shopping. Noelle hadn't mentioned anything about Harrison's call last night, or his baby, until Theresa was about to drop her off. Why she'd broken down in the end, she didn't know. She should've kept her mouth shut.

"Can't you be positive for once?" she asked, hanging her suede jacket on the antique hall tree in her small entry and stashing her purse right below it. "If Harrison and I can come to some sort of agreement, I have a chance to get a baby...*a newborn baby*...right away. That's a miracle!"

"A miracle?" Theresa didn't bother removing her coat.

Until Noelle told her about Harrison and their meeting this afternoon, she hadn't been planning on coming in. She had to take her niece to the orthodontist in fifteen minutes, but she wasn't about to let that stop her from trying to dissuade Noelle from making what she termed "a big mistake."

"The question is why you'd want to take on a baby right now," Theresa said, following Noelle so closely as they made their way into the kitchen that she nearly stepped on her heel.

Sometimes Theresa seemed to take Austin's death far too lightly. Her attitude triggered a rush of anger in Noelle, but she beat it back by reminding herself that Theresa didn't really understand. "In case you've forgotten, they gave me a hysterectomy when I lost Austin," she said. "I can't have children of my own, and babies don't grow on trees. I can't pass up an opportunity like this."

"Think about the risks!"

Theresa tried to get in front of her to capture her complete attention, and Noelle finally whipped around and propped a hand on her hip. "The only risks I'm thinking about are what might happen to the baby if I don't take him."

"For all you know, the baby could go to an ideal family. You can't say for sure that he won't."

Noelle had been up half the night, worrying about her decision, but she wasn't about to admit that to Theresa.

"I'll feel more assured of his safety and well-being if *I'm* taking care of him."

"What if this Harrison guy makes your life miserable?"

"I told you, he doesn't really want the baby. He's reacting to a sense of obligation. Once he realizes I've got everything under control, that the baby doesn't need him, he'll go on about his business. After a few weeks, I doubt I'll hear from him more than twice a year."

"And the baby will be yours."

"And the baby will be mine."

"What if it doesn't work out that way? What if Harrison changes his mind in a few years and wants to take his baby away from you? What will you do then?"

"A private open adoption is still an adoption. He can't do that. Besides, this baby's mother tricked Harrison into getting her pregnant. As I said, he's just looking for a good way out."

Theresa shook her head. "Haven't you ever heard of Murphy's Law?"

With an exaggerated sigh, Noelle circumvented her friend to start the coffeemaker. After her sleepless night, she needed a strong jolt of caffeine to get her through the rest of the afternoon. "What are my other options?" she asked. "I can't use an adoption agency. They'd put me on a list, a *long* list, and because I'm single, I have no doubt I'd be at the very bottom of it. And this baby needs me."

"Lots of babies need loving parents," Theresa said. "This

isn't the only one. Why not wait until later to adopt—like when you meet someone else and remarry?"

Noelle doubted she'd remarry anytime soon. She still hadn't recovered from her divorce. But Theresa hadn't heard the extenuating circumstances, didn't know about Steven's dark side. Noelle had kept his "little problem" to herself after he'd promised that he'd seek help—and because she didn't want to face the questions it'd raise among her friends and family. *Why didn't you say something sooner? Why didn't you get away from him? How could you let him treat you like that?* Asking herself those questions was painful enough.

"I'll just have to hope for the best," she said, and filled the coffeepot with water.

"That's a cop-out. You're telling me you're not willing to consider all the dangers."

Noelle understood the dangers. She just couldn't think beyond getting her arms securely around the tiny bundle in the hospital. "Maybe I'm not."

"I think you should. Harrison Ferello might be unsafe."

"He's a doctor. He's highly educated and driven, not dangerous." After her experience with Steven, she cringed at her own words, but she knew it was an argument Theresa would understand.

"You don't even know this guy," Theresa insisted.

"Harrison won't stick around!"

Theresa threw up her hands. "Steven said you could be stubborn, but this is ridiculous."

The note of familiarity in Theresa's voice when she mentioned Noelle's ex-husband was new—and nearly caused Noelle to drop the coffeepot. "What'd you say?"

A flash of something—Guilt? Alarm? Regret?—passed through Theresa's eyes, and she turned away. "Nothing. I've got to go. I'm late."

It was Noelle's turn to follow Theresa through the house. "Wait a minute. When did you talk to Steven?"

Theresa finally turned at the door. "A week or so ago."

"Where?"

She glanced down at her car keys as she opened the door, appearing more eager to leave by the second. "I bumped into him at the movies."

"Why didn't you mention it to me?"

"Because it was nothing. We said, 'Hello, how are you?' You know, the usual."

"That's it?"

"Yeah."

They stared at each other for a second, then Theresa mumbled goodbye and left.

Noelle leaned against the door. Something with Theresa didn't sit right. She suspected it had to do with Steven but couldn't imagine what or why. Steven and Theresa had always hated each other.

With a sigh, Noelle decided to let it go. The stress of what was going on in her own life right now was making her jumpy.

Harrison slowed so he could compare the numbers painted on the curb with the address on Noelle's card. This was it. He'd found her house, and it was everything he'd anticipated. A small English Tudor made of red burnished brick, with an arched entry covered in climbing ivy, it sat in the middle of a classy neighborhood of equally stylish homes and looked as clean as it was well-maintained.

Was it the perfect place to raise a child?

He couldn't answer that now, but he was hoping his meeting with Noelle would give him a better idea.

Parking his old truck out front so he wouldn't block the rather narrow driveway leading to a new Volvo and a detached garage, he got out and strode up a walkway littered with red and gold leaves. After hanging up with Noelle last night, he'd fallen into a troubled sleep, but what rest he'd managed to grab, combined with a hot shower and shave and a pair of comfortable jeans, made him feel almost new again.

Noelle answered the door before he could knock. "Hi," she said, a polite smile on her face. "Did you find the house okay?"

Wearing a black sweater and a pair of gray slacks, she was even prettier than Harrison remembered, but he told himself to ignore that. Looks didn't make a mother. His own mother was more than moderately attractive, but as much as he loved Rosie, he wouldn't wish her style of parenting on any child. "Your directions were easy to follow," he said.

"I'm glad." She opened the door wider. "Come in."

The interior of the house smelled slightly of fresh paint and was stylish yet warm and homey. Harrison could see Noelle had a knack for decorating, although he probably didn't have the most discerning eye. Anything was better than the stained Goodwill couches and tattered drapes he'd grown up with. "Nice place."

"Thanks."

"Is this where you lived when you were married?" he asked.

"Steven purchased the house while we were engaged. I moved in after we married. When we divorced, I bought him out." She waved to a picture window overlooking a well-tended garden. "My workshop is out there, to the left. I didn't want to lose it."

Harrison had come here determined to view everything from its worst possible angle, just to be safe. But he didn't see much to be leery about. "Your ex is the hospital administrator you mentioned last night, right?"

"Right. Can I get you a drink?"

"No, thanks."

She waved him into a living room with hardwood

floors, overstuffed green sofas, a circular area rug, distressed pine tables and plenty of candles. But it was the artwork covering the walls and the large sculptures blending in with the furniture that caught his attention.

"This is nice," he said, carefully studying the painting of a rocky cove over the fireplace.

"Thank you."

He recognized the style from the painting on his Memory Box and verified that it was her work by checking the name scribbled in the bottom corner. "So this is what you do for a living?"

"No. Painting's only my hobby."

He cocked an eyebrow at her. "Then…"

She motioned to a life-size sculpture of a small child doing a cartwheel between the sofa and chair. "This is what I do for a living."

He couldn't help being impressed. "You created this?"

She nodded. "Right now I'm doing a whole group of teenagers for the lobby of a new office building on J Street."

"No kidding." She was obviously talented. Her work looked worthy of the best galleries in New York and San Francisco—which lent her even more credibility. "You're good," he said.

"Thank you." She waved him toward the couch. "Please, sit down."

He did as she asked, but refused to let his reservations

disappear too quickly. She seemed normal, almost ideal, but there was so much to raising a child, and he had to take every precaution. He'd never be able to live with himself if she abused or neglected Jeremy. From working in the emergency room, he'd seen what some adults were capable of doing to children.

"Where do you want to start?" she asked, folding one knee beneath her and perching on the leather ottoman across from him.

"Maybe you can explain to me why you want a baby."

He'd been hoping to begin with something simple, but he could tell by the expression that flitted across her face that this question wasn't particularly easy. "Because I lost my own baby," she said shortly. "A year ago."

Of course. She'd mentioned grief and despair. He should have anticipated a tragedy in her recent past. But with postpartum depression, bipolar disorder, and a host of other maladies that sometimes compelled a mother to hurt her own child, this information ended up worrying him more rather than creating any kind of kinship between them. "I'm sorry to hear that."

Her gaze remained steady despite his scrutiny, but she didn't elaborate.

"How old was the baby when…"

"He was stillborn."

Harrison allowed himself a mental sigh of relief. If she was telling the truth—and he'd have to make sure, of course—her response ruled out his worst fears, including Shaken Baby Syndrome. "Were you married at the time?"

"Yes. But my husband and I split up right after I got out of the hospital."

"Losing a child is difficult on a marriage," he said.

Finely arched brows gathered above clear green eyes. "My marriage was in trouble before that, Mr.—"

"Call me Harrison." They'd been so informal with each other last night, but that was before they were considering some type of on-going relationship. Now they both seemed to have taken several steps away from each other.

"Harrison, then," she said. "I was trying to make my marriage work. I didn't realize until I lost the baby that I'd been stupid to hang on for the five years that I did."

"I see." He rested his hands on his knees. He was curious to hear the reasons behind the divorce, but he didn't feel justified in asking, at least not yet. The possibility of a future marriage, however, was a different story. "You know, I hate to pose such personal questions, but—"

She held up a hand. "I understand. You have to do what you can to protect the baby."

"Exactly."

She gave him a brittle smile. Maybe she didn't mind him *asking,* but anything that involved the loss of her baby was obviously a sensitive subject. "What else do you want to know?" she asked.

He searched his mind for a question that didn't pertain

to her marriage or her lost child. That way she could relax a bit before he returned to the hard stuff. "Do you know CPR?"

"No, but I'd happily take a class."

He knew this was coming off like a job interview, but wasn't sure how else to approach it. He couldn't make a decision without feeling reasonably secure that it was a good one. "Tell me a little about your background."

"I grew up in Chicago with three younger brothers. My parents divorced when I was starting high school, which is probably why I tried so hard to save my own marriage. I don't think I ever really forgave my mother for kicking my father out."

"You were close to him?"

"My life just wasn't the same afterward, especially once he remarried. My stepmother had two children of her own, and my brothers were such a handful, she didn't like having us over, so we rarely got to see my father."

"Unfortunately I think that happens all too often. Where is your family now?"

"Still in Chicago. Two of my brothers have married. The youngest is in high school."

"What brought you to Sacramento?"

"I went to UCLA. While I was there, I roomed with a girl who was born in Granite Bay. After graduation, Senator Rodriguez offered her a job here in Sacramento and she talked me into moving north with her."

"And you like it well enough to stay?"

"It's not as cold as Chicago or as crowded as L.A."

He rubbed his chin, trying to think of a delicate way to ask his next question. But there *was* no delicate way. "Have you—" He cleared his throat. "Have you ever been sexually molested, Noelle?"

Her jaw dropped. *"What?"*

"I'm sorry, but that kind of trauma would definitely affect your core values and beliefs, which might carry over into how you treat a child. I want my son to have a healthy view of human intimacy. It's an important part of life."

"I guess I can understand that," she said, but she spoke with some reservation and he got the impression she was evaluating him as much as he was evaluating her. "I've never been molested." She met his gaze more directly. "Have you?"

He recognized the flare of spirit that had motivated her to return the question. "No."

"Well, that settles that, I hope."

Not quite. "How would you handle the subject of sex when raising my son?"

She lifted her chin as if to say she could answer any question he thought to pose. "I'd teach him that sex is normal and enjoyable."

Their gazes locked, and an unexpected frisson of awareness zipped through Harrison. It had been eight months since he'd been with a woman. He was beginning to feel deprived—and Noelle was more than a little appealing. But now wasn't the time to experience any kind of arousal. If she was the decent person he thought she was, he needed her too badly to risk a romantic entanglement that could easily end badly.

"I'd also teach him to respect himself and the women he gets involved with," she continued. Her voice held just enough challenge to make him believe she'd felt the change in chemistry between them but was resisting any type of acknowledgment. "He needs to be aware of the dangers, both physical and emotional. And he should know that sex is never better than when two people are *fully committed and in love.*"

Had she emphasized that last point, or had he imagined it? He wasn't sure. Regardless, he felt his desire wane. After Lynnette, commitment equated with obsession and didn't rate high on his personal list of "must haves."

But what Noelle had said sounded excellent from a parenting perspective. Perfect, as a matter of fact. "That's a healthy response."

"I'm glad you think so."

"What about your future love life?"

"What about it?"

"Do you think there's any chance you might marry soon?"

"None whatsoever."

That had been stated strongly enough. "In a few years?"

"I can't predict something like that, can you?"

Even without a crystal ball, he felt fairly safe saying he wouldn't marry in the next ten years. But he took her point.

"Is there anything else?" she asked.

He had at least a million questions, but he was quickly coming to the conclusion that he wasn't going to find a better candidate to take care of Jeremy. Because he didn't want to scare her off, he decided to ask just a few more. "What type of discipline would you use if Jeremy—"

"Jeremy?" she said.

"That's what I've named him."

"I see. Jeremy what?"

"I don't know. I haven't decided on a middle name. I thought, if we came to some type of agreement about his future, that maybe I'd let you do that."

Another distracting, sexy smile curved her lips. "Okay."

He shifted to the edge of his seat and forced himself to regain his focus. "Anyway, about your style of discipline..."

"My methods would depend on the age of the child and what he's doing wrong," she said. "Time out, if he were younger. Loss of privileges if he were older."

Harrison remembered his mother beating him with a vacuum cord when he was eight years old. Rosie hadn't been particularly violent, but she'd been ill-equipped to raise a child, especially alone, and he'd pushed her too far once or twice. "Jeremy could do much worse," he said. "Are you ever planning to work outside the house?"

"As long as business is good, probably not. But situations change. I can't make you any promises there, either. Only that I'll do my best no matter what comes."

He liked her. She was honest and talented and intelligent. Could he have actually found a solution to his dilemma? "I believe you would."

She seemed to relax. "Great. Any more questions?"

"Don't you have a few?"

She rubbed her palms on her pants as if suddenly nervous again. "You indicated last night that you'd prefer to be involved in your son's life in some capacity. I'm still wondering *how* involved. Are we talking about weekend visits? Or a yearly Christmas gift?"

A yearly Christmas gift? She was obviously offering him the chance to play a very minimal role in Jeremy's life. But just because she seemed like the perfect caregiver didn't mean she was. And he hated the thought that one day there might be a little nine-year-old boy lying awake as he once had, wondering why his father hadn't cared enough to know him.

He took a deep breath. "I'm not sure how involved I want to be…yet. My schedule is pretty demanding. Can we play it by ear for a while?"

Her smile widened considerably. "Of course. I know

you're in a difficult situation, especially with the pressure of your residency and everything."

"Exactly." She seemed a little *too* accommodating in this area, but it was the first thing about Noelle that made Harrison the least bit uncomfortable, so he chose to believe she was only trying to be agreeable. "What about child support?" he asked.

"Child support?" She blinked at him as though she'd never heard of the concept.

"Surely you expect some kind of financial help from me."

"Actually, I hadn't considered it. I don't think parents who adopt a child get support, even if it's an open adoption."

What had sounded so ideal just moments before now seemed so...*permanent.* He wouldn't owe any child support, but he wouldn't have any parental rights, either. He'd be like a visiting uncle. "Is that the only arrangement you're willing to consider?" he asked, feeling conflicted again.

Her eyes narrowed. "What other type of arrangement did you have in mind?"

He raked a hand through his hair. "I guess for right now, I was hoping for something less formal."

She stiffened. "If we don't do a legal adoption, I'll have no protection. You could change your mind in a year or two and decide to cut me out of Jeremy's life. And I've already lost one baby, Harrison...." She didn't finish, but she didn't have to. She'd lost one, and she wasn't willing to risk losing another. He could understand her reluctance to trust him, especially on this, and yet he wasn't ready to give up his parental rights, not until he felt more confident in his decision and in her.

"Then we need some sort of trial period," he said. "I can't sign Jeremy over until I know you better."

Clearly not pleased, she frowned. "How long of a trial period?"

"Three months?" he offered hopefully.

She sank her teeth into her bottom lip. "I'll give you one month," she said at last. "But you *have* to be willing to make a decision by then."

CHAPTER
~FIVE~

A one-month trial period. Noelle had known right away she'd made a mistake bending on that issue. Once again she'd been too empathetic for her own good. But how could she expect Harrison to trust her with his child before he really knew her?

Besides, a month wasn't unreasonable, she decided as she headed in to Wee Ones, a shop specializing in baby furniture that was located a few blocks from her house. Thirty days would allow the shock of the situation to wear off and give Harrison a chance to recover, which was only fair. And Noelle didn't have too much to fear. He was in the first year of his residency, which meant he was as busy as he'd probably ever be. Chances were he wouldn't be able to come around much. If he did show up a lot, he'd learn just how needy a newborn was and how ill-equipped he was to deal with it; if he didn't visit very often, he'd quickly grow accustomed to letting her care for Jeremy while he devoted himself to his career, which was what he really wanted to do anyway. Soon he'd realize he was better off letting his son go. Then it would simply be a matter of filling out the paperwork.

Noelle's cell phone chirped as the Wee Ones saleswoman approached with a polite, "Can I help you?"

Noelle offered her an apologetic smile before glancing down to see who was trying to reach her.

Her screen read, "Unknown caller."

"I'll be with you in a second," she said, and pressed the talk button. "Hello?"

"There you are."

She gritted her teeth the moment she recognized her ex-husband's voice, frustrated that his name hadn't popped up on her screen so she could have let the call go to voice mail. "You've been looking for me?"

"I tried the house first. So how's my beautiful ex?"

The charm meant Steven wanted something. When he was this nice, he always wanted something, and he generally knew how to get it—at least from everyone else.

"My phone said 'unknown caller,'" she told him.

"I'm at a restaurant, using a pay phone. I lost my cell this morning and it hasn't turned up yet."

Lowering her voice, she pivoted away to spare the sales-woman their conversation. "What do you need?"

"Jeez, you're abrupt. Is it always going to be this antag-onistic between us?"

He was trying to disarm her, but she wasn't willing to be duped by his salesman-like tactics. "I'm busy right now, Steven. I can't talk."

"Come on, this will only take a second."

"What is it?"

"I want to quit counseling."

She didn't even need to think about it. "No."

"Come on, Noelle. It's been a year—*a year!* I'm better now. If you'd ever agree to let me come around, you might see that."

Noelle knew he couldn't have changed so fast. "Sorry. You promised to get me a letter from your therapist before you quit seeing her."

"So?"

"I haven't received anything."

"Are you kidding me? You're going to hold me to that? She makes a hundred bucks every time I show up. She'll never admit that I don't have a problem...anymore," he quickly added, but Noelle knew it was only for her ben-efit. Steven took no responsibility for his violent temper. When he'd caused her to lose their child a year ago, he'd actually had the nerve to tell her it wouldn't have happened if she hadn't made him so angry.

"We already agreed on this, Steven," she said, fighting to keep calm.

"I don't want to go back to that therapist."

"Then find a new one."

"Therapy is a total waste."

"I don't know of a better option."

"People at work are beginning to wonder where I disappear to every Monday afternoon."

"Then let them wonder."

"Screw you! I'm not going anymore."

Noelle clenched her jaw. "If I don't receive a copy of your canceled check for this month, as usual, you know what will happen."

"You're bluffing. You don't have any pictures. I never hit you hard enough for pictures to show anything."

"You're deluding yourself again, Steven."

He started shouting obscenities.

"I'm going to hang up," she said.

"Go ahead! You're the biggest bitch I've ever met. I should've knocked some sense into you when I had the chance—"

Noelle disconnected. Shaking, she stared down at her phone as the memories of her many altercations with Steven washed over her. There had been times when he'd knocked her around and, fortunately, she did have the photographs to prove it....

"Are you okay?" Noelle turned to see the saleswoman

hovering behind her, wearing a concerned expression. "You look a little pale."

"I'm fine." She forced a quick smile, but her mind was still on Steven. She was tempted to give up and let him quit counseling. She wanted him out of her life once and for all. But she was afraid of what he might do to the next woman to fall for his handsome face.

Biting back a groan, she realized, once again, that she had to remain strong. If only she'd been stronger a year ago and left him as she should have, as she almost did, she could have saved her baby. "I'm okay," she said.

"Can I get you a glass of water?"

"No." Noelle pumped up the wattage of her smile. "I just need to see your nursery furniture."

The following day, the pediatrician's office called Harrison to say he could come down and pick up his son, and he rushed off to buy diapers and other supplies first thing. Jeremy's release had come a day earlier than expected. Harrison wasn't prepared and had never been more scared of anything in his life. Jeremy seemed so small, so fragile....

"I can't believe they're going to let someone like me walk off with a baby," he told his mother, shifting his cell phone to the opposite ear as he pulled into the hospital parking lot.

"What do you mean *someone like you?* You're a doctor,

for Pete's sake," she laughed. "What type of training do you think a parent should require?"

He was too nervous to appreciate her confidence in him. "Some sort of basic baby care course would be a start."

"Oh, quit worrying. It's easier than you think."

It hadn't been easy for her. He could still remember all the mornings she hadn't been able to make herself get up and help him off to school. After he'd met his father and decided to change before he wound up just like him, he would pull on clothes from the discarded pile on his bedroom floor, eat potato chips, pretzels, or anything else he could find in the kitchen cupboards and hurry outside to catch a ride with Jimmy's mother. If he didn't make it to the corner by eight o'clock, he wouldn't reach school until noon, when his own mother finally dragged herself out of bed. Then she'd get into an argument with his teacher because he'd been late so many times already, and he'd have to miss his recess to catch up on his schoolwork.

But he didn't point Rosie's failings out to her. He didn't want to do anything to wreck her recent happiness. His life could have been worse. At least she'd always loved him and stuck by him. He couldn't say that much for his father.

"Why didn't you have that woman who will be helping out come with you if you're so nervous about picking up the baby?" Rosie asked. "You told me you already checked her character references."

Harrison had checked as many as he could in one afternoon. Not only had Noelle's friends and neighbors confirmed how her baby had died, they'd each said they'd trust her with a child of their own. One person he hadn't been able to reach was a woman named Theresa. But Noelle had said Theresa was her best friend, so he doubted Theresa would tell him anything different. "I did. She seems ideal. But she's gone for the day. I wasn't expecting the pediatrician to call until tomorrow."

"Where'd she go?"

"She has an appointment to show her sculptures to some commercial developers in Stockton."

"Sounds fancy."

Juggling his purchases and his phone, he locked the truck and strode toward the entrance. "She's talented."

"Are you still planning to attend Lynnette's funeral?" his mother asked.

He shifted the car seat he was carrying so he could see his watch. When he realized it was already noon, he frowned. The funeral started in an hour. "I'm trying, but I'll be late if I make it at all."

"That won't reflect well on you."

Light drops of rain began to fall, and Harrison picked up his pace. "Since when have you cared about appearances? Or being late, for that matter."

"I don't, but neither do I like anyone saying anything bad about my boy."

Harrison smiled despite his preoccupation with the funeral and the fact that he wanted to be there for Jeremy's mother and his twin, Tyler. He wanted to have that memory in addition to the small articles in the box Noelle had painted for him. "Lynnette's family isn't going to approve of me no matter what I do. They blame me for her unhappiness this past year, maybe even her death."

"What'd you have to do with her death?"

"She died giving birth to my children, remember?"

"She got pregnant on purpose, against your wishes!"

He entered the lobby and quickly moved off to one side, out of the footpath of the other visitors. "You and I know that, but we're talking about *her* family here." He put his packages down until he could finish his conversation. "They see the situation a little differently than we do."

"Has her mother or anyone else in the family offered to help you with the baby?"

"No."

"Have they even been to the hospital to see him?"

"Winona, her sister, came by when I was here last night. She said her mother's relapsed into depression and isn't up to visiting. She wanted to know what I planned to do with the baby."

"Did you tell her you're putting him up for adoption?"

Harrison fought the reluctance that gripped him at mention of the adoption, reminding himself of all Noelle could offer his son. She had more time *and* money than he did.

Everyone he'd spoken to had given her a glowing report. And she wanted a baby. "I told her that I've found a good home for him."

"Does Winona think you're doing the right thing?"

"She didn't say, but she seemed relieved I'm handling the situation. From what I can tell, Lynnette's family isn't in a position to do anything for Jeremy and—"

"You named him?" his mother broke in.

Harrison adjusted the tie he'd put on in anticipation of the funeral. "Yeah, actually I did."

"After my *dad?*"

"He looks like Grandpa."

"You didn't tell me."

"I didn't see the point. You're emotionally unattached right now. Why make this hard on you?"

There was a long pause. "Is it hard on you?"

"No," he lied.

"But if you've named him after my dad, you must really believe he's yours."

A large group of people came into the lobby, several carrying flowers. Harrison could smell the carnations as he moved the car seat off to one side. "I'm pretty sure he is, but I still ordered a paternity test. I can't spend the rest of my life with that 'what if' in the back of my mind."

"Isn't a paternity test expensive?"

"It cost three hundred bucks, but I found a lab online

that's overnighting me a tester kit. I'll do the cheek swabs myself, then send the DNA samples back."

"How long will it take after that?"

"A few days."

"It happens even quicker in the movies."

"Unfortunately this is real life, and the hospital lab, at least *this* hospital lab, doesn't do them." He peered through the window as the sky darkened and the rain fell harder. "I'd better go," he said. "It's starting to storm outside, and I don't want it to get too ugly before I buckle Jeremy into the truck."

"Okay. Call me later and let me know how it goes."

Harrison picked up the bag containing the diapers, diaper-wipes, undershirts and fuzzy sleepers he'd bought, but before he hung up, he had one last question. "Mom?"

"Yeah?"

"Did you ever hear from Duane after that day we... After we went to his house that summer?"

"God, you haven't mentioned Duane for twenty years. What makes you ask about him now?"

"I was just wondering what became of him."

"He worked at the same auto shop until you turned eighteen. I know that much because of his child-support payments. But since then..." She released a long sigh. "He could've left Yuba City. I sent him a notice of your college graduation and included a note that you'd been accepted into med school, but never got any response. It's been so long now, I guess he could be anywhere."

"Of course he could."

"Why? You don't want to see him again, do you?"

"No, I was only curious."

"He was the one who missed out, Harrison."

"Was he?" Harrison remembered how badly he'd longed for a father and found that very difficult to believe.

"Of course he was. Maybe I wasn't the best parent in the world, but now that I'm older and at least a little wiser—" her normally strident voice faltered "—I realize you were the best thing to ever happen to me. And you're the best thing I'll leave behind when I go."

"Thanks, Mom," he said. But her words—and the strong emotion they evoked—did nothing to make his decision easier.

If he let Noelle adopt Jeremy, he'd be the one missing out.

CHAPTER
⊶SIX⊷

The ringing OF THE cordless phone woke Harrison from a deep sleep. He was startled for a second, blinking against the darkness, wondering where he was and how he'd gotten there. Then something squirmed in the crook of his arm and he realized he was lying on the couch, holding a baby.

The full reality of the situation—the fact that this was *his* baby—connected in his brain a second later. But he still couldn't believe it.

Using his free hand, he fumbled under the pillows and between the seat cushions, but didn't reach the phone in time.

It was probably Rosie, checking up on him. Earlier,

Jeremy had cried so much that Harrison had placed three distress calls to his mother and two to the nurses at the hospital. He'd been positive there was something critically wrong, even though, from a medical standpoint, he couldn't figure out what that might be.

Fortunately the nurses he'd spoken to had confirmed what he thought—that sometimes babies cried for no apparent reason—and that everything was probably okay. Odd how different it was being on the receiving end of medical advice.

Thank God Jeremy had settled down at last. He was sleeping peacefully now, so peacefully that Harrison couldn't imagine how he'd caused so much trouble in the first place.

He considered calling his mother back to tell her the situation had improved, but he decided to let it go until morning. He was so tired....

He let his eyelids drift closed once more, only to have the phone drag him to consciousness again. Evidently Rosie couldn't wait until morning.

A new search yielded the handset before the ringing could subside. "Hello?"

"Harrison?"

"Yes?" It was a woman's voice, but not his mother's, and Harrison was too groggy to place it.

"It's Noelle."

Noelle! Clutching the baby, he sat up, trying to gather

his senses. He hadn't expected her to call so late. "Are you home?"

"I'm in my car. I just went by the hospital. Nurse Matheson told me they released Jeremy today."

He gazed down at the bundle in his arms. "I picked him up this morning."

The baby began to stretch, causing Harrison's stomach to knot in dismay. Would he start crying again? The past few hours had been harrowing. Harrison had never felt so helpless or inadequate. He needed Noelle even more than he'd thought.

Leaning closer to the table beside him, he squinted at the bottle he'd left there, trying to see if there was any milk in it. But between the darkness and the kind of bottle it was—the one with the plastic liners designed to keep the air out—he couldn't really tell. *Don't cry, kid. Come on, don't cry....*

"I left a message on your answering machine," he said, lowering his voice.

"I don't know how to check it remotely. Where's the baby now?"

"Here with me."

"I'm sorry I wasn't around to help. Are the two of you okay?"

For the moment, they were. But whether or not Harrison remained okay depended on what Jeremy did next.

"I think so." Still tense, he watched the baby squirm and yawn and squirm some more.

Finally, Jeremy seemed to settle once more, and Harrison released his breath. "He's going back to sleep."

She laughed softly. "Don't worry, I can take him now. Or would you rather I wait until morning?"

Harrison remembered the mess in the kitchen he'd made when he'd sterilized the nipples and rings and bottles; the bedding and clothes he'd washed, with a gentle detergent, that still needed to be moved into the dryer; the dirty diaper waiting by the door for a trip to the garbage; and the packaging he'd discarded as he opened the different items he needed, including the alcohol pads to clean around Jeremy's umbilical cord. The car seat sat overturned in the middle of the living room, where he'd stumbled over it, and the diaper bag was tossed to one side, its contents strewn across the floor because Harrison had been in such a hurry to get Jeremy changed in case that might stop the crying. He'd had his son only one day, and already his apartment had been transformed into a place he barely recognized.

Taking care of a newborn was every bit as difficult as he'd imagined. "I'll bring him over to you right now," he said.

"No, I'm already in the car and you sound tired. Tell me where you live and I'll come get him."

"Are you sure you don't mind?"

"Positive."

Harrison envisioned his father chuckling over the relief he felt that Noelle was on her way, but he was too tired to let it get to him. At least he'd picked Jeremy up from the hospital and cared for him all day. That was a step in the right direction—and a lot more than Duane would've done.

Noelle had trouble finding Harrison's apartment. By the time she arrived it was nearly one o'clock and raining again. Opening her compact umbrella, she stepped out of her Volvo, quickly surveyed the garden-style complex, and hurried across the puddle-ridden lot, moving as fast as she dared in high heels. It hadn't made sense to go home and change. She'd been too excited to get Jeremy.

Jeremy... She liked that name. She'd been searching her brain for a good middle name to go with it ever since Harrison had mentioned he'd let her choose one. She had yet to come up with anything. But she was sure she'd have better luck once she had a chance to get to know her baby.

Her baby... She could hardly believe the twist of fate that had given her this opportunity.

Or was it an opportunity? Was she being stupid to get involved?

She didn't think so. Maybe it would be different if she could have more children of her own, but Steven had made that impossible.

A little damp and definitely cold, she lowered her umbrella before knocking softly on Unit #31. She waited several long seconds, then knocked again. Finally she tried the door and found it unlocked.

"Harrison?" she called, poking her head inside.

"Noelle?"

The thickness of Harrison's voice indicated that he'd fallen back asleep, just as she'd suspected he might.

"Sorry to barge in on you," she said, "but you didn't answer my knock." Leaving her umbrella on the stoop, she stepped inside a utilitarian family room and kitchen area, lit only by the flicker of an old console-style television. A bike stood in the corner, and some shelves held several books, a few photographs and the Memory Box she'd made.

Harrison was lying on the couch, wearing socks, a T-shirt and faded jeans and holding the baby. "I thought I was dreaming." He yawned and scrubbed a hand over his face, then his gaze ran down to her feet and back up again. "You look nice."

"Thank you."

"What time is it?"

"Late. I got lost."

"Why didn't you call me?"

"I wanted to let you rest." She stared down at the baby in his lap and felt her pulse leap. "Looks like Jeremy's doing okay."

"You say that as though he's sweet. He's been a nightmare."

A flash of white teeth told her Harrison wasn't really upset, and Noelle couldn't help returning his smile. For someone who didn't want children, he'd taken his role as a father pretty seriously. His apartment was in shambles, but from what she could see, the mess was all baby-related.

The television changed colors, allowing Noelle a better glimpse of Harrison's clean, strong features. Stubble darkened his square jaw, but the thick blond hair sticking up on his head and his sleepy blue eyes gave his face a disarming, boyish look.

Jeremy could certainly have inherited worse genes, she thought. If he took after Harrison, he had every chance of being tall, well-built and too handsome for his own good.

"Did you make it to the funeral today?" she asked. She was eager to get Jeremy in her arms, but she was afraid, too—afraid she'd melt down the moment she touched him. Sometimes she felt completely recovered from the loss of her baby a year earlier. But there were other times when it seemed as though the passing months had only camouflaged the hurt.

Harrison shook his head. "I would've been *really* late, and I had Jeremy by then. I decided it might be better for Lynnette's family if we said our own prayers for her and Tyler—"

"Tyler?"

"Lynnette's sister named the other baby."

"I see."

"Anyway, I decided it might be better for them if we just faded away."

"They're not interested in seeing the baby?"

"It isn't that so much. Her mother suffers from depression and isn't doing well, and her sister's involved in a custody battle for her own child. They can't do anything for Jeremy. I was afraid it'd just make them feel worse to have a reminder that the entire situation didn't end with Lynnette's and Tyler's deaths."

Noelle was mildly surprised by Harrison's sensitivity. Lynnette had tried to trap him, yet he was doing his best to shield her family from the consequences?

"Can I hold him?" she asked at last, unable to wait any longer.

"Sure." Harrison sat up and motioned to the space beside him. "Have a seat."

Noelle could feel his residual body heat when she perched on the couch. But that had nothing to do with the warmth that rolled through her when he handed her the baby. This warmth came from somewhere deep inside, like a candle burning in her heart.

Closing her eyes, she rubbed her lips across the baby's cheek. He smelled so good, so…familiar. She'd known this moment might be difficult for her. But she'd had no idea that Jeremy would evoke such vivid memories of the day she'd had her own baby. Although she'd held Austin only briefly, her arms had ached for him ever since. And now, after so long, it felt almost as if she had him back.

She could sense Harrison watching her and tried to say, "He's so soft," to cover the depth of her reaction. But she couldn't speak. Tears welled in her eyes almost instantly, and her chest constricted until she could scarcely breathe. Her only escape was to bury her face in the baby's terry-cloth sleeper before she came apart.

Mommy's so sorry, Austin, so terribly, terribly sorry....

"Noelle?" Harrison said softly, unsure how to react.

She didn't move.

"Noelle, are you okay?"

She said nothing, but she didn't need to. He knew she was not okay. She was crying—if he had his guess, for the baby she'd lost.

Harrison hesitated, knowing she probably wished she were alone. But the sight of her bowed head made him want to protect her, to comfort her.

Moving closer, he put his arm around her. "You're going to be okay," he murmured.

Only the wind answered him. It howled outside, tossing rain against the large front window in great gusts that made Harrison feel isolated from the rest of the world—from everyone except this lovely woman who was struggling so hard with her inner demons. He understood her fight, understood how memories, experiences and losses of the past could sneak up in a dark moment.

Her shoulders shook beneath his arm as she cried silently. Rubbing his hand up and down her spine, he turned her slightly so he could draw her and Jeremy into a loose embrace. "Let it go," he said. "There's no one here but me."

He thought she might pull away and insist on coping alone, or even leave, but she didn't. "Do you want to talk about it?"

"No."

"It might make things easier."

"It's nothing."

"It doesn't seem like nothing."

Her eyes finally lifted. "I—I should've left him sooner, that's all," she said, her expression tortured. "It would have changed everything."

Harrison took Jeremy from her and put him in his car seat. Crouching before her, he covered her cold hands with his. "Who?"

"My ex-husband."

"Why?"

"It was my fault," she said.

Her fingers felt dainty, almost fragile beneath his touch. "What was your fault?"

Her next words seemed to require significant effort. "The baby's death."

Chills cascaded down Harrison's spine, and he couldn't help glancing at Jeremy. "How?"

"My ex-husband was…"

"What?" he prompted.

She closed her eyes. "A bastard."

A bastard didn't tell him much. "What'd he do?"

No response.

"Noelle?"

Her face suddenly seemed chalky white in the darkness.

"Did he hurt you?"

She nodded as the possibilities poured through Harrison's mind.

"Physically?"

As she opened her eyes, her large pupils reflected the light of the TV, but she didn't seem to see him.

"Noelle?" He lifted her hand to his mouth, brushed his lips across her knuckles to gain her attention. "Did he hit you?"

Drawing a ragged breath, she suppressed a shudder, and it was enough to confirm what he'd guessed already.

"Damn him."

Finally she spoke, but her voice sounded flat, unnatural. "He made me lose my baby. And…after that, I had to have a hysterectomy, which of course means…"

She didn't finish, but she didn't need to. Harrison finally understood why she might want a stranger's baby, why she might be willing to take Jeremy on almost any terms.

Reaching up, he wiped a tear from her cheek. "How is that your fault?" he asked.

Her forehead rumpled as she fought the emotions coursing through her, but another tear escaped her thick lashes. "I told you. I should've left him."

"You didn't know what he was going to do."

"I knew he wasn't what he appeared to be. I thought… I thought I could help him, that he'd try harder, that the baby would make a difference, but—"

"It didn't," Harrison said shortly.

"No." The word was barely a whisper.

"Then it was *his* fault, Noelle, not yours."

She started to shake her head, but he gripped her shoulders to make sure she'd listen. "If he struck you, he *is* a bastard, and it's *all* his fault."

She blinked at him with those large green eyes of hers, as though she longed to accept what he said, and he hoped she'd be able to. She was carrying a burden that was far too heavy for her.

"I wish I'd never married him."

"You can't change the past," Harrison told her. "You have to forget and go on."

"I can't forget."

"Sure you can, in time." He lifted her hand and rubbed her knuckles against his lips once again, trying to ignore the fact that his desire to comfort her was beginning to mix with other desires—like the desire to kiss her, to re-place the pain she was feeling with powerful, positive sensation.

He knew they were experiencing an unusual emotional connection, enhanced by the darkness in his apartment and the late hour. But he doubted she felt the same arousal that snaked through his blood. Letting go of her, he stood up, and she wiped her eyes with quick, impatient strokes.

"It's late—I'd better get going," she said. "I'm sorry for unloading on you. It was just…holding Jeremy for the first time—"

"Noelle…"

She looked up at him.

"I understand."

She nodded mutely, then stood and started gathering Jeremy's things, but he caught her arm. "Is there any chance I could convince you to stay the night?"

Evidently he hadn't done a very good job of concealing the sexual awareness he felt. Suspicion entered her eyes, and the color immediately returned to her face. "You can have my bed," he hurried to add. "I'll sleep on the couch. It's just that the storm's getting worse by the minute, and I'd rather not have you and Jeremy driving in these conditions."

"Right, the storm." She glanced at the window, as if she were only now aware of the slashing rain.

"It'd be better to get some sleep and leave in the morning, don't you think?"

She met his gaze and that intangible *something* he'd sensed in her living room arced between them again. "Sure, better safe than sorry," she said, then cleared her throat and looked quickly away.

Crying woke Noelle only a few hours later. At first she couldn't grasp the significance of it. It was just noise. Loud. Foreign. Intrusive. And she couldn't figure out where the heck she was. The bed was comfortable, but the room was strange, sparsely furnished. No pictures on the walls. Nothing but a blind on the only window.

Suddenly she remembered. She was sleeping in Harrison's bed, she was wearing Harrison's clothes, and his baby, Jeremy—no, *her* baby—was crying. He needed her.

Springing out of the tangle she'd made of the blankets, she fumbled through the darkness to where she'd left Jeremy wrapped warmly in his infant seat. "I'm coming, sweetheart...I'm here," she cooed.

His cries quieted to a whimper as soon as she scooped him to her. "You're okay, honey. I'm right here." She settled him in the crook of her arm. "Better late than never, huh?"

The moment she kissed his soft cheek, he twisted toward her, innocent, trusting, searching for food. The solid feel of him in her arms seemed to fill the massive emptiness in her chest that had been there since her own baby's death. And the pain she'd experienced earlier when she'd held Jeremy drained out of her, at least for tonight. Now she was actually able to smile. "Don't fuss. I'll get you a bottle."

She opened the bedroom door to head out into the hall and bumped into Harrison coming from the other direction. It was too dark to see him, but her arm had definitely grazed the warm bare skin of a flat, tightly muscled stomach.

"Sorry, I didn't mean to frighten you," he said, steadying her when she let out a startled gasp. "I thought I'd get the baby so you could sleep."

"I should have gotten up sooner. For some reason his crying didn't wake me right away."

"You haven't had much sleep."

"What time is it?"

"Four o'clock."

"The door was shut. How did he manage to wake you?"

"I'm a light sleeper. It comes from working through the night at the hospital."

"Then you probably need your sleep more than I do."

"I'm getting used to the hours."

It *would* be hard for a single person in his situation to raise a baby, she thought.

"I already made a bottle," he said. "Do you want me to take Jeremy?"

"No, I've got him."

Harrison's hand slipped down her arm. He was only guiding the bottle, but his touch, the darkness, his scent on the clothes she was wearing and the knowledge that she was sleeping where he slept every night caused a giddy, breathless sensation to shimmy through her.

"Here you go."

She thanked him, but she didn't turn back to the bedroom. For the moment, she stood transfixed between the bed at her back and the man standing in front of her.

Finally Harrison muttered, "See you in the morning," and the floor creaked as he moved away.

CHAPTER
∽SEVEN∽

Harrison had to work hard not to stare. Noelle was wearing the gym shorts he'd given her last night to sleep in, only she'd rolled them up at the waist so they wouldn't slip down over her hips. Now they revealed a pair of the shapeliest legs he'd ever seen.

After washing and drying her bowl, she put it in the cupboard and came toward the table. Harrison dragged his attention back to his cereal.

"Did the pediatrician say when I'm supposed to bring Jeremy in for a checkup?" she asked, adding another spoonful of sugar to her coffee as she sat down.

Jeremy was sleeping again. Fortunately he did that quite often. But Harrison thought it would be nice if the baby would wake up, so he'd have something more demanding than cereal to distract him from Noelle's nicely sculpted legs. "In two weeks."

"Do you have his name and address?"

Legs… What was wrong with him? He had other problems to worry about, *big* problems that were never going to go away. And here he was, watching every move she made and fairly salivating. The male sex drive sometimes surprised even him. "I'll call you with it later."

She took a sip of coffee. "Would you also let them know of our arrangement so I don't surprise anybody when I show up instead of you?"

"Of course."

When she finished her coffee and got up, he allowed himself another admiring glance at her legs. "When can I see you again?"

She pivoted to face him, her eyebrows arched in apparent surprise. "What?"

He cleared his throat. "I mean, when can I see *Jeremy* again?"

She glanced at the baby as if she hadn't done so a million times already this morning, and Harrison hid a smile. She couldn't keep her eyes off Jeremy; Harrison couldn't keep his eyes off her. It was almost laughable.

The moment she saw that Jeremy was still sleeping peacefully, she turned to Harrison. "When would you like to?"

"I have six twelve-hour shifts at the hospital this week, but I'm off on Wednesday. Will that work?"

She started making a bottle, presumably for the road. "That's fine, but…"

"But?" he echoed.

"I understand how stressful a residency can be, so if it doesn't work out, don't worry. Work, sleep, play softball. We'll be fine on our own."

Play softball? She sounded as though she didn't care if she ever heard from him again. And of course she probably didn't. Then she'd have the baby all to herself. "It'll work out," he said.

"Well, if something comes up and you can't get away for a while, I hope you know it'll be okay. I'll love Jeremy as my own, give him everything he needs—"

"Noelle."

She ignored him and checked her watch. "Oh boy, is it that late already? I'd better get changed." She started for the bedroom, but he stood up and cut her off.

"I'll see you on Wednesday," he repeated, more pointedly.

She stood only inches away. His clothes fell baggy and shapeless on her smaller frame, and her mascara was slightly smudged, but she looked more beautiful than she had the night he'd first seen her at the hospital. Fresh, casual, warm and real…

The hand he'd placed on her arm itched to explore the

warm skin beneath his touch—and elsewhere. But he let go of her and merely allowed himself to run a finger along her jaw. "I'm going to be part of Jeremy's life, Noelle," he said softly. "That was our agreement."

Her neck muscles worked as she swallowed, and if he wasn't imagining it, her breathing grew shallow. "Of course. I was just letting you know that I have no expectations. Visit only when you want to," she said, then slipped past him.

"You wanted to *what?*"

Noelle held the phone a little farther from her ear, cringing at the shock in Theresa's voice. "You heard me. I wanted to sleep with him. If he'd come back into the bedroom with me when he brought me Jeremy's bottle, or when I was getting changed to leave, I'm honestly not sure I would have sent him away."

"But you'd barely met him!"

"I know. It's crazy, but also…exciting, hopeful. It's the first time I've felt anything like that since my divorce." Noelle hugged Jeremy closer and continued to rock him gently in her arms while he slept. She'd scarcely gone out in the two weeks since she'd brought him home, but she didn't mind being cooped up. She loved having a new baby, and that night at Harrison's—and the nights she'd seen him since—had given her a lot to think about. Now she knew she could desire a man again, that after the hysterectomy, her body wasn't the numb, empty shell she some-times feared it was.

"Why didn't you tell me about this before?" Theresa asked.

"You haven't really been by, except that once when you came to see the baby."

"Sorry, I've been...busy lately." Noelle wondered what was suddenly taking up so much of her time, but Theresa rushed on before she could ask. "I've called you a few times. You could have mentioned it then."

Before, Noelle hadn't wanted to talk about that night at Harrison's. "I don't know why I didn't tell you. I was embarrassed, I guess, wasn't sure *what* I thought of my re-action."

"And now?"

Noelle laughed. "I still don't know what to think, but like I said, I'm happy that I seem to be healing."

"Do you ever feel that way when you're with him now?"

"Sometimes," Noelle admitted.

"You should let him know," Theresa stated bluntly.

"I can't. What if he feels the same way? We'll wind up in bed together."

"Then you'll have what you want."

"You think I should sleep with him?"

"You bet I do. Since you and Steven split up, you've been walking around like the living dead. As far as I'm concerned, it would be good therapy."

"That's some kind of therapy, Theresa."

"Besides, he's not much of a stranger anymore."

That was true. Harrison had spent several evenings with her since she'd brought Jeremy home. He was usually on his way home from work or, if he was working graveyard, just heading back to the hospital after trying to grab a few hours' sleep in the afternoon, but they'd spent a lot of time talking, watching TV and eating dinner together.

"At least the tension between you would have an outlet," Theresa added. "Once it's over, maybe you can concentrate on other things. This way—"

"I can't risk getting involved with Harrison," Noelle interrupted briskly. "If the relationship didn't work out, I couldn't very well expect him to walk away and leave me his son. And you know this baby is more important to me than anything."

"I agree that Jeremy is wonderful. But love and desire are an important part of a woman's life, too."

"Thank God I'm beginning to believe that again. I'm thrilled just to *want* to feel a man's hands on me."

"So...the attraction's merely physical, or—"

"Oh yeah," Noelle said, but she knew that wasn't true. Harrison had been the only person capable of reaching that cold dark place where she harbored her feelings about her lost baby and her divorce. His support had helped her deal with some of the debilitating guilt, and because of that, she'd been tempted to trust him to bring her body back to life, too. That night, at his place, she'd felt healthy and normal for the first time in twelve months. She was grateful to him and liked him a great deal. But she didn't want to make Theresa feel like less of a friend for not being the one to help her through Austin's death.

"How do you think *he* feels?" Theresa asked.

"I don't know. It's been two weeks since that night and he hasn't even touched me."

"How many times have you seen him?"

"At least ten. He comes over for dinner whenever he can. Sometimes I cook, sometimes he brings takeout." She went to lay Jeremy down because she needed to do a load of laundry. "What about you?" she asked. "Your love life must be hopping, considering how scarce you've been around here. Are you still seeing that guy from work?"

"Not anymore."

Noelle turned on the mobile over Jeremy's head while waiting for Theresa to expand on her answer—but she didn't. "So what happened?"

"The attraction fizzled out before it got off the ground. And…"

"And?"

"I've met someone else."

"Really?" Noelle straightened in surprise. "When?"

"I've known him for a while, actually."

A strange tension sprang up that hadn't been there just moments before, but Noelle couldn't figure out what, exactly, had changed. "And you think *I've* been keeping secrets?"

"I wasn't expecting the relationship to come to much, but I...I think I really like him," Theresa admitted.

"So who is he?"

A strained pause. "Noelle..."

"What?"

The doorbell rang in the background. "Never mind. He's here. I've got to go, okay? I'll call you later."

The phone clicked in her ear, and Noelle sank into the rocker near Jeremy's crib. She wasn't sure what was going on with her best friend, but she had a feeling it wasn't good.

Exhaustion weighed heavily on Harrison's back and shoulders. He'd just spent one of the longest days of his life. His shift at the Med Center had seemed to drag on for an eternity. He had a headache, his nerves were on edge, and he felt like he wanted to sleep for a month. Yet here he was, calling Noelle the moment he walked into his apartment. It had been two weeks since he'd let her take Jeremy home with her, but he thought of her when he was at work, late at night, first thing in the morning.

What was going on? He'd never been so preoccupied with a woman.

It was because of Jeremy, he told himself. He hadn't been able to stop thinking of his son, either. He'd gotten the results back from the paternity test a week ago, and they'd been positive, just as he'd expected.

When the fourth ring went unanswered, Harrison figured the answering machine would kick in. He was about to hang up when he heard a breathy, "Hello?"

"Noelle? It's Harrison."

"Oh…hi."

He glanced at the Memory Box she'd painted for him, which had come to represent Noelle as much as his lost son, and smiled. "How's Jeremy?"

"Good. I just bathed him and was drying him off when the phone rang. That's what took me so long to pick up."

"Do you need me to call you back?"

"No, he's here in my arms."

"Can I see him tonight?" Harrison asked the same question almost every night. He wanted to see his son, but he wanted to see Noelle, too. There was something comforting about her home and the way she took care of his baby. And sometimes, when he looked up at her, he could imagine taking her in his arms and—

"Can I fix you some dinner?"

He forced his wandering mind back to the conversation. What had he eaten so far today? A package of Pop-Tarts he'd found in the employee lounge and a gallon of coffee. But she'd cooked last night. "Why don't I bring pizza?"

"I've already defrosted a couple of pork chops."

He smiled. She was beginning to expect him. "Are you sure you'd rather cook?"

"I'm sure."

"Okay, I'd appreciate it." He hung up and immediately started giving himself the usual pep talk about continuing to keep things impersonal with Noelle. He didn't want to blow what seemed like a perfect situation for Jeremy. But where Noelle was concerned, he was finding it more and more difficult to keep his hands to himself.

Harrison stopped at the closest convenience store for a bottle of wine to take to dinner and a cup of coffee so he wouldn't nod off on the way. Then he hurried onto the freeway. He had a fifteen-minute drive. He wanted to enjoy being away from the Med Center and relax to some good jazz on the radio while he anticipated seeing Noelle and Jeremy. But Lynnette's mother hadn't returned his call when he'd tried to apologize for missing the funeral, and he thought he should let her know the results of the paternity test.

Setting his coffee cup in its holder, he retrieved his cell phone.

"Hello?"

Harrison didn't recognize the voice of the person who'd answered. "Is Connie there?"

"One minute."

A few seconds later, Lynnette's mother came on the

line. Harrison wasn't surprised to find that she sounded extremely subdued.

"Connie?"

"Yes?"

"It's Harrison."

A long pause. "What do you want?" she asked at last.

He couldn't put a name to the emotion in her voice but the undercurrent wasn't positive. "I wanted to tell you... the baby's mine."

"I thought so."

Ignoring the vindication in her voice, he forged on. "I also wanted to say..." What? How could anything he said make the smallest difference to her? She'd lost her daughter three weeks ago. "I'm sorry about Lynnette. I never meant to hurt her. I hope you'll believe me."

Silence followed, then he thought he heard her sniffle.

"I know you're going through a miserable time," he went on, "but I wanted to put your mind to rest about the baby. I'll make sure he has everything he needs, and...if you ever want to see him, just give me a call."

"You're keeping him?" she asked in surprise.

Harrison's heart jumped against his chest. He hadn't meant that he was keeping him. He couldn't keep him. With his hours, Jeremy would be raised by day-care personnel.

But if Noelle insisted on adoption, he wasn't sure he

could live with scheduled visits and no real involvement, either.

"Um...I'm not sure exactly what'll happen. At least not yet. But whatever I do, I'll make arrangements so that we can both be part of his life."

"Thank you, Harrison," she said softly. "I have to admit that I'm starting to see why Lynnette loved you so much."

Harrison smiled and hung up. His call had made a difference, at least to Connie. But *he* was feeling more unsettled than ever. He hadn't chosen to have Jeremy; he wasn't the best person to raise him. Yet the moment Connie had asked if he was keeping his son, he'd suddenly known, in a bone-deep way, that he could never give him up. Not completely. Not even to Noelle. Which meant he had to tell her...tonight.

CHAPTER
～EIGHT～

Noelle watched Harrison park from her kitchen window, then drew a steadying breath as he dodged a soggy pile of leaves in the gutter and strode up the walkway. She'd thought of him far too much since she'd seen him last, and it had only been one day.

She waited for him to knock before she answered the door. Although she'd told herself she wasn't dressing up for him, she'd pulled her hair back, applied makeup and changed into a nice pair of jeans, a black sweater and leather boots with heels high enough that she and Harrison were almost at eye level.

"That was quick," she told him as she stood in the doorway.

"I'm getting pretty familiar with the trip." He grinned, looking great in a brown sweater and chinos. But small lines at his eyes and mouth showed fatigue.

"Come in." She held the door for him. "Jeremy's getting fussy. I think he wants to be fed."

Harrison turned his shoulders so he could fit past her, bringing him close enough that she could smell his cologne. The scent immediately carried her back to the night she was in his clothes and his bed, and all the nights she'd spent with him since then.

"Smells good," he said.

She'd been thinking the same thing, but not about the food. "Dinner's almost ready. Why don't you sit in the living room and feed Jeremy while I finish up?"

"Sure, no problem."

While he settled in with the baby, she turned off the stereo in favor of ESPN so he'd have something to watch. But when she returned from the kitchen fifteen minutes later, she found both Harrison and the baby asleep.

Harrison had dozed off a time or two in the past, but never *before* dinner. She was disappointed they wouldn't be eating together, but she was also relieved to see he was finally getting some rest. He needed to slow down. And he looked perfect on her couch.

Lifting Jeremy from his lap, she put the baby in his crib, turned on the monitor and closed the door. Then she brought a blanket and a pillow from her bedroom.

Harrison opened his eyes when she pressed him to lie down. "We need to talk," he mumbled.

"We'll talk in the morning. Get some sleep."

She thought he might argue, but the doorbell interrupted.

"Are you expecting someone?" he asked, coming more awake.

She checked her watch to see that it was only seven o'clock. "No, but I'm sure it's Theresa. She said she might drop by tonight."

He started to sit up, but she nudged him back down and covered him with the blanket. "Relax. I'll talk to her in the kitchen."

"This isn't going to work, you know that, don't you?" he said before she could leave the room.

"What isn't going to work?"

"Keeping everything so…polite and formal between us."

"It has to work," she said.

He shook his head but closed his eyes, and she went to answer the door.

She was so sure it was Theresa that she didn't bother checking the peephole, something she immediately regretted when she saw Steven standing on her front porch.

"What are you doing here?" she asked before he could say hello.

He put a hand on the door so she couldn't close it. "I've come for the pictures."

"Steven—"

"Get them. I won't let you blackmail me any longer."

"Blackmail you! I'm trying to make sure you get some help, you ungrateful jerk."

"I don't need any help."

"You need lots of help, Steven. You caused me to lose a baby—and the chance of ever having another one."

"That's bullshit. I'm tired of you blaming me. It was an accident."

"An accident that wouldn't have happened if not for your violent temper!"

"You'll see the meaning of violent if you don't get me those damn pictures."

"What I have are only copies. They won't do you any good."

"Bullshit." He started shoving his way into the house but came to an abrupt halt when he realized that Harrison had just blocked his way.

"Who's *this?*" Steven's gaze darted suspiciously between the two of them.

"Harrison Ferello, meet my ex-husband," she said.

Harrison didn't bother with any niceties. "I don't re-member hearing Noelle invite you in."

Steven's expression turned sulky. "She has something of mine. As soon as she gives it to me, I'll leave."

Harrison raised a questioning eyebrow at Noelle.

"That's not true," she said. "He wants some pictures I have, but they belong to me, and the originals are somewhere else anyway."

"I guess that settles it—now get out," Harrison told him flatly.

Steven's eyes narrowed, but he focused his attention strictly on Noelle. "You'd better shut up your new boyfriend or there'll be hell to pay for this."

Hearing the not-so-subtle threat in his voice, Noelle put a hand on Harrison's arm. "Harrison, don't. When he gets angry, he loses all control, and this isn't your problem—"

"He doesn't scare me," Harrison replied. "As a matter of fact, I'd like to show him what happens when he loses control with someone his own size." He looked Steven up and down, wearing an expression of disgust. "But I don't think he's got the guts."

Noelle saw Steven's hands ball into fists and felt her heart leap into her throat. "Look out!"

Harrison stepped closer instead of backing away, his eyes hard and glittery. He hadn't fisted his own hands, but the tension thrumming through his body told her he was ready for a fight. "Are you thinking about throwing a punch, big man?" he asked, shoving Steven in the chest.

Surprisingly Steven didn't do anything but back up. "I'm just trying to resolve something. It doesn't have anything to do with you."

"It does now," Harrison said. "You ever touch Noelle again, and you'll answer to me, understand?"

Steven glared at Noelle. "And this asshole's the guy you told Theresa you wanted to sleep with? Hell, if you're that hard up, you can come to me." Whirling around, he stomped off, pausing only long enough to throw a few parting words over his shoulder. "This isn't over, Noelle," he shouted, then he got into his car and peeled off.

Noelle stared after him, her knees weak.

"He's gone," Harrison said, once the sound of Steven's car had died on the night air.

Slowly she nodded, but she didn't move. It was more than Steven's threats and the narrowly averted fight that upset her. Theresa had told Steven about Harrison. They were in close contact....

I've met someone else...I've known him for a while, actually....

God, Theresa was seeing her ex-husband.

Noelle continued to stare down the empty street until Harrison pulled her inside and closed the door. "Are you okay?"

She nodded and folded her arms to help her stop shivering. Steven and Theresa. She almost couldn't believe it, not after the many arguments she and Steven had had over Theresa. Steven had been so opposed to the friendship that Noelle had finally tried to distance herself from Theresa just to keep peace. And Theresa had definitely resented it. She'd never had a nice thing to say about Steven....

"Maybe you should show me those pictures," Harrison said, watching her closely.

Steven had just told him she wanted to sleep with him, which made her cheeks blaze hot. But they were both ignoring that, pretending it hadn't happened. Thank God. Noelle couldn't handle the embarrassment along with everything else. The pictures made her look pathetic enough.

She couldn't understand why she hadn't put a stop to what was happening sooner, except that Steven would always start crying and insisting that he was sorry. She'd believe him, believe it would never happen again. It took time to kill the hope. Too much time. But she knew Harrison, or anyone else for that matter, wasn't likely to relate.

"They're humiliating," she said.

He shoved his hands in his pockets and leaned against the opposite wall, watching her. "You've already told me the truth. Seeing the pictures won't change anything."

"I'm not the same person I was," she said. "I'd never let a man do that to me now."

"I'd never let a man do that to you, either," he said softly.

She remembered Harrison holding her while she cried. As humiliated as she was by the past, and by what Steven had blurted out, Noelle realized she was trying to shut out the one person who had really comforted her. He'd been there for her—and he was here for her now, if she'd let him be.

"Just a minute," she said, and went to her bedroom to retrieve the copies she kept in her dresser.

When she returned, she handed Harrison the manila envelope before she could change her mind.

He frowned as he slowly shuffled through date-marked photos that showed her with a split lip, a nasty bruise, a mark on her leg.... "Who took these?" he asked when he'd gone through them all.

"I did. I have a tripod and a time-delay on my camera." She chuckled humorlessly. "I'm surprised I even bothered. I was so heavily into denial that I half-believed the lies I told to cover for him."

"These make me regret that I didn't break his jaw," he said frankly.

Noelle smiled. "Be glad you didn't. He's not worth it."

Harrison tapped the pictures. "So who's he afraid you're going to show these to? The police?"

"No. It's too late to take them to the police. I have no proof that he was the one who caused those injuries. He's worried I'll go to his mother. She'll believe me, even though she's had nothing but praise for him since the day he was born."

"From what I've seen, you should've sent them to her long before now."

"I know, but she's old and sick, and I love her. I'm not

out to hurt her by ruining the image she has of her 'perfect' son. I only want to see that he gets help."

"What kind of help?"

"Weekly visits with a therapist."

His eyes ran over her, and suddenly all she could think about was feeling his lips on hers. She was in the middle of a crisis. She needed to protect her relationship with Jeremy. And yet Harrison made her breathless at the thought of one kiss. It was worse now that he *knew*....

"Has he been fighting you on the counseling issue ever since your divorce?" he asked.

"No. At first he felt badly enough about what happened to our baby that he didn't balk. But the past few months he's managed to convince himself that he doesn't have a problem. And now I think he's seeing my best friend."

"Theresa?"

She nodded. "But I won't let him get away with hurting her the way he hurt me. I'll show her the pictures if I have to."

"And you'll keep insisting Steven see this therapist?"

She considered her options. "I have to."

"Why?"

"What if he hurts someone else?"

"God, do you think you have to take care of *everyone?* You're not responsible for his actions, Noelle. You've done your best to help, now let it go so *you* don't get hurt again. And what about the baby?"

"He'd never purposely hurt a baby. He didn't mean to do what he did to Austin."

"Accidents happen."

She knew that, knew what an accident could cost. She rubbed her eyes, feeling tired—tired of worrying about Steven, and tired of fighting her attraction to Harrison. "You're right. Now that I've got Jeremy, I can't risk Steven showing up angry again. I'll have to get a restraining order."

An odd expression crossed Harrison's face, one that sent talons of fear through Noelle. "Don't you think that's enough?" she asked.

"Maybe." He shoved the pictures back into the envelope and handed them to her.

She waited, watching him closely. "Harrison?"

Raking a hand through his hair, he sighed. "What?"

"Earlier you mentioned that we needed to talk."

He didn't respond.

"Steven hasn't changed your mind about Jeremy, has he?" *He might have made me look like a fool, but please say he hasn't changed your mind....*

"No," he said. "I know you'd never let anything happen to the baby."

Noelle's fear eased and she managed a tremulous smile. Maybe he'd forget the part about her wanting to sleep with him. "Then what?"

"Never mind. It's nothing. We can talk about it later."

* * *

Home cooking held a special place in Harrison's heart. Probably because his mother had done so little of it. He'd grown up on cold cereal and drive-through, and until he'd met Noelle, he'd still been surviving on anything instant. But as good as Noelle's grilled pork chops probably were, Harrison couldn't taste anything. He was too preoccupied with the images floating through his head—images of Steven standing on Noelle's front porch, saying she wanted to sleep with him, threatening her; images of Noelle in those pictures; images of Noelle at dinner, shyly telling him that she'd decided Jeremy's middle name would be Dane, after a beloved English teacher she'd had in college who had inspired her.

What now? Harrison wondered. Part of him wanted to carry her down the hall. The other part knew he couldn't take advantage of her, then tell her what he'd decided about Jeremy. She'd be better off if he kept his distance. But there was something about Noelle that really got to him. That she could still hope Steven would change told him how deeply she believed in the goodness of others. Being more of a cynic himself, he admired her idealism, especially because she hadn't let Steven harden her, even after all the bumps and bruises. The respect Noelle had for her ex-mother-in-law also impressed him. She wasn't out to hurt others simply because she'd been hurt. She'd borne the brunt of Steven's problem in silence and demanded, on her own, that he seek help. How could he take Jeremy—Jeremy *Dane*—away from her after everything she'd already been through?

He couldn't. But neither could he risk that a restraining order would be enough to keep Steven away, or relinquish his parental rights by going through with a formal adoption. They'd have to figure out how to protect the baby and share him...somehow.

"I can pack the leftovers for you to take home, if you want," she said.

This is the guy you told Theresa you wanted to sleep with? His gaze traveled over her. The later it got, the more difficult it was to ignore the fact that, despite the baby issues and the ex-husband problems and Harrison's fatigue, he felt the same way about her.

"Harrison?" she said when he didn't answer.

"I don't think I'm going home."

"Excuse me?"

His cell phone interrupted. Glancing down, he saw his mother's name on his caller ID.

"Just a sec," he said, and answered.

"How's it going?" his mother wanted to know.

Harrison thought of the mess he was in, which had only worsened over the past two weeks. "Fine."

"You don't sound fine."

Because he wasn't. He was sexually frustrated and exhausted and his orderly, ambitious life was spinning more and more out of control. "I've got a headache."

"You need to get more rest."

"That's easier said than done."

"So have you seen him lately?"

"Who?"

"The baby, of course."

"I saw him an hour or so ago, when he was awake. I'm at Noelle's right now."

"Again?"

"Yeah."

"But if he's been asleep for an hour, what are you still doing there?"

A very good question. Except, as he'd been about to tell Noelle, he couldn't leave. Not when there was a chance that Steven might return. "Noelle's ex-husband is causing some trouble. I'm hanging out to make sure he understands that playtime is over."

"What do you have to do with Noelle's ex-husband?"

Harrison recalled his hastily uttered promise. *You ever touch Noelle again and you'll answer to me.* Where had *that* come from? He'd said it as though he had a stake in her life, in her future...

"Remember Vince Boyd from around the corner?" he said.

"How can I forget? You knocked out his front tooth, and

when his mother came crying to me to pay the dental bill, I had to tell her——"

"I remember what you told her," he interrupted, chuckling. Half the people in their old neighborhood could probably recite what his mother had told Mrs. Boyd, because Rosie had chased Mrs. Boyd out of their house and screamed it down the street.

"At least he quit trying to stir up trouble with you after that," she said. "And Mrs. Boyd never had the nerve to contact me again."

"Exactly."

"You're saying Noelle's ex-husband's a bully?"

"More or less."

"And you're taking care of it."

"Someone has to."

"Normally you can't be bothered with anything that isn't a patient or a textbook...."

He glanced at Noelle, who'd gotten up and started the dishes. He considered denying what his mother was implying—that he had deeper motives for protecting Noelle—but he didn't dare. Rosie knew him too well, had hinted about it before. And he had to admit, as crazy as things were, he wanted Noelle badly enough to let them get a little worse....

CHAPTER
~NINE~

"So what are you trying to say?" Theresa snapped.

"I'm not *trying* to say anything," Noelle replied, curling her hand more tightly around the phone. "I'm telling you that I know something is going on between you and Steven."

"He called you?"

"He came over."

"What for?"

Noelle could hear the jealousy and confusion in Theresa's voice and felt sorry for her. Theresa dated a lot, but for some reason, she had trouble establishing serious relationships. "He wants something I have."

"Which is..."

Noelle craned her head to see down the hall. Harrison had disappeared while she was feeding Jeremy, and she suspected he was sleeping in her spare bedroom. Fortunately, he hadn't said anything about what her ex-husband had announced to him at the door.

"Some pictures," she said, heading from the baby's room back toward the kitchen.

"So give them to him. You don't care about him anymore. You haven't had one nice thing to say about him since the two of you broke up."

"There's a reason for that," Noelle said.

"Yeah, you don't love him anymore. Which means he should be fair game, and you shouldn't be upset if we go out."

Noelle frowned at the defensiveness in Theresa's voice. "Theresa, I don't love him anymore, I love you."

A long pause. "So you're doing me a favor."

Sarcasm. "I'm warning you not to get involved with him. He's got serious problems."

"Everyone says that about their ex-husband," Theresa said. "So what if he leaves the cap off the toothpaste or doesn't pick up his boxers? I don't care. I think Steven's someone I could love, and he seems just as interested in me."

Noelle took down the pictures she'd stashed on top of the fridge before dinner and started going through them. With each photo came a memory she'd rather forget, but she had to save Theresa from making the same mistake. "He's abusive, Theresa."

"Oh, come on. Maybe he's a little aloof emotionally, but I don't think I'd call that abusive—"

"I mean *physically*."

Silence. Then, "I don't believe it. You would've told me."

Noelle released the breath she'd been holding. "I was ashamed, embarrassed. Beyond that, I was planning to get our relationship straightened out and didn't want everyone I know to hate my husband. I knew I could probably forgive him, but I was afraid it would be asking too much of the people who care about me to do the same."

"I'm your best friend."

"I didn't tell *anyone*."

"Probably because it wasn't that bad."

"It *was* bad." Noelle opened her mouth to explain what had really happened to their baby, but in the end she couldn't do it. She'd finally put her pain over Austin to rest. She was working on forgiving herself and moving on, and she had a fresh start with Jeremy Dane. She wouldn't dredge up her most painful memory again. Fortunately she didn't feel as though she needed to. If Theresa would only lower her defenses enough to listen, Noelle had all the proof she needed. "I have pictures."

"What? I don't believe it. You're just jealous. You don't like it that I've found value in someone you've tossed away."

"Theresa—"

"Don't ruin this for me, Noelle," she said vehemently, and hung up before Noelle could respond.

Closing her eyes, Noelle pressed her forehead to the refrigerator door. Theresa wasn't listening....

The moon filtered through the blinds, outlining Harrison's profile in silver. After what Steven had said, Noelle knew she was crazy to be standing in the open door of her spare bedroom, admiring Jeremy's father. She should try to get some sleep, too. There was no telling how many times Jeremy might get up in the night. But she couldn't quit worrying about Theresa or wondering if Steven would come back, and she wanted Harrison to wake up and be with her. His support changed everything.

Telling herself not to succumb to her need for a little more solace, she turned to go, but his voice stopped her. "Don't tell me you're chickening out."

"What?" she said, surprised that he wasn't asleep after all.

"You've been standing there for ten minutes."

Noelle clung to the shadows so he couldn't see her blush. "So?"

"So now you're leaving?"

"Don't you think that's a good idea?"

"I think it's a better idea for you to stay, or I wouldn't have left the door open."

She smiled. "Said the spider to the fly."

"How do you know *I'm* the spider?"

"Because I can't seem to move from this spot."

He chuckled softly. "Fighting only makes it worse." He fell silent for a few seconds. "So, did you mean it?" he asked at last.

"Mean what?"

"You told your best friend that you wanted to sleep with me."

What a mess. Theresa, Steven, Harrison… "Our situation is difficult enough already, don't you think?" she said.

"Definitely."

"My climbing into bed with you won't make our lives any easier."

"That may be true, but at this point, I'm not sure it'll hurt anything, either."

After the year she'd spent, she was beginning to agree. How terrible could it be to feel good for a change?

"We'd be taking a chance."

"On what, specifically?"

"On each other."

"Maybe I'm not as bad a gamble as you think."

Folding her arms tightly, she leaned against the door frame. "Or maybe you're even worse."

"Come on. Life is full of unknowns. That's what makes it fun."

"You wore a condom even when you thought Lynnette

couldn't have children. You don't appear to be a big risk-taker to me, Dr. Ferello."

"Regardless, my life is veering out of control, and I don't seem to mind as long as you're around. Can you explain that?"

"Um—" she pretended to think "—you like my cooking?"

"I like more than your cooking." He sat up and patted the bed beside him. "Come here."

Noelle stared at the empty spot he indicated. Her heart was pounding in her ears, egging her on, and her body was growing warm, responsive, reminding her that she was still very much alive.

Tentatively, she stepped closer. "This is crazy."

"Some things are meant to be crazy," he said, and captured her elbow, pulling her down on top of him as he fell back on the bed.

"I like the way you smell," he said, sweeping his nose up her neck and kissing the indentation below her ear. "And..."

Noelle shivered at the sensation. "And?"

He slipped his hands beneath her shirt and touched the bare skin of her waist. "And I like the way you feel."

Bracing her hands on the pillow at either side of his head, she stared down at him. The huskiness in his voice and the expectant glimmer in his eyes seemed to curl through her veins like smoke. "And?"

"And I want to make love to you. I've wanted to since you were in my apartment—no, since I first saw you in the hospital."

Even when she was married to Steven, their problems had loomed so large that Noelle had experienced little passion. She couldn't remember the last time she'd felt like this, the last time she could actually say she burned for a man.

Maybe it wouldn't last, but she'd at least have this night.

"Then, what are you waiting for?" she breathed.

She felt his hand slip up her shirt, over her bare back as he rolled her beneath him. Yes! This was what she wanted. She could quit worrying, let go. One night with Harrison couldn't hurt anything. She couldn't even get pregnant anymore. She was normal, healthy....

"Harrison?" she whispered.

He'd just fisted his hand in her hair. "Hmm?"

She gazed up at his face, inches from hers. "Just promise me you won't change your mind about Jeremy. I can risk everything else, but I can't risk losing him."

He'd been about to kiss her. Now he froze. Noelle could smell a hint of the wine they'd had with dinner on his breath, could almost feel his soft, warm lips moving over hers. She wanted to taste him, to finish what they'd started. But her words had thrown up an unexpected barrier. "Noelle, I..."

"What?"

His forehead creased in a pained expression, he rolled off her, and sat up. "I don't know how to say this, but I have to tell you the truth, especially now."

That hesitancy she'd noted earlier was back, and so was her fear. She couldn't look at him; she could scarcely breathe. "What truth?" she said softly.

He took her hand, which suddenly seemed cold and foreign to her body. "I'm sorry. I can't let you adopt Jeremy."

She felt as though he'd slugged her. The confrontation with Steven ran through her mind, along with the meals and late-night talks she'd shared with Harrison over the past two weeks. What had changed his mind?

Finally she managed to speak. "Because of Steven?"

"Not just Steven. I can't let him go. I'm afraid I'd regret it the rest of my life." He shot her a troubled glance. "I hope you can understand."

Of all reasons, she could understand that one best. But it didn't make the reality any easier. She'd lost another baby, just when she'd found hope.

Numbly, she nodded. "Okay."

"I'm sorry."

She blinked back the tears that threatened. She would *not* cry. She would not make him feel guilty for making a decision he had every right to make—for making essentially the same decision she would have made in his shoes. "Don't be sorry," she said. "You're his father."

"Maybe if you're willing to explore other options, we can—"

"No." She held up a hand. "I—I can't. Not right now."

He sat on the edge of the bed and hung his head. "I feel terrible about this."

"Don't. Jeremy's a beautiful baby." Her voice wobbled in spite of her attempt to control it. Gritting her teeth, she fought against the crushing pain in her chest. She'd come so close…. "You can raise him just fine," she continued. "You don't need me. Find someone you can trust to look after him while you work, and spend every minute you're not at the Med Center with him, loving him. You won't regret it."

He seemed encouraged by her words. "It'll be a challenge, probably the biggest one of my life."

She forced a smile. "But you're good at challenges. Look what you've accomplished already."

The decision had been made. There was no turning back.

Harrison took a deep breath as he packed up Jeremy's belongings. He was sure he was doing the right thing. The peace he felt inside told him so. He was keeping his son because he wanted to—even though he knew the future wouldn't be easy.

"What about all this…baby stuff?" he asked, motioning to the crib and changing table and rocker she'd purchased.

She hovered at the entrance to the nursery she'd created as though she didn't dare venture inside. "You can buy it from me, if you want. Or I can take it back. It doesn't matter."

He needed baby furniture, but he was pretty sure he should visit Goodwill to get it. With his student loans and the added expense of caring for a baby, he needed to be frugal. He still wasn't sure how he was going to pay for childcare. He might have to start tutoring Med Students on the side. "You should probably try and take it back. If the store won't return your money, let me know. I'll reimburse you." *Somehow....*

"I don't think that'll be a problem. I still have my receipt and it hasn't been thirty days."

"Okay."

Noelle folded her arms as if she had to physically hold herself together or she'd come apart. Harrison wished he'd been able to make a decision sooner so he could have saved her the false hope. He'd put what she wanted most inside her grasp, only to snatch it away again. But he'd come to terms with fatherhood as quickly as he possibly could.

"Are you sure I should leave you here alone?" he asked when he had the baby buckled in his car seat. "I'm afraid your ex-husband might—"

"With the baby gone, there's nothing to worry about," she interrupted quickly. "If Steven comes back, I can handle him. This time I'll know better than to open my door to him, and if he tries to force his way in, I'll call the police."

"That's good," Harrison said, but her words hardly made him feel better. He was only leaving because he knew the night wouldn't be any easier on her if he stayed. She was obviously trying to deal with his decision the best way she could, but it had affected her deeply and he suspected she'd crumble the moment she had some privacy.

He winced as he remembered her reaction when she'd first held Jeremy...Jeremy Dane. He decided right then that he'd keep the middle name, in honor of her.

"I guess that's it, then," he said.

"I guess so."

"Thanks for everything."

"You bet."

He started out with the baby, but his feet grew heavier and heavier as he neared the front door. Finally he turned back. "Maybe we can get together and grab a bite to eat this weekend, or——"

"No," she said firmly. "But thanks for the offer."

Jeremy let out a squall and Harrison couldn't help noticing how quickly Noelle's gaze dropped to him.

"Do you want to hold him one more time?" he asked.

She shook her head in an abrupt movement that told him she couldn't handle it.

"Okay. Well..." He wanted to get his arms around *her*

one more time, but knew she'd rebuff him. "Dinner was great, by the way."

"Be careful driving home," she said, then he stepped out into the cold and she closed the door behind him.

CHAPTER
~TEN~

Harrison glanced over at his sleeping son as he drove home. He was just as frightened as when he'd retrieved Jeremy from the hospital, but he swore that, regardless of the problems he encountered in the future, he wouldn't give up on being a father. That's all he had to offer—his determination to stick around, as Rosie had, and do his best.

Unfortunately all the determination in the world couldn't make him feel better about Noelle. He'd only known her a few weeks, but he'd felt a spark the moment he laid eyes on her in the hospital nursery. When he imagined making love to a woman, *she* was the one he pictured. The one he wanted....

But Harrison didn't believe in love-at-first-sight. He wasn't even sure he believed in plain old "love," at least not the kind depicted in the movies, where two people became so enthralled with each other that nothing and no one else mattered. Other things always mattered to Harrison. His freedom, his work, staying in control of his emotions and protecting—

He cut off his thoughts because he didn't want to look quite that closely. He was simply feeling a sense of obligation, along with compassion for Noelle's loss, and guilt for his part in making that loss worse. Even his mother would tell him that.

He decided to call Rosie immediately, before his doubts could undermine his intentions any further.

"Is everything okay?" Rosie asked as soon as she picked up.

The worry that resonated in her voice nearly elicited the truth: *Yes and no. I know I'm doing the right thing by Jeremy, but I still feel as though someone has blown a hole right through my chest.* But he managed to catch himself. "Fine."

"You're fine," she repeated, her tone going flat.

"Yes, of course."

"Then do you think you could call me in the middle of the day next time?"

He'd been thinking so much about Noelle that he hadn't realized it was after midnight. "Sure. Sorry. I just wanted to let you know… I called to tell you that I'm taking Jeremy home."

She hesitated. "You mean for the night, right?"

"No, I mean forever."

The silence grew strained.

"Mom?"

"It won't be easy," she said softly.

"I know that."

"How will you get by?"

"I'll figure out a way. You did, right?"

Another long silence. "Okay," she said at last. "I'm coming home."

Harrison turned down the radio. "You are? For how long?"

"Forever, if that's how long you need me."

Harrison's eyes began to burn, and a lump so large it nearly choked him rose in his throat. "Mom, don't. You deserve a life of your own. You're newly married and happy in Vegas. You own a home for the first time. I don't want to be responsible for—"

"Harrison," she interrupted.

"What?"

"You mean more to me than this home, and Bill and I will be just as newly married and happy in Sacramento, where we can help take care of our grandson."

Harrison remembered all the days his mother hadn't climbed out of bed to help him get off to school, the way

she'd embarrassed him by cussing like a sailor in front
of the other PTA moms, the fast-food wrappers that had
stacked up on their kitchen table and the general mess in
their house. Maybe Rosie hadn't done an exemplary job of
raising him, but she'd always been there when it mattered
most.

Noelle sat in the nursery she'd created for Jeremy,
gently rocking in the wooden rocker. The silence felt pro-
found. She knew she needed to pack up the baby furniture
and return it. She couldn't let herself dwell on another
loss. For one thing, she had to get back to work or she'd
blow her deadline on the ceramic teenagers she was under
contract to create for the J Street office building. For another, she knew from experience that focusing on the pain
didn't help. Life would go on, eventually.

Yet even though she knew all of that, she couldn't make
herself get up. She'd been sitting there for hours; it was
nearly midmorning.

The cordless phone that rested in her lap rang. Noelle
turned it over to view the screen, hoping it was Theresa.
She'd left several messages, begging her friend to come
over and talk, but the Caller ID read, "Grantham Hospital." Noelle almost let it go to voice mail. She didn't want
to talk to anyone, especially someone who might have bad
news—until a terrible thought crossed her mind.

"Hello?" she said.

"Noelle, this is Charlene Matheson."

Fear clutched at Noelle's stomach. "Is something wrong with Jeremy?"

"With who?"

Noelle reminded herself that Charlene and the other nurses had no idea she'd been involved with Harrison or Jeremy. "The baby who lost his mother. He's okay, isn't he?"

"As far as I know. I'm calling about something else."

Noelle closed her eyes and sank deeper into the chair as the tension drained out of her. *Thank God.* "What's that?"

"Good news. Sutter General across town called earlier, asking about our infant bereavement program. I told them about the Memory Boxes, and they want to be included. Do you know how to get them on the list?"

"Of course. They can call the coordinator or log on to the website to add their information."

"Do you have the URL?"

"It's www.memoryboxes.org," Noelle said and nearly let the conversation go. Another artist could supply the boxes Sutter General required. Noelle couldn't do it. Without Jeremy, she wanted to crawl in a hole and hide from the world again, just as she had when she'd lost Austin.

She stiffened. Wait a minute... The reason she'd become involved with the Memory Box Artist Program in the first place was to forget about her own problems by helping others. How could she let herself backslide now?

Standing up, she let her eyes sweep the nursery one final time. Then she walked out in the hall and closed the door behind her. One day would lead to the next....

"Never mind," she said. "I'll give them a call and take care of it myself."

Theresa held her breath as she knocked on Steven's door. Noelle had to be lying. Sure, Steven had been a jerk when he was married to her. Theresa would be the last person to argue that point. But Noelle and Steven were split up now, and he seemed to have changed for the better. He was educated, had lots of friends, his family adored him, and he had a high-powered, well-paying job. A person like that didn't beat his wife. If he was violent, she would have known by now. Noelle would have told her. She wouldn't have kept something like that from her best friend.

Surprise registered on Steven's face when he finally opened the door. "Theresa? I thought we were planning to hook up later."

"I couldn't wait."

His eyebrows shot up at the urgency in her voice, but Theresa couldn't hide her concern. She'd been stewing about this all night and all day, wondering what to do.

"Is something wrong?" he asked.

"Tell me it isn't true."

"I don't know what you're talking about."

"Tell me you didn't hit Noelle. Ever."

Disgust swept across his face. "She's telling you I caused her to lose the baby, isn't she?"

Theresa's heart thumped heavily in her chest. Noelle hadn't mentioned the baby.... "Tell me what happened," she said. "I want to hear it from you."

"Nothing happened. We argued, I tried to leave, she got in the way of the car, that's all. Accidents happen, you know?"

Accidents happen? Noelle had been suffering over the loss of her son for a year, and Steven could stand there and act as though it was nothing?

"So you never struck her with your fist or—"

"Of course not," he interrupted.

Theresa longed to believe him. For a second, she told herself she *did* believe him. But there was a slight tic in his cheek and something else, something in his eyes, that betrayed him. Deep down, she knew that Noelle was telling the truth.

"What about the pictures?" she asked, her anger growing at the thought that Noelle had suffered in silence while this man—this man Theresa had thought she was beginning to care about—showed no remorse.

His face grew mottled. "Did you see them? Did she show them to you?"

Theresa briefly closed her eyes and shook her head. "She didn't need to," she said, and turned away.

"So what's going on?" he called after her. "You're not cutting things off between us just because I lost my temper a few times with my ex-wife. She's the one who caused it. She provoked me."

Theresa couldn't believe her ears. How could she have almost fallen in love with this man?

"You're pathetic—don't ever call me again," she shouted back. Then she walked away, swiping at the tears she hadn't realized were falling.

The next morning, Harrison stood in the supervisor's office of A-B-C Daycare. He'd managed to survive his first day as a full-time father without too much trouble. He'd wanted to pass his second day sleeping as much as possible, but Jeremy had other ideas. And since Harrison had to work tomorrow, that left only today to make arrangements for his son. Rosie wouldn't be arriving for another few weeks, and even after she moved back to town, he'd need some type of fall-back babysitting for the times she wasn't available.

Painted in bright primary colors, the day care had looked nice enough from the outside. It was located in an upscale part of town. But Harrison didn't like it any better than the other four he'd already visited—at least not for a newborn. There were too many kids, some with runny noses and coughs, and the place *smelled,* even though it appeared clean. He couldn't imagine leaving Jeremy here with strangers. Jeremy was too young.

"Dr. Ferello?"

He blinked and returned his attention to the woman who'd been telling him all about A-B-C's child-care philosophy.

"What do you think?" she asked, obviously at the end of her spiel. "Would you care to fill out the paperwork?"

She'd assured him that the new babies were separated from the older children, but that placed Jeremy in a tiny room with three cribs. Was that where he wanted his son to spend a good portion of his first year? Had he taken him out of Noelle's cozy home for this?

Noelle.... He pictured her smiling down at him when they were on the bed together—just before he'd delivered the news that must have ripped her heart out again. He'd almost called her a dozen times since he'd left her house, but unless he could give her Jeremy Dane, he knew he'd only wind up hurting her more.

"Dr. Ferello?" the young woman repeated. "Did you want to fill out the paperwork?"

"Sure." With a sigh, he sank into the chair she'd offered him once before and set Jeremy on the floor in his infant seat. What other choice did Harrison have? He had to work tomorrow, and this day care wasn't any worse than the rest. In any case, beyond gut instinct, he had no way of telling which one would be best for his son.

"It doesn't take long," she said, obviously pleased. "Here are the first forms. There's actually a couple more, but it looks like I'm running low. I'll make a few copies while you get started."

She handed him a pen and a clipboard from her desk, then went into a small back room where he could soon hear the hum of a copier.

Harrison started filling out the first form but hesitated once again when he saw the financial commitment he was making. Day care was outrageously expensive. He'd be spending nearly one-third of his total income to put Jeremy in a place he didn't want him to be. But it wasn't the expense that bothered him so much. What he was doing just wasn't right. He could feel it.

He looked down at Jeremy to find his son wide-awake and gazing up at him.

"What do you think?" he murmured, running a finger over his baby's downy head.

Jeremy continued to stare up at him as though transfixed, and Harrison finally attached his pen to the clipboard. He wasn't going to put Jeremy in day care. He wasn't going to let his mother watch him day after day, either. Jeremy belonged with Noelle, and Harrison belonged with Jeremy. Which meant there was really only one answer—and outlandish though it was, Harrison liked it.

SMALL PACKAGES

* * *

Harrison's heart pounded as he carried Jeremy through Noelle's gate, then made his way along the garden path to her workshop. He'd knocked at the front door several times and received no answer, but her car sat in the driveway, so he knew she was home.

Leaving Jeremy around the corner of the little building, where Harrison could see him, but Noelle couldn't, he knocked on the workshop door.

"Who is it?"

Harrison drew a deep breath. "It's me."

The door opened slowly. Noelle had her hair pulled back in a ponytail and wasn't wearing any makeup or even a bra. Just an old T-shirt, a pair of faded jeans and slippers. Silver paint was smudged on her hands and one cheek, but she looked absolutely beautiful to him.

"Hi," he said, and had to work to convince himself that he wasn't about to have a heart attack. After all, he should know the symptoms.

"Harrison. What are you doing here?" She glanced around, obviously looking for Jeremy. Harrison knew that if Noelle agreed to his proposal, she'd be doing it largely for Jeremy. But he needed to feel as though at least a little part of her cared about him, too. Or that she was *open* to caring about him.

Clearing his throat, he jammed his hands in his pockets. "I have something I want to ask you."

In his mind, this whole exchange had gone much smoother. But now that he was here, facing her, he felt awkward, and very nervous. His future—and Jeremy's—hinged on his next question.

She eyed him suspiciously. "I can't babysit for you, Harrison. I'm sorry. I—"

"I know. That's not it. I—" He took her hand and met her gaze. Now that he'd made his decision, he was going to do this right. "Will you marry me, Noelle?"

Her jaw dropped and so did his stomach. He'd expected to feel a flood of remorse at this point. He'd never taken such a daring emotional plunge before. But he felt fear instead—fear that she might not say "yes."

She blinked several times before answering. "Harrison, you can't be serious. There are easier ways to get the help you need."

As if that was her last word on the subject, she tried to pull away, but he wasn't finished yet. "There's no other way to get Jeremy a mother."

"So this is for Jeremy?"

"Not just Jeremy."

"Think about your goals, Harrison. If you marry me, you'll have a wife *and* a child. That pretty much constitutes a family, which is something you've told me you *don't* want."

"I know what a family is."

"Well, I can't have any more children. If you've changed your mind, you'd be better off to find someone—"

Harrison had heard enough. Stepping closer, he gripped her shoulders and drew her to him. She lifted her paint-speckled hands as if she might protest, but her resistance disappeared the moment he bent his head and kissed her. Then she molded herself to him the way he'd dreamed she would, and let him deepen the kiss. She stirred his blood, made him forget how to be passive or indifferent about love or life. "I want *you*," he said.

Noelle was drowning in a sea of muscle and warmth and titillating sensation—and didn't want to come up, even for air. A moment before Harrison had shown up at her door, she'd thought it was all over. No Harrison. No Jeremy.

"What do you say?" he murmured, trailing kisses down her neck. "Will you marry me, Noelle?"

She didn't know how to respond. Harrison and Jeremy were everything she'd ever wanted, which meant there had to be some reason she couldn't have them. "Where will we live?" she asked.

"Here, for now. I don't make a lot of money yet, but in a few years I'm hoping I'll be able to buy you the house of your dreams."

In a few years... He was serious about making a life with her.

A startled sound drew Noelle's attention before she

could respond. Glancing over Harrison's shoulder, she saw Theresa standing just inside the back gate.

"I'm sorry to interrupt," she said, twisting the strap of her purse.

Harrison kept one arm around Noelle's waist but turned as Noelle made the introductions. "Harrison, this is Theresa."

"Your best friend?" he said.

Noelle studied Theresa, wondering what she'd come to say. Their last conversation hadn't ended well, and Theresa hadn't returned any of her calls. "She used to be my best friend, but I'm not so sure how she feels anymore."

A tear rolled down Theresa's cheek and she quickly wiped it away. "I'm still your best friend."

"What happened with Steven?"

"I told him to hit the highway."

"How did he take the news?"

She chuckled shakily. "He's left me some pretty angry voice mails, calling us both all sorts of nasty names."

Noelle slipped away from Harrison long enough to hug Theresa. "It's better to find out now," she said. "There'll be someone else for you."

"I know." As Noelle stepped back, Theresa sniffed and jerked her head toward the side of the workshop. "What's your baby doing over there?" she asked Harrison.

He gave Noelle a sheepish look. "Waiting for Noelle to say yes."

"To what?"

He grinned and pulled a small box from his pocket, which he held out to her.

The sight swept Noelle's breath away. She took it and opened the velvety lid. He'd bought her a *ring*.

"Oh, my gosh!" Theresa cried. "You two aren't… You're not getting *married,* are you?"

Noelle couldn't take her eyes off the ring. She knew Harrison didn't have a lot of money. That he'd taken such a chance where she was concerned touched her. "I don't know. I really need some advice from my best friend."

A broad smile split Theresa's face. "Do it."

Noelle glanced up at Harrison to find him watching her closely. "But we've only known each other a few weeks."

Theresa laughed and shrugged. "So? That baby was meant to be with both of you, and you know it."

Noelle did know it. Even better, she knew she was already in love with Jeremy's father. Sliding the ring on her finger, she rose on her tiptoes to give Harrison a kiss. "When should we have the wedding?" she asked.

ᗒ—EPILOGUE—ᗕ

There was something familiar about the old guy in the gas station. Harrison hesitated the moment he caught sight of him, wondering where they'd met before. Had he seen him as a patient? If so, Harrison doubted it was during the past five years since he'd started his own practice. He knew most of his patients pretty well. It might have been during his residency....

"Dad, can I have this?"

Harrison turned to see Jeremy holding up a candy bar. "That doesn't look like a very healthy snack," he said.

"Aw, come on. You and Mom make me eat too many vegetables. We're going to the cabin for a whole week. One candy bar won't hurt, will it? *Pleez?*" He screwed his face up into the pleading expression Harrison and Noelle both had such a hard time refusing. They were planning to

264

roast marshmallows later, which would be treat enough, but Harrison knew he might as well give in. He would in the end, anyway.

"I guess so. But you'd better eat your dinner tonight... and brush your teeth a little longer before bed."

Jeremy grinned, revealing the gap in his smile where he'd lost his two front teeth. "What teeth?"

"You know what I mean."

"Okay, I promise."

Harrison followed his son to the cashier and ruffled the boy's dark hair before letting his gaze stray back to the man pulling a six-pack of beer out of the cooler. The old guy straightened and came toward them, and suddenly Harrison knew exactly where they'd met.

"Those cars are cool, aren't they, Dad?"

Harrison didn't know what Jeremy was talking about, and couldn't bring himself to glance away long enough to find out.

"I bet they can go two-hundred-thousand miles an hour. They have a book at the library——" Jeremy finally seemed to realize that Harrison wasn't paying attention because he paused to look behind him—and followed Harrison's line of vision to Duane Ferello. "Who's that, Dad?"

Harrison wasn't sure how to respond. This man was a stranger; this man was also his father.

Duane scowled when he found himself the object of

their attention. Keeping his eyes fastened mostly on the floor, he shuffled down the aisle to get in line behind them.

The bell jingled over the door as the person in front of them left.

"That'll be $33.75," the clerk said.

Jeremy pulled on Harrison's shirt. "Dad? It's $33.75."

"Oh, right." Harrison fumbled in his pocket for his cash and set the whole wad on the counter.

"Wow, look at all that money," Jeremy said. "That's too much, isn't it, Dad?"

Harrison was vaguely aware of the cashier counting out his change. Jeremy collected the money and the receipt and started for the door, but Harrison couldn't bring himself to move.

Duane reached around him to put his beer on the counter. "Excuse me," he said gruffly. When Harrison *still* didn't move, Duane drew his eyebrows together. "Do you *mind?*"

"Duane?" Harrison said.

Jeremy stood at the door, waiting for him. "You know that guy, Dad?"

Duane stiffened. "That's my name," he said, "but I don't think I know you, do I?"

Harrison felt Jeremy move closer to him. He put his arm around his son's shoulders and squeezed. Since he'd had Jeremy and married Noelle, he hadn't thought much about his father. His life had been too full to worry about

Duane anymore, to bother accounting for old losses. But now he realized that there was more to his peace than the love he received from his wife and son. He no longer felt any anger. The difficult decision he'd made eight years ago had helped him understand the fear a man might have about taking on a child. Harrison was finally able to forgive and know that Rosie was right: Duane was the one who had missed out. He was still missing out because of Jeremy, who had to be the greatest kid on earth.

"No, you don't know me." Harrison offered his hand and Duane tentatively took it. "But I wish you well."

With a smile at the bewildered expression on his father's face, Harrison walked out with Jeremy. Noelle was waiting for them in their Ford Expedition, along with Theresa, Theresa's husband, Ben, and their new baby. Glancing up, Noelle caught his eye and mouthed, "I love you." And not for the first time, Harrison thanked God that he'd chosen differently than his father.

* * * * *

GRACIE CAVNAR
❧ Recipe For Success Foundation ❧

E ver tried to feed a child quinoa with grilled chicken, roasted root vegetable soup, whole-wheat muffins and a green salad? Gracie Cavnar has, and not only did the kids try it, many cleaned their plates.

Gracie is the energetic and passionate founder of the Recipe for Success Foundation, a Houston-based charitable organization with the singular goal of combating childhood obesity by changing the way children eat and think about the food on their fork. More than 4,000 children spend several hours each month planting gardens at school, tending to their plants and cooking up a batch of healthy, delicious food they eat together come harvest time.

This Seed-to-Plate Nutrition Education™ program Cavnar designed has transformed the lives of more than 12,000 of Houston's most needy kids, one carrot at a time.

In an era when nearly thirty-two percent of American children are overweight or obese, Gracie is certain she couldn't have chosen a better time to take action.

"I'm all about food. Love, love, love it," she says. "But we're getting away from food—real food. Instead, we're left with Frankenstein food."

This highly processed food, filled with additives, chemicals and little nutritional value, is the first thing she wants to see kicked out of children's diets. And she's convinced—through her personal experience and by watching students change their eating habits since launching the Recipe for Success Foundation in 2005—that all children have the capacity to eat well. Eating patterns and lifestyle habits can be changed, especially if children are reached before the sixth grade.

"I've lived my whole life this way, so I know you can get kids to eat good food," she says. "They don't just automatically turn it down. It's all about presentation and making it fun."

Vending machines out, good food in.

Gracie's life before Recipe for Success can be described as a mixture of high fashion, entrepreneurship and "California hippy mom." Born and raised in San Antonio, Texas, she has worked as a fashion model, been a residential and commercial architect and owned a hospitality marketing and public relations company. She is also a mom to three kids who ate baby food she made herself and never knew a can of soda until they turned eight and started visiting friends' houses.

But Gracie doesn't come across as a health-food zealot; instead, she acts more like a cheerleader of good living and even better eating. She has recruited many dozens of high-profile chefs to create the centerpiece of her program—Chefs in Schools™. And she is delighted to count the president and first lady as fellow advocates who share her sensibilities about nutrition. In fact, Cavnar now serves on the first lady's national task force focused on childhood obesity.

It was when she started toying with retirement and deciding what to do next that she stumbled across a newspaper article that would change not only her life, but thousands of Texans' lives, too.

The article described the many elementary schools that had installed soft-drink vending machines. Granted, they used the proceeds to pay for programs such as soccer and the arts, but still, Gracie was shocked.

"It wouldn't matter how you raised your kids," she says now. "If little Johnny is in kindergarten and has seventy-five cents in his pocket, all of a sudden he's drinking a sugar-filled soda."

When Gracie started to make the connection between unhealthy food choices and depressing studies claiming that an epidemic of overweight and obese children was on the way, she finally decided to take action. It was the mid-nineties and people were only beginning to see what a problem childhood obesity might become.

"The more I found out, the more I became incensed. By then the fire was lit and I couldn't put the genie back in the bottle."

For ten years, Gracie talked to experts and met with officials, teachers, principals and chefs. She envisioned her role would be as a yenta, a matchmaker who would connect volunteers and health and nutrition organizations to turn the epidemic around. Eventually, it became apparent she needed to do more.

"I realized that if I really wanted to make something happen, we had to be the ones spearheading and managing it," she admits. "So here we are."

Today, the foundation has eighteen employees and several hundred volunteers, including more than seventy-five top chefs who donate their time to the Chef's Advisory Board and work with the children through the Chefs in Schools™ program. Classes have also expanded to include after-school and summer camps.

"I never thought that one hour a month would have such an effect on children, but after one year I could see a change in how they spoke about food," says Randy Evans, an area chef. "It wasn't just something that came from a box, but it was produce that came from the earth and needed respect."

At least eighty-five percent of the children in five original Recipe for Success participating schools are part of the federal free or reduced lunch program and often their only meals come from school. Now the program is available in a broader range of communities, but Gracie remains particularly focused on lower-income neighborhoods.

For the first year, Gracie taught all the classes, but now most of her time is spent behind the scenes. She is hard at work fine-tuning and designing a new curriculum, developing a related television show, writing her cookbooks and expanding Recipe for Success to more schools and community centers across the country. She's also finalizing details to build a 100-acre urban farm overlooking Houston's skyline. In 2010, she had more than 120 schools and districts on her waiting list to bring the program to them, too, and she and her board launched a national push to put Recipe for Success's Seed-to-Plate Nutrition Education™ in every community in America.

Busy, yes, but children will still find Gracie rolling up her sleeves and digging in the dirt with them. Her philosophy—if people cared as much about food and cooking as she does, they would treat it with care and moderation—drives her to be hands-on, too.

She thinks back to a little boy who refused to participate in the program at first, a boy who turned up his nose at anything green. Every day, his mother would show up at school with his lunch in a fast-food bag. But on the last day of the program, as he gleefully cut, stirred and diced vegetables with his friends, he waved his mother and the takeout lunch away.

"He wouldn't even touch it," says Gracie. "This is a huge gulf that we crossed." She admits that she has so many other success stories she doesn't know where to begin. "What we teach is a lesson they'll have for life."

For more information on the Recipe for Success Foundation, please visit their website, www.Recipe4success. org.

MERYL SAWYER

⟨Worth the Risk⟩

◦—MERYL SAWYER—◦

is a *New York Times* and *USA TODAY* bestselling author of twenty-five romance-suspense novels, one historical novel and one anthology. Meryl has won an *RT Book Reviews* Career Achievement Award for Contemporary Romantic Suspense, as well as an *RT Book Reviews* award for Best New Contemporary Author. Meryl lives in Newport Beach, California, with her three golden retrievers. She loves to hear from readers and may be contacted at her website at www.merylsawyer.com.

CHAPTER
~ONE~

Lexi Morrison swept through the doors of Stovall Middle School along with a gust of spring wind. She waved at the secretary as she sailed down the hall to the cafeteria to volunteer in her sister's class. She hated being late, but it couldn't be helped. Professor Thompson had kept her behind to compliment her work. It would have been unspeakably rude not to listen, especially since she was counting on him to give her a reference once she'd completed her MBA.

"Lexi, there you are," called Mrs. Geffen as Lexi shouldered her way through the double doors into the cafeteria.

"Sorry I'm late," she whispered to the teacher. The second the words left her lips, Lexi realized the room was silent, which was unusual when over thirty teenagers were assembled in one place.

Then Lexi saw why. At the front of the room was a tall man with dark hair and striking blue eyes. He wore a navy shirt with Black Jack's emblazoned in red on the pocket. He must be the guest chef who was scheduled to demonstrate today.

"Mr. Westcott was just telling us that he learned to cook in the CIA," Mrs. Geffen told her in a voice everyone could hear.

Lexi nodded and understood what he meant, but she couldn't imagine the students would catch on. No doubt they assumed he'd been in the Central Intelligence Agency.

She quickly glanced around the room to locate her younger sister, Amber. Volunteering once a week in Amber's culinary arts class was the commitment Lexi had made to encourage Amber with her studies. This cooking class was an elective and the only subject that interested her. Unlike Amber, Lexi had always been in advance-placement classes and loved school as much as her sister hated it.

She spotted Amber in the front row. Her sister was always so eager to get to this class that she'd probably been waiting for the doors to open. Her honey-brown head tilted slightly toward the guest chef, then she turned and caught Lexi's eye. "Hot," she mouthed.

So that's why her sister had been in such a rush to get here. Lexi thought the guy looked arrogant. He was frowning at her. She'd obviously interrupted and he didn't appreciate it.

"Class," Mrs. Geffen said as the group began to whisper, "Mr. Westcott was telling us about his training. Let's listen to what he has to say."

The teacher was short and packed into a moss-green suit that she'd worn almost every Wednesday that Lexi had volunteered.

"Someone asked where I learned to cook," the chef repeated.

Lexi recalled Brad Westcott was the owner and executive chef of Black Jack's, one of the most successful restaurants in Houston. It was also one of the few that didn't purchase produce from City Seeds, Lexi's gourmet-vegetable operation.

"Like a lot of you," he said in a voice that indicated he was at ease with inner-city kids, "I used to think cooking was tossing something in the microwave."

The students chuckled and elbowed each other, especially the boys. Many of them came from Mexico or South America and regarded cooking as women's work. They were in this class because their other elective choices had been filled.

"Then I went into the army," he continued.

That statement got the boys' undivided attention. Many of them would join when they were old enough.

"I was assigned to the officers' mess hall. That's what they call the kitchen—the mess hall. Mostly I peeled potatoes, carrots—"

"What about the CIA?" yelled one of the boys.

"The army is where I became interested in cooking," Brad continued, ignoring the interruption. "When I got out, I had enough money to enroll in the CIA. The Culinary Institute of America right here in Houston."

Lexi smiled, but it took a few seconds before the light dawned on the rest of the students. The girls giggled while the boys rolled their eyes or elbowed each other.

Their reaction didn't bother Brad Westcott. "Over half the students at the culinary institute were men. Top chefs in many restaurants are men. Lots of the celebrity chefs on television are men."

The boys seemed more interested. "A good chef can make a lot of money," Brad continued. "Plus, you meet lots of interesting people, especially women."

Now they were impressed. Money was a never-ending concern in the inner city. The word *money* got the boys' attention, but mentioning women didn't hurt. They might try to deny their interest in the opposite sex, but they didn't fool anyone.

"Something to think about," Brad told them with a

canted smile that made him look mischievous. "Today, I'm going to show you how to make an easy treat. Has everyone washed their hands?"

Lexi was sure they had. It was required before any class where food was to be prepared, and special monitors at the door checked the students. In addition, the tables had been covered with clean butcher paper to prevent spreading germs.

"You're going to learn how to make chocolate-truffle balls."

There were a few snickers from the boys and Lexi groaned inwardly, but not for the same reason. No doubt they thought truffles sounded like a sissy word, even though most of them probably had no idea what it meant. Lexi knew her little sister adored desserts—especially chocolate.

Amber had been diagnosed with juvenile diabetes when she was just seven. She realized sweets weren't good for her, but she often ignored the doctors' warnings. The girl loved to cook and she especially liked to bake.

Lexi and Aunt Callie had tried to encourage Amber to prepare healthy food, but since Aunt Callie's death, she had become more difficult. She indulged her sweet tooth even though she was aware of the health risks. If a hyperglycemic attack resulted, her blood sugar would suddenly spike, and she would need a dose of insulin or a trip to the E.R.

Amber resented Lexi being named her legal guardian. Lexi couldn't understand her younger sister's attitude. After all, since the death of their parents, Lexi had been more of a mother to Amber than Aunt Callie. Their aunt's death and the judge's decree had merely formalized the arrangement. But at fourteen, Amber believed she was old enough to take care of herself.

Seeming to realize Lexi was thinking about her, Amber turned and flashed playful green eyes that were exactly like Lexi's. Then she turned back to the two boys who would be her partners for the cooking assignment. How could Amber be so sure of herself? Lexi wondered.

Lexi was almost ten years older than her sister and had excelled in school, especially in math. Amber never worried about her grades or about having diabetes. She took everything with an "oh, well" attitude. She didn't seem to realize—or care—that they lived one step from being homeless.

When Aunt Callie died, she'd left them the house. It no longer had a mortgage, but there were property taxes and utilities, plus college tuition to be paid. Lexi worked two jobs to make ends meet while she attended college. The last thing she needed was for Amber to become ill from an improper diet.

"Do you sell vegetables to Mr. Westcott?" whispered Mrs. Zamora. She was one of the mothers who regularly volunteered to help Mrs. Geffen on cooking days.

"No. I think Black Jack's is more casual, less gourmet," Lexi responded, although she wasn't really sure. She couldn't afford to eat out so she'd never been in the trendy restaurant.

"That's too bad," Mrs. Zamora said almost wistfully, with a glance at the visiting chef.

Lexi didn't need to look at him again to know that most women—not just girls Amber's age—would find the guy attractive. He was tall and powerfully built with a ready smile and blue eyes that radiated a certain sparkle.

"Black Jack's probably doesn't serve baby vegetables and exotic greens," she told Mrs. Zamora. Lexi was justifiably proud of the unusual vegetables she raised in the backyard behind the house they'd inherited. It was in an older part of Houston where homes had large yards. Most of the neighboring houses had been split into multifamily homes with shared rear yards.

Luckily, Aunt Callie had kept the family home intact and used the yard to raise market vegetables to sell. After her death, Lexi had realized there was more money to be made in smaller baby vegetables that could be sold directly to restaurants.

"I was at Black Jack's once," Mrs. Zamora said. "For my husband's company party. Great ribs."

"Right," Lexi responded, her eyes on the chef. Ribs and steak. Texas food.

Right now Brad was showing the class how to roll the chocolate mixture into small balls. "Does anyone know what a truffle is?"

Lexi doubted many of the students would, but to her surprise Amber's hand immediately shot up. Brad nodded at her and Amber answered, "A truffle is in the mushroom family. It's brown and grows mostly in deep forests. Pigs hunt them by sniffing them out. They're *very* expensive."

The class laughed uproariously, as if Amber had just told an off-color joke.

"That's right," Brad's voice cut through the noise. "Truffles are hard to find and rare. That's why they're so expensive."

Amber must have read about wild truffles in one of her cookbooks. Why she couldn't devote as much attention to her other studies mystified Lexi.

"We call this chocolate a truffle because it's brown and roundish," Brad continued. "You don't have to roll a perfectly round truffle. Just make them about the same size."

Lexi, Mrs. Zamora and Mrs. Geffen walked around the room helping any students who were having problems. It was a simple assignment. The only ones who asked for help really wanted attention. Lexi often found this true when she volunteered.

After they formed the truffle balls, the class was shown how to roll them in cocoa powder and place them on cookie sheets for cooling in the commercial-size refrigerator. It was a simple assignment, considering some of the more intricate recipes guest chefs had prepared, and everyone seemed to be having a lot of fun. Of course, that meant the noise level in the cafeteria shot into the stratosphere.

Brad Westcott didn't seem to mind. He made his way around the room to speak encouragingly to the students. Lexi caught him looking at her several times.

"I hear he's one of the chefs being featured on a television program about rising stars in the restaurant business," Mrs. Geffen whispered as the students lined up to put their cookie sheets into the refrigerator.

"Really?" Lexi said, but she wasn't surprised. Black Jack's had opened to rave reviews and become an overnight sensation.

What Lexi didn't understand was why the chef had chosen to demonstrate chocolate truffles. Mrs. Geffen's class was supposed to feature healthy food.

Many students, like Amber, had chosen culinary arts as an elective because of their previous experience in Recipe for Success back in elementary school. The program had given them an appreciation for growing and preparing food.

"How many of you know about my restaurant Black Jack's?" Brad asked after the students had gone back to their seats.

Most of the group raised their hands. Lexi considered it tactful of him not to ask how many had eaten there. Fast-food places were the extent of most of their dining experiences.

"Good," Brad said. "We're known for ribs and steaks, but also for fabulous desserts. I'm sponsoring a contest for middle school students organized by the Chefs' Association. The grand prize will be a thousand dollars and a summer internship with my pastry chef for the student who creates the best new dessert."

"An internship is an opportunity to work alongside a professional," Mrs. Geffen told them. "You learn by doing."

"You won't get paid for your work," Brad added.

There were some moans from the boys, but most of the students were interested. Especially Amber. She was beaming and whispering to the students seated beside her.

Great. Just what Lexi needed. Summer was her busiest season in the garden and her most profitable. She wanted Amber to go to summer school to boost her grades and help with City Seeds in her free time. Spending hours in the kitchen creating a new dessert would be catastrophic for her health and no help in raising the money they needed so much. Besides, as far as Lexi was concerned, the world had too many desserts.

CHAPTER
∼TWO∽

L exi groaned inwardly as Brad Westcott described the two rounds of the contest. Each school would have a winner; then the winners would compete in a final round for the grand prize. She could just imagine the hours Amber would spend in the kitchen.

"Who'll judge?" Amber wanted to know.

"Chefs from restaurants in the area," replied Brad. "They'll be looking for something different...unique. A dessert that's healthy and lower in calories."

"They'll taste like...yuck," protested one of the boys.

Just then the timer went off, signaling the truffles were ready to come out of the refrigerator. The leader of each team went to retrieve their cookie sheet. Naturally,

Amber was a leader. She proudly displayed the collection of quarter-size brown truffles to her teammates.

"Amber's a natural cook," commented Mrs. Geffen. "You can teach the basics but there's a certain flair some people have that others lack."

Lexi couldn't help saying, "I just wish she was as interested in her other subjects as she is in cooking."

"Her grades are average," Mrs. Geffen said quietly. "Maybe you expect too much."

"I want her to have the opportunity to go to college."

The teacher looked thoughtful for a moment. "Amber might do better to attend junior college first."

Lexi didn't want to disagree with Amber's teacher, but she believed that if her sister applied herself, she could be in advance-placement classes. Lexi was afraid that junior college might be too much like high school and Amber would become bored, drop out and take any job she could get.

"Speaking of school," Mrs. Geffen said, "how are you doing?"

"Very well. I'll complete my master's in business administration soon, and this summer I'll prepare to take the CPA exam in the fall. I need to get a part-time job in an accounting department. Firms hire grad students and let them work until they pass the exam. I'll start interviewing next week."

"That's fabulous," Mrs. Geffen said. "You've worked really hard."

Lexi watched as the class devoured the chocolate truffles they'd made. Even Amber ate both of hers, knowing her blood sugar level would spike. Did she engage in such risky behavior to provoke Lexi or because she couldn't resist sweets?

"You rolled those truffles in cocoa powder," Brad said, raising his voice to get their attention. "Does anyone know where cocoa powder comes from?"

That was a great question, Lexi thought. A lot of kids believed food came from a package in the supermarket. Amber's class had learned about planting and harvesting in the Recipe for Success program back in the fourth grade.

"It's ground-up chocolate," called out one of the girls. "Like from a Hershey bar."

Brad chuckled, a deep masculine sound that took Lexi by surprise. It made her want to laugh along with him. For some reason she hadn't expected the chef to have a sense of humor. "Not exactly, but you're on the right track."

Amber was waving her hand furiously. Brad nodded at her.

"Cocoa powder comes from cocoa beans, not from a candy bar. Candy bars are made from cocoa."

"What does a cocoa bean look like?" Brad asked.

"Like a coffee bean... I think," Amber replied.

Lexi silently admitted that's what she thought, too. She'd seen pictures but never actually held a cocoa bean.

He pulled a foot-long yellow pod out of a shopping bag. "This is where chocolate comes from. Before it's processed it grows on trees in warm, wet places in Africa and South America.

"You open the pod." He demonstrated by splitting the plant with his pocketknife. "Inside are the smaller pods that make up the cocoa that becomes chocolate when processed."

"Who do you think was the first European to see cocoa beans?" Mrs. Geffen asked the class.

No one had an answer and Lexi wasn't sure she knew. She guessed it must have been one of the Spanish explorers.

"Who discovered America?" Brad asked.

"Columbus—1492!" a boy shouted.

"That's right. Later he met some natives who had cocoa beans in their canoe. He thought they were a new type of almond because no one in Europe had ever tasted chocolate."

"Get out!" someone cried.

"Seriously," Brad responded. "Columbus didn't taste it either. The Spanish conquistadors tried it in 1519 when it was served to Montezuma as a drink. That's over twenty years after Columbus saw it."

Interesting, Lexi thought. The students had given him their full attention. Brad Westcott knew the right buttons to push: money, girls, television, chocolate.

"The Aztecs used cocoa beans as a form of money," added Mrs. Geffen.

"When chocolate was taken to Europe, it instantly became popular," Brad explained.

This was the best demonstration she'd seen, Lexi decided. The kids were so animated, so interested. They'd really learned something today.

"The truffles you made are actually low-calorie treats," Brad told them. "The recipe I used cuts down on the fat and sugar but still tastes good."

From the low buzz that hummed through the group, this was a surprise to the students.

"That's what I'm looking for in the contest," Brad said. "We want desserts that taste great and are also healthy for us."

Lexi endorsed the idea of healthy desserts, but she still didn't want Amber spending hours in the kitchen for a contest.

The bell rang, signaling the class was over. "Clean up your workstation before you leave," instructed Mrs. Geffen.

Most of the students hastily gathered the butcher paper and wiped down the tables, then stampeded toward the door. But a few hung around to talk to the chef while the monitors washed and put away the cooking utensils.

Amber charged up to Lexi, her face flushed with excitement. "I'm going to enter that contest."

Now was not the time to have a discussion about her grades and the work she was responsible for in the garden.

"I'm sure you'll come up with a really unusual dessert," Mrs. Geffen said.

Lexi tried for a smile, but didn't quite manage. She reminded herself that Amber needed to build self-esteem when it came to schoolwork. The culinary arts class would earn her a good grade. It would probably be the only A she received, but it might also encourage her to pay more attention to her other classes.

"I'm gonna enter the contest," Amber informed the chef as he walked up to them.

Brad smiled. "That's great! I'll look forward to tasting your dessert."

Lexi had to admit the guy was charming. Too charming. No doubt Amber would be talking about him for days. She was going through a boy-crazy stage.

"Are you going to be a judge?" Lexi asked Brad.

Brad turned to her with a captivating smile. "Actually, the chefs from the Chefs' Association are judging, but I'll want to taste the winning recipe."

"Brad, this is Alexis Morrison," Mrs. Geffen said. "She's

Amber's older sister. She helps me on the days we're pre-paring food." The teacher turned to Mrs. Zamora and in-troduced her as well.

"Everyone calls her Lexi," Amber said.

An early warning signal from Lexi's brain said to get away from this man before Amber was even more in-trigued. Lexi had to admit that even she was conscious of his virile appeal. A young girl would find him irresistible.

"I'm going to win the contest," her sister assured Brad before Lexi could drag her away.

Brad smiled encouragingly. "If you win, you'll be up against students from all the other middle schools in the final round."

"Not a problem," Amber assured him with her usual confidence.

"Lexi owns City Seeds," Mrs. Geffen said.

Lexi stifled a groan. "Mr. Westcott has probably never heard of us."

"Please, call me Brad," he responded as he gazed at her with intriguing blue eyes. "I've seen City Seeds' produce. You specialize in baby vegetables, right?"

"And upscale greens," Amber answered for her. "I help grow them."

"Really?" Brad's assessing glance stayed on Lexi. "My sous-chef is in charge of purchasing our produce."

"Do you use baby vegetables?" Lexi asked. They were two or three times more costly than regular ones.

"We haven't, but you never know. Our menu is always changing."

"Thanks for the demo," Mrs. Geffen said. "My students really enjoyed it."

Lexi nodded her agreement, then nudged Amber. "Time to go." She turned to Mrs. Geffen. "I'll be back next week."

"Thanks for your help," the teacher said as Lexi walked away, Amber in tow.

"That was, like, so mean," Amber said once they were out in the hall. "I wanted to talk to Brad. Get some hints about how to win the contest."

"I have a paper due," Lexi told her. "And before I even begin, I have to water and weed."

"Whatever," Amber replied with an exasperated sigh.

Brad Westcott watched the attractive brunette walk away. He'd noticed her the minute she'd walked into the room. She looked just like her sister. Who would have thought Lexi Morrison owned City Seeds? Brad wasn't sure who he had expected to own the premier local produce company, but not someone so young or so pretty.

"Did Lexi start City Seeds herself?" he asked Mrs. Geffen.

"Her aunt had a backyard garden. The girls came to live with her after their parents were killed in an automobile accident."

How terrible, Brad thought with a pang of sympathy. His own youth had been difficult, but both his parents had loved him, and he'd always had them for support.

"Lexi's aunt sold produce at the local farmer's market, and Lexi noticed baby vegetables brought a higher price," put in Mrs. Zamora.

Enterprising, Brad thought.

"She did all that while getting straight A's and a scholarship to the University of Houston." The teacher smiled proudly as if Lexi were her own child. "She's about to get her master's degree in business administration. Then she'll take the CPA exam."

"Impressive," Brad said and he meant it. Not many people could juggle so much at once. No wonder she'd been in a hurry to leave.

He left the school and drove to Black Jack's. Although he had three restaurants in the Houston area, he concentrated on this one. It was the largest and most profitable.

Lexi Morrison drifted out of his thoughts as he strode through the back door. As usual, the kitchen was controlled chaos. Slabs of beef ribs were smoking and huge pots of barbecued beans simmered on the industrial-size stoves.

"Hey, Brad," called Charmayne Collins, the pastry chef. "How was the demo?" She was piping whipped cream around a tiramisu mousse.

"Great," he replied. "The kids seemed to enjoy it." An image of Lexi Morrison flashed across his mind. "Where's Allen?"

Charmayne kept her eyes on the ceramic dish in front of her. "He's not here."

Brad stopped and spun around, nearly bumping into a waiter carrying a tray. "What? Where is he? Did something happen?"

It was late in the afternoon. The sous-chef should have started preparations for the evening crowd. If the assistant chef hadn't stepped up, Brad would have to hustle or every dinner would be late tonight.

"I don't know what happened to Allen," Charmayne told him. "He spoke with Trevor."

There was an undertone in her voice that he didn't like. Something was wrong. He charged across the busy kitchen and into the bar area, where Trevor, the head mixologist, was setting up for the evening rush.

Just when bartenders became mixologists, Brad couldn't say, but they did deserve the more impressive title. The bar was the cash cow of most restaurants and Black Jack's was no exception. Like most mixologists in successful bars, Trevor had created his own specialty, the snakebite.

"Where's Allen?" he asked the short fireplug of a man.

Trevor looked up and said, "He quit. There's a message in your office. He took the job as executive chef at Valentino's."

The air left Brad's lungs in a dizzying rush. "Without giving me notice?"

Trevor shrugged one shoulder. "Allen told you more than once that he wanted to move up."

"True," Brad conceded. He was Black Jack's executive chef and didn't intend to give up the position. Since his other restaurants already had executive chefs, he didn't have anywhere to move Allen. "I assumed he would have given me more notice."

Trevor shrugged again in his laid-back way. "The position came up unexpectedly and they needed him ASAP. They offered him a bundle."

Unbelievable, Brad thought. He was going to have to do the work of two people until he could find another sous-chef.

CHAPTER
~THREE~

Lexi walked through the front door of her house, her new briefcase under her arm. She'd just interviewed at a fourth accounting firm. Another cube farm, she thought. She might as well become a factory worker. Calculating people's taxes wasn't what she'd had in mind when she started her MBA, but in this weak economy, it seemed to be where the jobs were.

Once she'd gained some experience to add to her résumé, she could look for a smaller firm.

"Amber," she called when she didn't see her sister at the dining room table doing homework.

The delicious scent of chocolate hung in the air. Lexi wasn't surprised. Since Brad Westcott had announced his dessert contest, Amber had been obsessed with creating a winning recipe. She tried to hide her efforts by meticulously cleaning up after herself and donating the "experiments" to the senior center nearby, but Lexi wasn't fooled. The telltale scent of baked goods was impossible to hide.

Lexi changed into work clothes and went out into the garden. Spring was here, but heat shimmered up from the ground in visible waves as if it were the middle of summer. Netting shaded the more sensitive plants, but everything desperately needed water.

Naturally, Amber had been too busy baking to water the plants. Baby vegetables were very sensitive. They could easily wilt in the scorching heat even though they were shaded. Once a baby veggie flopped over, there was no reviving it. Lexi uncoiled the soaking hoses from their bins and placed them so they would slowly fill the dry trenches that snaked through the garden.

The yard wasn't big compared to a real farm, but it was large for the area and entirely devoted to gardening except for a small locked shed that held the equipment. In this area of Houston, what wasn't locked up was stolen.

Even the gates to the backyard had industrial padlocks on them. The neighborhood children weren't inclined to steal the vegetables, but they'd been known to tear up the garden beds just for fun.

Three hours later, she left her muddy sneakers on the

back porch and went into the house. Still no sign of Amber. She was probably kicking back at a friend's or had taken the bus to the mall.

What would become of the garden when Lexi found a job at an accounting firm? She certainly couldn't trust Amber to run the operation alone. Chefs at several of the most prominent restaurants in the city counted on City Seeds' produce.

Lexi would need to find an assistant. She thought about Urban Plots, a community garden several blocks away. Local people planted and tended their own spaces in a lot provided by the city. Maybe someone there would want to make some extra money by helping Amber.

The front door suddenly burst open, bringing with it a gust of heat. Amber rushed into the house. "I've got it! I've got it!" she shouted.

Her sister was so excited that Lexi hated to scold her for not having watered the garden. It seemed lately that all they did was argue.

"What have you got?" Lexi asked with all the patience her tired body could muster.

"I know what I'm going to bake for the contest." Amber collapsed onto the sofa that had been ancient years ago when they'd come to live with Aunt Callie. She swung her feet up onto the scarred coffee table. "A to-die-for chocolate-raspberry tart. I made it for the third time today and everyone at the senior center said it was the best. A real winner."

Lexi doubted the seniors would criticize a free treat, but she had to admit Amber was a good cook.

"Don't forget this is just the first round. If—and it's a big if—you win, then you'll have to compete against the winners from all the other middle schools."

"I know," Amber replied with her usual self-confidence. "I'll invent something new for that round."

Swell, Lexi thought. More baking, more sampling. Too many sweets for a diabetic. "Have you tested your blood sugar?"

Amber swung her feet to the floor. "All right. All right. I'll test, but I didn't have a piece of the tart. I relied on people to tell me if it was good." She stomped off toward her bedroom, presumably to test her blood sugar. Lexi resisted the temptation to follow her. Amber had been giving herself insulin long enough to be able to do it on her own. Having Lexi hover over her only made Amber more difficult.

In a few minutes, Amber reappeared. "While I was waiting for the tart to bake, I made a chicken salad for dinner. The kind with Granny Smith apples that you like."

Lexi thanked her sister. She could hardly berate her for not watering the plants now.

"How did your interview go?"

Lexi was amazed Amber remembered that she'd had one. She rarely paid attention to anything unless she was directly involved.

"Okay, I guess."

"What do you mean—you guess?"

"They didn't offer me a job on the spot, but they may. I'm just not sure I want to work there. Everyone's jammed in like cigars in a box."

"What else can you do until you take the CPA exam?"

"Good question," Lexi admitted. "Not much. Keep City Seeds going and continue to work at Millard's."

Millard's Upholstery was a small business nearby where Lexi did the payroll as a part-time job. There was no chance to move up in the family-run business, so it made sense to join a large CPA firm until she passed the exam. It would also pay better.

"It sounds as bad as school," Amber complained. "At least you're earning money. What use is geometry and history?"

"It'll help you get into college." They'd been down this road too many times to count.

"So I can end up like you, with a master's and nothing interesting to do with it?"

Lexi hoped the anger that surged inside her didn't register on her face. Amber was baiting her, and reacting would just encourage her sister. She repeated her usual explanation. "A college degree will give you more options. If you settle for being a cook without a college education, you may end up slinging hash at a drive-through fast-food joint. Would you like that?"

"Maybe," Amber huffed.

Brad hesitated outside the old Victorian house. This couldn't be City Seeds. The home was in one of Houston's oldest areas. It was in the DMZ between a lower-middle-class district and a neighborhood overrun by gangs and the homeless. Once the neighborhood had belonged to the city's elite, but over time people had moved to more desirable enclaves. Most of the homes had subsequently been split up to accommodate multiple families.

He checked the address on the note he'd written. This was the right place. He assumed its large backyard was intact or there wouldn't be room for a garden.

When he rang the bell, he heard a girl yell that she would get it. Amber, he guessed. The door swung open.

"Oh my gosh!" she cried. "What are you doing here?"

Before Brad could answer, Lexi appeared in cutoffs and a faded navy blue T-shirt. A sexy outfit, but he doubted she realized it.

"Mr. Westcott?" she said, obviously not thrilled to see him.

Lexi had been on his mind a lot since he'd met her, but he'd been so busy at work that he hadn't found a chance to see her again. Finally he'd hired another sous-chef, a woman this time.

"I've heard such good things about City Seeds that I thought I'd come see for myself."

"That's great," gushed Amber, but Lexi didn't look too pleased. "I've come up with a winner of a dessert for the contest."

"Really?" It took a second for him to recall that the contest's preliminary round was next week. "That's wonderful."

Lexi moved around her younger sister. "What sort of vegetables are you interested in?"

Brad shrugged. "I'm not sure. I'm creating several new dishes for the summer menu."

"This way," Lexi said as she walked by him.

They headed down the front steps then followed a stone path around the old Victorian. Amber trailed behind them. He watched Lexi move and decided she was one of those women who could be provocative without trying. Something he found extremely appealing.

Lexi unlocked a metal gate then swung it open to reveal a lush backyard full of plants and vines. There didn't seem to be an inch that wasn't under cultivation. Rows and rows of plants covered the ground. Long containers were set on stepped racks that lined the fence, creating space where there was very little. Ingenious, he thought.

"We grow a lot of unusual lettuce," Amber told him.

"I can see that," Brad replied, a little ashamed he didn't recognize the varieties.

"Some of these greens are native to Asia," Lexi said.

"Really?" Brad was impressed. Houston had a sizable population of Asians. He had been experimenting with some Chinese and Thai dishes in his spare time.

"You should taste this." Lexi picked a curly red leaf off a plant and handed it to him. Brad didn't particularly like lettuce. He wasn't a salad kind of guy, but he took it anyway. He popped it into his mouth and chewed thoughtfully.

"Good, really good," he said, and he meant it. The lettuce had a slight taste of nuts.

"You could design a special summer salad with red wave lettuce," Amber said.

"True."

"It also goes great with chicken," she added.

"I'm sure I can come up with something," Brad said. "May I buy a box of red wave lettuce?" That would give him a dozen heads to use. If he created a luncheon special, he'd go through that much in a weekend.

"Yes, but there's a limited supply," Lexi responded.

"Great," he said. He could use the exclusive aspect to promote the dish.

"I'll box it up for you."

"How much per head?" Brad asked, and almost choked when she told him the price. The new salad would cost as much as a seafood salad.

"I'm dying to see how you use our lettuce," Amber said.

Lexi was filling a wax-coated box with lettuce that she was pulling directly from the ground.

"Do you have anything else that you think might work with it?" he asked.

Lexi raised her head and looked at him, but it was Amber who answered.

"What about beets? The yellow variety is incredibly sweet. Everyone loves them. They serve them as a side dish at Marché."

That got him. Marché was one of his chief competitors. Their food appealed to an upscale crowd that was willing to spend a lot of money dining out. "That's a possibility. Could I try some?"

"I'm not sure we have enough," Lexi responded. "Marché buys almost all the specialty beets we grow."

"Is that right?"

Again Amber answered for her sister. "Most of what we grow is already promised to restaurants who've been buying from us for years."

"I see." Why hadn't he known more about City Seeds? Obviously, letting his sous-chef buy all the produce had been a mistake. He'd lost touch with the local market.

"We do have an Asian type of baby squash that might work," Lexi suggested.

"Really?"

"They're over here." She left the half-full box of lettuce and walked across the yard to a small hothouse. "I grow them hydroponically."

Lexi plucked a small green squash the size of his little finger off a vine growing from a cylinder of water. At the top of the baby squash was a bright orange bubble-shaped blossom.

Brad bit into the veggie and an unusual savory flavor filled his mouth, unlike any squash he'd ever had. "Wow! This is good."

"I thought you might like it," Lexi said with the first smile he'd seen from her.

"I'm going to go with them instead of the beets."

"Awesome!" squealed Amber. "I can hardly wait to taste your special."

The girl had more confidence than three kids her age, Brad decided. Lexi was more reserved, but Amber's interest gave him an idea.

"Do you two have plans for lunch on Saturday?" he asked. He really wanted to know about dinner, but decided anyone as attractive as Lexi would have plans for the evening.

"No, we don't," Amber answered.

Lexi didn't look half as pleased as her sister. She was about to say something, when a horn blared.

"That's my ride." Amber dashed toward the gate. "See you tonight, Lexi." She stopped, hand on the gate, then spun around and called out to Brad, "I'm going to win your contest. Count on it!"

Lexi waited until Amber slammed the gate shut. "I hope she doesn't win."

Her reaction surprised him. "Really, why?"

Lexi hesitated for a moment. "I want her to get a college education. I don't want her slaving over a hot stove only to find out the job's not as glamorous as she thinks."

"She could do both," Brad responded, a little shocked at the frustration he detected in her voice.

"Not Amber. She's got a one-track mind. Right now all she can think about is winning that contest and she's neglecting her schoolwork. I want her in summer school, not tagging around after some pastry chef."

"I wouldn't worry about it," Brad said, attempting to assure her. "What are the chances she'll win?"

"She's an excellent cook. Baking is Amber's specialty." Lexi sounded defensive. "And if she loses, she'll be disappointed, crushed."

Cripes, Brad thought. There was no reasoning with women.

"I have an idea that might solve your problem."

CHAPTER
❧ FOUR ❧

L exi followed Amber through the double-wide doors into Black Jack's on Saturday. Amber had been so excited about lunch that she'd changed outfits at least six times. Brad had persuaded Lexi that a visit to his restaurant and a tour of the kitchen during the hectic noon rush would show Amber that working in a restaurant wasn't glamorous. But what if he was wrong? Suppose the chaos and hair-trigger tempers Brad had so vividly described actually energized Amber?

"Wow! This is awesome!" Amber made no attempt to hide her enthusiasm.

The place had a Caribbean style to it with dark wood floors and plantation shutters that filtered the light. High above their heads, ceiling fans shaped like palm fronds circulated the air above the wicker and bamboo furniture.

Lexi hadn't dated a lot, but she had been out enough to know there were ritzier restaurants in Houston. Amber had only eaten at fast-food places, so this had to seem highly sophisticated to her.

"You must be the Morrisons," said a perky blonde hostess when they walked up to her.

"Yep. That's us," Amber responded with a beaming smile.

Lexi hoped they were suitably dressed. She'd worn a tan pair of slacks and a coral blouse with a thin tan stripe running through it. A conservative outfit but one that looked nice, she thought. Amber couldn't be talked out of a very short raspberry-pink skirt and a matching tank top that revealed her midriff whenever she raised her arms.

The hostess picked up menus the size of wall posters and led them to a corner table. "Brad will be right out."

"Look at this menu! A-mazing!" Amber exclaimed after they'd been seated. "Ribs, steaks, chicken and zillions of yummy desserts."

"Interesting salads and chicken dishes," Lexi said. If she came out and told Amber to make a healthy choice, her sister would balk.

Amber didn't reply as she intently read the menu word for word. Great, Lexi thought. Amber would study a recipe or cookbook or menu as if it was a treasure map, but she could barely find the time to scan her schoolbooks. But now was not the time for that discussion, Lexi reminded herself.

"I don't see our red wave lettuce on the menu," Amber whispered, even though no one nearby was paying any attention to them.

"The waiter usually tells customers what the specials of the day are," Lexi said. "That way they don't have to reprint menus all the time. It would be too expensive."

Amber gazed at her with something akin to respect—a first. "How do you know? Do your dates bring you to places like this?"

Lexi had been receiving more and more questions from Amber about boys and dating. Aunt Callie hadn't allowed Lexi to date until she was sixteen. Lexi thought that was a good rule, but Amber insisted all the girls she knew were already dating. Soon some boy would ask Amber out and Lexi would be forced to make a decision. "I've been to nice places like this a few times, but young guys mostly take you to fast-food places."

"Oh, yuck!"

"Think about it," Lexi said. "It costs a lot to have dinner and go to a movie. Most guys can't afford anything fancy."

"Matt could."

Matthew Hastens. Lexi's former boyfriend. She'd broken up with him because he'd gotten too serious. At the time she'd been barely nineteen and Aunt Callie had still been alive. "It's easier to marry money than make it," Aunt Callie kept telling her.

Lexi intended to marry for love—not money. And she hadn't loved Matt.

"When we went to nice places like this—" Lexi looked around "—Matt didn't pay. His parents did."

Amber shrugged. "Whatever. Hey!" She waved frantically. "There's Brad."

Lexi had to admit the man was attractive, but for some reason he disturbed her. She wasn't sure why. Perhaps because she knew he was too worldly and sophisticated to be interested in her.

"Hey, glad you could make it." He came up to the table and pulled out a chair.

"Great place," Amber said before Lexi could utter a word. "Where did you get the idea for the decorations?"

Brad shot them an engaging smile that seemed to be second nature to him. "I liked the tropical feel they have in Key West restaurants. I told the decorator that's the look I wanted."

"I read you have other restaurants," Lexi said.

Brad turned toward her. "True. I have two more. One is done like a Paris bistro—"

"What's that?" Amber wanted to know.

"A small café about a quarter the size of this with lots of wood paneling, soft lights and white tablecloths."

"That's what it's like in Paris?" she asked.

Paris sounded so exotic, Lexi thought. A must-see place—a world away from Houston. She intended to visit one day—after she'd completed her education, landed a good-paying job and sent Amber through school. Maybe then she'd have enough money to travel.

"You've been to Paris?" she heard herself ask. Dummy! Of course Brad Westcott had traveled extensively.

"Yep. Courtesy of Uncle Sam. In the army I was stationed in Germany. On leave a bunch of us went to Paris. The food was awesome. Paris bistros are like our coffee shops. They're everywhere. But unlike some of our coffee shops, it's hard to get a bad meal. Owners take great pride in what they serve."

A cute redhead sashayed up to their table with a flirty smile for Brad. "I'm Tiffany. I'll be your waitress. What can I get y'all to drink?"

They decided on tropical ice tea and their waitress swished away to fill their order. Out of the corner of her eye, Lexi watched Amber. For once she didn't seem to know what to say.

"What's the theme of your other restaurant?" Lexi asked.

Brad settled back in his chair. "Jo' Mama's is a

backwoods-style rib joint. Southern barbecue. Picnic tables, checkered tablecloths, mugs for beer."

"Sounds like a winner," Amber said. "Everyone loves barbecue."

Another food that Amber loved but needed to limit, Lexi thought.

Brad must have detected the concern on her face. "We offer plenty of healthy choices at all my restaurants." He pointed to the oversize menus in front of them. "The hearts in front of a selection mean it has less fat and sugar."

"You'd be surprised how much sugar is hidden in food," Amber said.

This insight was a direct result of the nutrition classes she had taken after she'd been diagnosed with diabetes. Sugar was in an amazing number of foods—especially prepared foods in the grocery store.

"You two into healthy eating?" Brad asked.

Lexi waited for Amber to answer. Sometimes she felt uncomfortable discussing her diabetes.

"I *always* watch what I eat. I have diabetes."

"Interesting." He grunted the word, obviously not knowing how to respond. Lexi waited for his captivating smile, but it didn't come.

"*Interesting* is a word people use when they don't have a clue what to say," Amber responded.

As usual, Amber's thoughts moved directly from her

brain to her mouth. But to give her sister credit, Lexi thought, she accepted her diabetes even though she sometimes ignored the food restrictions.

Uncertainty shadowed Brad's eyes. "Actually, I was thinking that's a lot to have to deal with at such a young age."

"You learn to handle it. That's why I'm going to win your contest. I want to create a dessert even diabetics can eat."

"I know the feeling," Brad said, his expression intent. "When I was your age, I was overweight. Obese, probably, but we didn't say that back then."

Lexi couldn't believe this buff guy had ever been overweight, but the earnestness in his voice said he was telling the truth.

"Did the kids tease you?" Lexi asked.

"All the time," he admitted.

"I get teased about having to take insulin," Amber said in a sharp tone. "I just ignore them."

"That's what I did. I developed my own interests."

"Cooking?" Lexi asked.

Brad shook his head. "No. Like I told the class when I did the demo, I didn't get interested in cooking until I was put on mess duty in the service. I was interested in stamp collecting. My grandfather had left me a dozen boxes of loose stamps that he'd purchased but had never sorted and put into collector's books."

"Fascinating," Lexi said, and she meant it.

Brad focused his blue eyes on her with a penetrating gaze. "After I went into the service, discovered my interest in cooking and lost the flab, I sold the stamp collection to finance my first restaurant."

Wow, Lexi thought. Brad had a depth to him that she hadn't suspected. It gave her new respect for him and his accomplishments. The information also made him seem more accessible somehow. He wasn't as perfect as she'd imagined.

"Let's order," said Brad. "While we're waiting for our meals, I'll show you around the kitchen." He signaled to the waitress and she approached with a practiced smile to tell them the specials.

"We're featuring an awesome red wave lettuce salad. That's a really unusual but yummy Asian lettuce that's in limited supply. We serve it with grilled chicken on top."

The server rattled off a few more specials. Lexi and Amber went for the special, but Brad ordered a grilled-vegetable salad.

"What?" cried Amber. "You're not having the red wave salad you created?"

Brad winked at her. "Nope. Coming up with a new dish means lots of combinations, lots of tasting. I've had more than my share of the special. Let's see what you two think."

"What if we don't like it?" Amber asked.

Brad shrugged. "Be honest. Let me know. I haven't been serving it that long. I'm still evaluating it."

"It's a deal," Amber said.

Brad rose. "Let's tour the kitchen while they're preparing our lunch."

CHAPTER
❦ FIVE ❦

"We're in the beverage center," Brad informed them as they walked into an alcove where built-in stainless-steel coffee urns were marked Decaf and Regular. A wall-mounted unit dispensed soft drinks, and pitchers marked Tropical Iced Tea were nearby. A huge ice machine dominated the corner. Off to one side was a computer terminal.

"The server inputs the drinks ordered and the table number," Brad explained, pointing to the computer, "then serves the beverages except for alcohol. That has to come out of the bar."

They moved through swinging doors into what Brad called the lion's den. It was a fitting description for the hurricane of activity in the huge commercial kitchen. Everyone seemed to be moving at once without—miraculously—bumping into each other. Most of them were shouting at someone else.

A mist of steam from the simmering pots and smoke from the nearby grill filled the air. A thousand different, delicious smells swirled around Lexi. She couldn't help wondering if there was some order in this chaos.

If any of the crew noticed Brad, none of them showed an interest. Everyone seemed to have a job to do, and by all appearances, they were behind schedule and frantically attempting to catch up.

The three of them stood there a moment, watching in amazement. Lexi caught Brad's eye and he smiled, lifting his chin just slightly to indicate Amber. The girl was gazing awestruck at the scene before her. Like Lexi, Amber had naturally curly hair. A few minutes in this kitchen and she would look like Frankenstein's bride, but Amber didn't seem to notice. She stood, silent and trancelike.

And loving every second, Lexi would bet.

"Looks pretty high-tech," Lexi said to Brad. "Aren't those minicomputer terminals above each station?"

"That's right," he said. "The server enters the selection at a terminal just outside the kitchen and it appears in front of the chef. That way we don't have any extra people in the cooking area, creating a traffic jam. The completed dishes are put on the ledge for the server to pick up."

"Doesn't the heat and steam make the computers short out or something?" Lexi asked.

"Nah. These are special computers."

"It's a miracle a meal comes out of here," Lexi said.

"Everyone has a job," Brad assured her, "and they're doing it. As long as food's not backed up, the kitchen is running smoothly. Right now, things couldn't be better."

"What's the woman in the corner doing?" Amber asked, speaking for the first time.

Lexi immediately saw who Amber meant. A woman with a white gauze bandanna wrapped around her head like a turban stood in one corner. A crate of pomegranates was on the counter beside her. A large stainless bowl full of water was in front of her. Was she washing them one by one? Lexi wondered.

"Come on," Brad told them. "Let's take a closer look."

They wriggled their way between the workers and came up behind the woman laboring over the stainless bowl. Nearby a mound of glistening pomegranate seeds stood on a platter.

"Emily is prepping pomegranate seeds to be used as garnish," Brad said. "She's doing *mise en place*—that's prep work for the chef."

Emily looked over her shoulder with a toothy grin. A

bristle of bangs like a whisk broom stuck out from under her bandanna, a casualty of the steamy kitchen.

"Removing pomegranate seeds is easily done underwater," Brad said. "The membranes float to the top while the seeds sink. You skim off the membranes, then drain the water through a strainer to save the seeds."

"Awesome!' cried Amber. "I hate taking out pomegranate seeds." She twirled around to face Brad. "I never read this in my cookbooks."

Brad laughed. "Some things aren't in books." Then he looked pointedly at Lexi. "Learning doesn't just take place in the classroom either."

Amber turned to Lexi. "That's why I want to win and be an apprentice to the pastry chef. I'm gonna find out inside tricks."

Just my luck, Lexi thought. Amber didn't view the kitchen as a trip through hell. No. She was intrigued and wanted to learn more.

"Where is the pastry chef?" asked Amber.

"In the next room." Brad pointed to a door that opened off the side of the kitchen. They walked into a cool passageway with racks of fruit and cheese lining the walls.

"This is a semicool room," Brad said, "like they use in Europe. Cheese and fruit is best when it's close to room temperature. Americans tend to whisk everything straight from the refrigerator to the table. The food's too cold to really appreciate the flavor."

They entered another kitchen where a soft buzz of conversation filled the air. Unlike the pandemonium of the main kitchen, this smaller area had fewer people and was more orderly.

"Charmayne, got a minute?"

"Sure," the petite blonde said with a smile.

Lexi realized most of the female staff had a thing for Brad. He possessed an easy kind of charm and the good looks women appreciated. She wondered what kind of boss he was. Brad introduced them and told Charmayne that Amber was entering the baking contest and hoped to serve as her intern for the summer.

"Great," said the pastry chef with genuine enthusiasm. "I was just about your age when I decided I wanted to become a pastry chef. Mother made me go to college first."

Lexi silently blessed Charmayne's mother. Amber's smile faltered, but the woman kept talking.

"I worked part-time in pastry shops. You have to get up at three in the morning to bake and be ready for the morning coffee crowd, but it pays really well and leaves plenty of time for classes."

Had Brad coaxed the pastry chef into mentioning her education? Lexi wondered. He was working hard to relate to Amber, and Lexi appreciated the effort. What she thought made little difference to her sister, but Amber looked up to these professionals.

"Didn't college just eat up time you could have spent learning your trade?" Amber wanted to know.

Charmayne shook her head. "No. I studied hotel and restaurant management. The world is a really technical place these days. You need to know how to run your own kitchen. That takes as much business know-how as it does cooking skill."

"Really?" Amber sounded doubtful.

"You'd be surprised." Charmayne pointed to something creamy she'd been whipping. "How much cream should you order for a weekend? How long does it keep? Is there anything else you can do with it if no one orders a certain dessert and you're stuck with too much?"

"Making one recipe of anything is easy," Brad said. "Multiples take time and planning."

"Right." Charmayne turned to a set of double-wide coolers. "Some desserts can be prepared in advance. You can estimate how many to make by checking your computer and seeing what was consumed previously. Other desserts have to be put together when the order hits the kitchen."

"We better let you get back to work," Brad told Charmayne.

"Thanks," Amber said. "Look for me this summer."

After they left the pastry kitchen they passed another bank of computers where a young man was working. "This is the check station," Brad said. "The final bill showing all you've ordered is printed out here. The cash and credit cards are processed here by one person—Jake."

"That would be me," the young man said with a bow.

"Why one person?" Lexi asked.

"There's a lot of credit card fraud these days," Brad told them. "When you allow all the waiters to use the machines, one bad apple could be using a swiper to record the card numbers. This way just one trusted person is responsible."

They arrived at their table just as Tiffany and a helper brought their lunches. They were silent for a few minutes while they began to eat. Lexi waited for Amber to give her opinion first.

"This red wave lettuce salad is scrumptious." She munched enthusiastically. "It's bound to be a hit. Watch your computer and see."

"What do you think?" Brad asked Lexi, catching her off guard.

"I agree. The blend of flavors really works."

"Honest?" He kept aiming his blue eyes at her, making her even more uncomfortable.

"Absolutely," she assured him as a warm flush crept up her neck.

"How did you come up with it?" asked Amber, oblivious to the intimate moment between them. "I know we suggested the lettuce and the baby squash, but I think you made your own dressing and marinated the chicken in lime and something, right?"

"Correct. I had to experiment a lot because this is my first Asian-fusion salad. I wanted a simple dressing that wouldn't taste like some kid's chemistry experiment."

Amber giggled. "This salad dressing is great. I taste... balsamic vinegar."

Brad nodded. "Balsamic vinegar from Spain infused with ginger. I use the KISS method. Keep It Simple Stupid. Balsamic vinegar, ginger, Vietnamese herbs and—"

"Sesame oil not olive oil."

"You've got a knack for taste," Brad said with an approving smile. "Sesame oil is best in this salad. It allows the unique Asian flavor to come through."

"You marinated the chicken before it was grilled." Amber speared a sliver as she spoke.

"Again. Keeping it simple is the secret of most chefs' success. I marinated the chicken in lime juice for an hour before draining it and patting it dry. Too many people use enough marinade to pickle a bull and leave it on too long. An hour, two, tops, for chicken, or it gets mushy and all you taste is the marinade."

"I'll remember that."

"What did you think of my kitchen?" Brad asked Amber.

"Hectic. Much more frantic than I imagined." She played with her fork for a moment. "But it was really exciting. Not boring like some jobs."

I told you so, Lexi silently said to Brad.

"Most people in a kitchen work for minimum wage," Brad added. "It's stressful and pays poorly."

"Not the sous-chef or executive chef or pastry chef."

"True," Brad conceded, "but that's a few people out of—what?—two dozen."

"I want to be one of the few," Amber assured him. "You know, the few, the proud, the brave. Like the Marines."

Lexi didn't know whether to laugh or cry. Instead she nearly choked when she looked up and saw Rick Fullerton, executive chef from Marché, heading toward their table.

"Out slumming, Fullerton?" Brad greeted his competitor.

"Hello, Lexi," Rick said to her.

"Hi," she managed to reply in what could pass for a level voice. Rick was her biggest customer. He personally picked out produce from her garden twice a week. She'd never had enough money to eat at his restaurant. How could she explain being here?

"Actually," Rick said with a barely perceptible smile, "I came to try your special salad. I'm hearing great things about it."

"It's fabulous," Amber said. "Lexi gave Brad the idea."

Lexi had the urge to dive under the table.

"Interesting."

She didn't like the sound of Rick's voice. She hoped she hadn't lost her best customer over a lunch that had done absolutely nothing to change her sister's mind about pursuing a career as a chef.

CHAPTER
∽SIX∾

"You're not going to believe this!" cried Amber.

Lexi was stooped over a row of baby squash and plucking out the weeds that seemed to have sprouted since she left this morning for a job interview. She stood up, her back aching. How had Aunt Callie done this when she'd been over eighty? "Believe what?"

Amber clutched her backpack to her chest and kept talking. "Today Mrs. Geffen had us draw lots for the proctors for the cooking contest."

"So?" Lexi yanked up another weed. "You knew there would be a proctor who would watch you prepare and bake your dessert. They just want to make sure the contestants don't buy it somewhere or have their mother make it."

"Yeah, right, but talk about luck. Guess who I drew?"

Lexi could tell from Amber's tone it wasn't good. According to the contest rules, a pastry chef or a pastry chef's assistant would be a proctor. "Who did you get?"

"Monsieur Broussard. He's the pastry chef at Marché."

Lexi didn't know him, but since her encounter with Rick Fullerton at Black Jack's, she'd been concerned about her relationship with the chef/owner. He'd come this week as usual to select the best of her baby vegetables, but hadn't been very friendly and he'd purchased fewer vegetables than she'd expected. She wondered if he had found another supplier. With baby vegetables in such demand, a number of local farmers were now cultivating them.

"What's wrong with Monsieur Broussard? After all, Marché is known for its fabulous desserts. I understand he comes from France."

"You weren't there the day he did the demo of crème brûlée. He was mean and snobby and hard to understand. And he didn't even try to make a healthier version for our class like he was supposed to." Amber sighed, the deep exasperated sound she made when she was really frustrated. "He's going to make me so nervous I'll goof up."

Lexi sympathized; she didn't like anyone looking over her shoulder while she worked either. "You won't make a mistake," she assured her sister. "You've prepared the recipe many times, right? You know how to do it by heart. Just relax. The chef is merely checking to make sure no one cheats."

"Easy for you to say." Amber stomped off toward the house. It would be nice to believe she was going to study, but that would be wishful thinking.

"I have some news," Lexi called after her sister.

Amber turned, the sullen look still on her face. "What?"

"I've been offered a great summer position with Gilfoy and O'Malley. They're one of the biggest firms in the city. It could lead to a permanent position when I pass the accountant's exam."

"That's awesome!" Amber sounded as if she was genuinely thrilled for Lexi. "When do you start?"

"Next Monday." A lot of people had been interviewed yet she'd been selected.

"Who's going to take care of the garden?" Her sister's surly expression had returned.

"I'll work every weekend. I've hired Joey Tran to help you during the week."

"Help me?" Amber said it like it was a crime.

"You know what to do. Train Joey. He'll be fantastic." She doubted Joey would need much training. All he had to do was follow a watering schedule and weed. He worked with his mother at the community garden. He was probably better at it than Amber, but Lexi thought giving her sister a little responsibility would help her mature.

"I'm going to win the baking contest. When I'm interning with Charmayne, I won't have time for the garden."

"If you win," Lexi replied with all the patience she could marshal, "I'll figure out something. We can't just let the garden—"

"You don't think I'm going to win, do you?" Amber's voice teetered on hysteria.

"I hope you do."

"No, you don't. You want me to lose so I can be a slave in your precious garden."

Lexi battled the impulse to say something sarcastic. "It's not my garden," she replied in as level a tone as she could muster. "Aunt Callie started it long before we came to live with her. The money it generates allows us to live here and go to school."

"But you'll be working, making plenty of money," Amber retorted. "We don't need the garden."

"Yes, we do," she replied matter-of-factly. They'd been over this too many times to count. "I have to repay student loans and save money for your college education. If we keep the garden, *you* won't have to take on costly student loans."

"Like I care!"

Lexi watched her sister bounce off. A minute or two

later, music loud enough to rupture eardrums screeched from Amber's room through the open window. Lexi wanted to ask her to turn it down, but didn't fell like another confrontation.

The portable phone rang barely loud enough to be heard over the music, and Lexi scooped it up from the ground and pushed the button to answer. "It's Brad Westcott," said a deep male voice.

Her heart jitterbugged beneath her ribs. She'd been thinking about him more than she wanted to admit. "Hi," she said as lightly as she could manage. "What's happening?"

"Not much," Brad responded. "But I hired a new sous-chef."

"That's great."

"I've been a little slow to let anyone else assume responsibility in the kitchen. That's why my last chef left. Tomorrow night, the new sous-chef is taking over for me."

"You're letting him run the place?" Why was he calling her? Did he want to purchase vegetables or was the call more personal?

"The new chef is a woman. Alice Blankenship has three new entrées that will be available tomorrow evening. We'll see how it goes."

There was a moment of silence; Lexi was tempted to speak, but still wasn't sure what to say.

"I'm getting out of Black Jack's so I don't make Alice nervous," Brad finally said. "I was wondering if you might want to join me at the annual mixology contest."

"Mixology contest." She nearly choked on the words. Brad Westcott was asking her out on a date.

"Bartenders compete for most original drink. It's being held tomorrow evening at the Silver Spoon. Trevor, my head mixologist, has come up with a concoction he calls Black Jack's Snakebite."

"Is it black?" she asked, her mind scrambling for a way to phrase her response to his invitation. She wanted to go out with him more than she'd wanted anything in a long time.

"No. Black drinks don't sell. This is a pale amber. The ingredients are a secret, but it's topped with foamed egg whites."

"Eggs?" Lexi asked, a little surprised. "In drinks?"

Brad chuckled. "Whipped egg-white drinks are the latest. Started out in California. People are always looking for the unusual. Gives them something to talk about."

"That should work."

"How about it? Would you like to join me?"

Would she ever! But it was impossible. Why did it have to be tomorrow evening? "It's the first meeting of my board study course. I can't miss it." Despite her best efforts, her voice wavered. "I really wish I could, but I have to pass the accountant's exam to keep a job I just found."

"You have a job besides City Seeds?" Brad sounded surprised.

"Yes. I've been doing payroll for a family-owned company. I'll receive my MBA in a few weeks, so I've been hunting for a job in that field. Gilfoy and O'Malley offered me a position. In this economy, I'm lucky to get it. I want to be sure I pass the exam the first time I take it."

"I've heard of them. Supposed to be a really good firm."

"It is a good firm, but there's a lot of pressure to pass the exam. I just can't skip class tomorrow evening."

"I understand," Brad assured her.

Lexi wanted to suggest the following night instead, but she didn't have her sister's bold personality. "Thanks for asking. I hope your guy wins."

"I guess I'll see you next Saturday then," Brad said.

It took her a moment to recall what was going on then. "Yes, at the baking contest. My sister is still determined to win."

Brad laughed. "I'm sure she is. See you then."

Lexi hung up with a surge of disappointment and she wasn't sure why. Brad Westcott was out of her league. Going out with him would only lead to more disappointment. Still, she couldn't help feeling an inexplicable sense of loss.

* * *

Brad hung up the phone in his small office at the rear of Black Jack's kitchen. Since his divorce, he hadn't dated much. His restaurants occupied all his waking hours. But Lexi was different. He kept thinking about her even though he didn't have time for a woman in his personal life.

He put his feet up on the desk and looked out at the kitchen through the glass that formed half his office wall. When he wasn't out there himself, he often watched the lion's den from his desk. This afternoon, though, he was deep in thought, wondering why Lexi appealed to him when no other woman had in a long, long time.

Maybe it was because she was as devoted to her work as he was to his. And besides running City Seeds, she would soon be holding down an accounting job. He hoped she would learn to manage better than he had. A satisfying career was only part of a fulfilling life.

Brad assured himself that by hiring Alice and allowing her to take part of the responsibility for running Black Jack's, he would have more time to himself. Who was he kidding? Taking one day a week off didn't make a balanced life. He'd been unable to ask Lexi if she could go out another night because he didn't have any time available.

His next free day was Saturday, which he would spend going from one baking contest to another. Of course, he would have to work Saturday night. It was the busiest night of the week—make-or-break time in most restaurants.

He thought back to his failed marriage. He'd been too wrapped up in his work to devote the necessary time to a relationship. If he wanted to try again, he would need to make some real changes in his schedule and allow the sous-chef more freedom.

CHAPTER
∽SEVEN∼

Lexi leaned toward Amber so her sister could whisper in her ear without having anyone in Stovall Middle School's auditorium overhear them. The contestants had baked their entries for the contest in the cafeteria and the desserts had been brought here for judging. They were on display at the front of the room. Each entry had a number beside it but no name was attached. There were about a dozen, Lexi noted.

Most were fairly professional, considering middle school students had baked them, but a few others weren't so good. One was a chocolate layer cake that listed like the Leaning Tower of Pisa. Another looked like a sticky caramel bird's nest.

The contest rules stated that entries had to use healthy ingredients. Nothing was mentioned about presentation, but Lexi suspected appearance would influence the judges—at least a little. Amber's Ali Baba Tart looked as good as any dessert Lexi had ever seen. It was a simple raspberry-chocolate tart garnished with plump raspberries from their garden.

"I'm not going to win," Amber whispered, a note of despair in her voice. "Monsieur Broussard watched every move I made. He didn't smile or even blink. He made me *sooo* nervous, I know I messed up big-time."

"Don't worry," Lexi reassured her sister as she glanced around the crowded auditorium, looking for Brad. He hadn't arrived yet, which wasn't unexpected. Since he wasn't a judge, he didn't need to be here when the chefs sampled the desserts. His job was to award the prizes at the various schools.

Still, she kept hoping to see him. She wondered what would have happened if she'd gone out with him.

Don't go there, she warned herself. She had too much on her mind, too many things to do. She couldn't waste time mooning like a teenager over a man.

Suddenly, Brad came through the side door with Charmayne at his side. A few people noticed him, but most seemed to think he was just another parent or friend here for the contest. He glanced around the auditorium, spotted

Lexi and... Had he winked at her? It happened so fast she couldn't be sure. He opened the backstage door for Charmayne and disappeared before he saw the special smile Lexi flashed at him.

Be cool, she told herself, knowing she would see him after the contest.

"Brad brought the pastry chef, Charmayne," whispered Amber, who obviously hadn't noticed the wink. "I wonder why. Do you think she's going to sample the entries?"

"I'm not sure, but he may want to introduce her as the person the winner will work with this summer."

"Makes sense," Amber replied. "Look! There go the judges. That was so fast."

Lexi saw the judges leaving by the same side door that Brad had used. "They're probably on their way to the next contest. This is their second today. They have six in all."

"Right," mumbled Amber.

Lexi could tell her sister was getting nervous. It wouldn't be long now. The endless rounds of chocolate-tart making would be over. She wanted Amber to win and knew how devastated she would be if she didn't at least place in the contest. But if she did win, it would mean yet another series of baking experiments and tasting sessions and less work in the garden.

Mr. Rodgers, the principal of the middle school, walked up to the microphone. He tapped on it twice and silence fell across the large crowd. "Earlier I introduced the judges, chefs from local restaurants. They had to leave for another contest, but they have chosen two runners-up and a winner of the first annual Light-and-Healthy Bake-Off at Stovall Middle School. Here to announce the winners is Brad Westcott, owner and executive chef at Black Jack's. Mr. Westcott is also the sponsor of this contest."

Brad emerged from the side of the stage, a smile on his face. "Thank you, Mr. Rodgers," he said, and the older man stepped to the side while Brad stood in front of the microphone. "The judges told me their decision was *really* difficult. Everything was so delicious that they had to taste each entry twice before reaching a decision."

Lexi imagined a silent drumroll as he paused and removed a three-by-five-inch card from the pocket of his sports jacket. Amber clutched Lexi's arm with fingers like steel bands. "Don't worry," Lexi whispered.

"Before I announce the winner and runners up, let me introduce my pastry chef, Charmayne Collins."

Charmayne walked up beside Brad. She beamed and waved at the crowd.

"I know this is just round one," Charmayne said, "but I can hardly wait to find out who will win the cash prize and be my intern this summer. All I do is create desserts, so you know it'll be a lot of fun."

The audience laughed politely, but Lexi could tell they

were as anxious as she was to hear who'd won. Amber's hand was still on her arm, and she was facing forward, her eyes fixed on the podium. Lexi could feel the tension in her sister and realized how much this meant to her. It hadn't been that long ago when Lexi had sat in an auditorium and waited for the winners of a scholarship contest to be announced. She'd felt as if her very life hung in the balance.

Then her name was called.

Lexi said a silent prayer for her baby sister and hoped she, too, would experience the joy of winning despite the problems it would cause.

"Learning about food—where it comes from, how it grows and when to harvest it—can lead to careers in the food industry," Brad continued. "This contest highlights just one possible career—becoming a pastry chef."

"I think many of our parents and guests grow crops in the community garden, Urban Plots," added Mr. Rodgers.

Lexi recognized people in the audience from the community garden, including Joey Tran's entire family. They were known for their high yield of lemongrass.

That's where she'd first met Joey and his parents. Lexi had been looking for locals to help plant exotic vegetables to sell to restaurants through City Seeds. The Trans couldn't help because they needed their six plots to fill their lemongrass orders from chefs, but she'd gotten to know them and they'd taught her about Asian vegetables.

Charmayne held up a plaque. "The second place winner goes to the Lemon-Rosemary Cake created by Shelby Tibbets," Brad announced.

Above the round of applause, Amber said, "I knew she would at least place. She's a really good cook."

Shelby walked up to the podium, all smiles, to receive the plaque.

"The judges really liked the delicious flavor of your cake," Brad told Shelby and the audience.

Shelby bowed slightly, beaming at her parents, who were seated in the second row. "Thanks," she said as the audience clapped.

Brad waited a minute for Shelby to leave the stage before saying, "First runner-up goes to Peter Nguyen's Lemongrass Panna Cotta."

Amber dug her fingers into Lexi's arm. "He's Joey Tran's cousin. Guess where he got the lemongrass?"

Lexi had never heard of lemongrass until she visited the community garden. Peter had used it to give traditional Italian panna cotta a creative spin.

The Trans and Nguyens stood, clapping and stamping their feet as a short boy with glossy black hair gelled up like a rooster's tail shuffled up to the podium. His lackluster smile revealed his disappointment.

"Peter's good and he expected to win," Amber told her. "He bragged about his 'invention' for weeks." Amber made it sound like a crime.

As Peter was congratulated, Lexi was alarmed by the fierce look on her sister's face. She knew Amber was stubborn and difficult to deal with at times, but she'd never been this determined before. Lexi wasn't sure how she should respond if Amber lost. How did you encourage someone when they were confronted with failure?

Lexi realized she knew very little about mothering. How could she give Amber advice the way a mother would when she had had so little mothering herself? Aunt Callie had been loving, but she'd had no parenting skills.

As Peter left the stage, Lexi ventured a sideways glance at Amber. Her back was rigid, her eyes focused straight ahead.

"Please," Lexi whispered to herself, "let Amber win."

Brad held up a gleaming gold-colored metal plaque that was much larger than the others. Even from the midsection of the auditorium where Lexi was sitting she could make out the words: Winner of the Light-and-Healthy Bake-Off. "This year's winner..."

For a second the room froze. Then Lexi realized Brad had said, "Amber Morrison. The chefs chose her Ali Baba Chocolate-Raspberry Tart as the best entry in this contest."

Amber spun around in her seat to bear-hug Lexi. "I can't believe I won!"

"You deserve it," Lexi assured her. "You worked really hard."

Lexi's heart filled with pride and wonder and she blinked back tears as she watched her sister walk up to Brad and Charmayne. How thrilled their parents would have been, Lexi thought. When they'd died, Amber had been so young. It would have been difficult to imagine the self-assured girl that Lexi saw on the stage.

"The chefs commented on the delicious flavor of this tart," Brad told the audience. "It uses unsweetened chocolate and whole fresh raspberries. Amber used unsweetened coconut, which gives the tart a unique texture. She also used a sugar substitute and whole wheat flour, which cuts back on the calories and is healthier."

"Amber will now represent Stovall Middle School in the final round," said Charmayne. "The winner will receive a thousand-dollar cash prize and an internship as my assistant for the summer."

There was an enthusiastic round of applause, then Brad said, "Amber, do you have anything to say?"

Amber stepped up to the mic with such confidence that Lexi was certain she'd practiced this speech many times. "Gee, it feels like the Academy Awards," she joked, and the audience laughed politely. "I want to thank Mrs. Geffen for all her support and her wonderful cooking class. I also need to thank my sister, Lexi, for all her help."

Lexi hadn't really helped except to taste the last few Ali Babas. But still, she was touched by the acknowledgment.

"Most of all I want to thank the Recipe for Success program," Amber said. "Back in the fourth grade, I planted, harvested and cooked in their program. Until then, I hadn't really appreciated how food was grown and how to prepare it.

"You see, I'm a diabetic. I have to be careful what I eat. Their program gave me a new appreciation for foods I'd never tasted. That's why I enrolled in Mrs. Geffen's class."

Amber paused, then smiled at Brad. "I'm sure I speak for all the contestants in thanking the Chefs' Association for sponsoring this contest."

Tears welled in Lexi's eyes. She'd never heard her sister speak about her diabetes so passionately or in front of such a large group. That took true courage.

Brad strode up to Lexi. He projected such an energy and power, and Lexi was almost embarrassed by her instinctive response to him.

"Your sister outdid herself," Brad told her.

"Amber deserved to win. She tried hard. I can't tell you how many tarts she baked."

"She didn't taste them all, did she?" Brad sounded concerned. That made her like him even more.

"No. She was good. The seniors at the center sampled them and offered opinions."

"Hey, that's a smart move." Brad touched her arm lightly. "You're both very enterprising."

"I guess." Lexi had never thought of herself as anything other than a survivor. She did what she needed to do, even if she often felt as if she was on a treadmill.

"I've got to rush off to another contest," Brad said. "How about going out for coffee around five—before I have to get back to the restaurant for the dinner rush?"

Lexi's heartbeat throbbed in her ears and she felt heat creeping up her neck. "I'd like that."

"Good. I'll pick you up at four."

She watched him walk away. A strange excitement filled her as she turned to find Amber.

CHAPTER
EIGHT

"So you're a runner." Brad flashed his engaging smile. "So am I, when I have the time."

"Same here," Lexi responded. "I was on the track team in high school, but now I'm lucky if I can find the time to run a couple of days a week." An unexpected glow warmed her. They had a lot more in common than she'd thought.

They were sitting at a small corner table at Brew Ha-Ha, having iced caramel-flavored coffee drinks and sharing a blueberry scone.

"What about movies?" Brad asked.

So many questions, she thought. Most men liked to talk

about themselves or their work, but not Brad. He wanted to know all about her.

"I don't have much time for movies lately," she said. "When I do go, I look for foreign films."

"Hey, so do I."

"I don't mind the subtitles. I like to see how people in other countries view life."

"Exactly!" He leaned forward and lowered his voice in a way that added to the intimacy she already felt. "I'm not interested in films that are nothing but car chases and shoot-outs."

Lexi nodded. Most of her dates had taken her to "guy" movies because they liked them or silly "chick flicks" to please her. She'd rarely been asked what she wanted to see. "I like to talk about films after I see them. That means there has to be something to discuss."

His look was galvanizing. What was he thinking? Did she sound pretentious?

"I like to talk about films, too," he told her. "I find I dissect a lot of things to see what makes them work. This place, for instance." He examined the last bit of the scone they'd been sharing. "The coffee is great, but there are other places with coffee that's just as good. What makes Brew Ha-Ha special is their pastries."

"Right," she agreed. "Their scones are tastier than

others even though they're low fat. At least that's what the sign says."

"They are. I've spoken at length with the owner." He stared at her thoughtfully for a moment. "You analyze the world around you, too."

It was a compliment, but Lexi wasn't sure how to respond. Finally, she said, "I guess that's why I'm a numbers person. I like to come up with definite answers."

"That's where we're different. I don't mind not coming up with an exact answer. I like to consider the opportunities for creativity in each situation." He gestured to the room around them. "Pastries set this place apart, but there's more—"

"Great ambience," Lexi cut in, "and really friendly service. They always remember your name."

"Right! The world is so impersonal these days that folks appreciate a friendly attitude. I tell my servers that all the time." He checked his watch. "Speaking of servers, I've gotta run."

Lexi stood up. "I have rows of veggies screaming for water."

She thanked him for the coffee, feeling way more relaxed than she had when they'd come here.

"Let's get together again—soon. I'd like your opinion on a pizza place people have been telling me about."

"Sure. I'd like that." She said this in an offhand tone,

but as they walked out she admitted to herself just how much she wanted to see Brad again.

They'd enjoyed a "working" dinner because Brad was considering adding pizza to his menu. Lexi had liked the deep-dish house special and had several ideas that he seemed to take seriously. They'd met at a park twice to run. And each time Lexi found herself relaxing more.

Since she'd started her new job at the accounting firm she wasn't around the house as much as she should be to help Amber with her schoolwork. From what Lexi could tell, her sister spent most of her time working on her new recipe, which she was positive would win her the final round in the competition.

Joey Tran was helping in the garden. Lexi had spent all day each weekend there, as well, but getting Amber to help remained a struggle. Lexi didn't nag her about it. That only made Amber more stubborn. Besides, Lexi had to prepare herself for the possibility Amber would win and not be able to help over the summer. Anticipating this, Lexi gave Joey more responsibility.

"I'm home," yelled Lexi after she closed the front door.

Silence answered her, but the scent of chocolate swirled around her like a heavenly mist. What did she expect? Amber had prepared another Diva's Red Velvet Torte. No doubt she'd taken it to the center for the seniors to sample.

Lexi put down her purse on the sideboard and flopped onto the sofa. She was too tired to pick up the remote control and switch on the television. She would just rest a minute before changing shoes to go out and check on the garden.

"Lexi, Lexi. Wake up."

Lexi heard her sister speaking, but it took a few seconds for the words to register. She gazed around and realized she'd fallen asleep on the sofa. "What time is it?" she asked.

"Almost seven," Amber replied.

Lexi walked toward the kitchen. "Did you eat?"

"No." Amber waved a sheet of paper in front of her. "I have my grades," she said, joy bubbling in her voice.

"Already?" Lexi knew the school year was drawing to a close, but didn't expect a report card for a week or so.

"They came out today. I got mine in homeroom," Amber informed her with a smile.

Good news, Lexi thought. Amber wouldn't be this happy if she was failing a class. Her sister handed her the computer printout that served as a report card. Lexi scanned it, then reread it slowly.

"Not bad, huh?"

"Excellent. Really great, Amber. You pulled up your grades."

"Except for math. I'm going to get a head start on algebra by studying at home this summer."

Problem was—Amber didn't have Lexi's self-discipline. She had good intentions but no follow-through. She had to attend summer school.

As if guessing her thoughts, Amber said, "I worked really hard this term to bring up my grades. I worked even harder after I found out about the contest. I'll study at night after I work with Charmayne."

Lexi didn't want an argument right now. After all, the report was good. Now was not the time to harp on Amber's shortcomings. Or to suggest she might not win the contest.

"There is bad news. I saved it for last."

Uh-oh, Lexi thought. "What's wrong?"

"Rick Fullerton is going to be one of the judges in the final round."

"That's not so bad. I think he'll be fair."

"Ha!" Amber grunted. "He isn't buying as much from us, is he?"

"No," Lexi agreed. Rick had been giving her the cold shoulder since their meeting at Black Jack's, but at least he was still buying some of her baby vegetables.

"If I don't win, will I *have* to go to summer school?"

Lexi wanted to say losing might be a blessing in disguise, but she didn't. No sense in burdening Amber with another worry. They could deal with this when the contest was over. "We'll see. I'm not making any promises."

The next morning was Saturday, the busiest day for City Seeds. Chefs or their helpers appeared before she opened the gates. They were anxious to select produce for weekend specials. As usual Rick Fullerton was at the head of the line. He personally selected produce. Brad had been coming, too, but he wasn't here yet.

"Hi. Looking for anything special?" she asked Rick with her warmest smile.

"Just looking," he replied. After poking around for about half an hour, Rick left with two boxes of her best baby vegetables.

There was still no sign of Brad, and she was a little concerned—not about him buying produce elsewhere. She was unnerved by how much she wanted to see him.

The group had thinned as most chefs raced back to their kitchens. Her cell phone vibrated, and she pulled it out of her pocket. The caller-ID screen read, Black Jack. Brad was calling!

"Hello."

"Hey," he said in his husky voice. "How's it going?"

She mustered a level yet friendly tone. "Fine. Most of my regulars have already been here. I'm down to half a box of Asian red wave lettuce. You can have it if you want it." She'd warned him that the heat was ending the season, so he wouldn't be able to prepare his highly successful salad much longer.

"I'll take it. Got any of that baby squash left?"

"Yes. Probably enough for the available lettuce."

"I'll send someone by to pick up the produce."

"Okay," she replied in a voice that seemed to come from some distance away. All she could think was that she wouldn't get to see him for another week. How had she allowed this man to mean so much to her?

"I'm giving the new sous-chef special training this morning. I should be through by three or so. Could I come by and take you with me to sample some gelato that I'm thinking of using?"

A sigh of happiness nearly broke from her lips. "Sounds like fun."

"What do you think?" Brad asked as they sampled strawberry gelato at Gelato Paradiso. The Italian shop had been open for more than a year, but Lexi had never tried it.

"Great." She licked the ice cream in the waffle cone. "Sensational, actually."

"I'm thinking of cutting a deal with the owner to exclusively supply Black Jack's with several flavors of gelato."

"How would you serve it? Alone? With fresh fruit?"

"I'd take vanilla to put with our flourless chocolate cake or whatever else Charmayne thinks will work. I'll also use it with seasonal fruit. Baci could stand alone."

"Perfect." Lexi had already sampled the chocolate and hazelnut gelato called baci and knew it was unique enough to stand alone. She smiled at Brad and allowed herself to bask in the shared moment. He was asking her opinion; she had to mean more to him than just a quick date.

They were sitting at a table for two hardly bigger than a briefcase, eating the gelato. An undeniable magnetism had built between them. What would she do if he kissed her? Kiss him back came the immediate answer.

"How's the summer job?" he asked.

Lexi had conditioned herself to give a reply like "good." But that wasn't the truth, and considering how Brad treated her, she needed to share her feelings with him. "I'm a little bored. No, actually, I'm really bored. I'm working on taxes. It's the same stuff over and over every day."

"Aren't we beyond tax season?"

"Yes, of course, but you'd be surprised how many people missed the deadline and had to ask for an extension. We're working on those now."

"You must have known what it would be like to work for an accounting firm," he said, leaning closer.

"I did, but I guess being at a small private company for so long made me think I'd be doing lots of things, not just taxes. I find I'm in a rut. Taxes are the bread and butter of the firm."

"You could go elsewhere and do something more challenging with your degree."

"True," she agreed. "But first I have to pass the exam. So I'm stuck here until the fall at least."

He took her hand and rose. Her skin prickled at his touch. As they walked toward the door, he put his arm around Lexi and she couldn't resist leaning against his powerful chest. "Life's too short to get stuck in a job you hate. It's worth the risk to follow your dream."

"True," she agreed, but she also had a sister to put through school.

He stopped outside the shop, his arm still around her. "Speaking of dreams. I have an idea."

Something in his tone alerted her. "Oh? What's your idea?"

"Amber is determined to win, isn't she?"

"Yes. Obsessed is a better description," she reluctantly admitted.

"What if she doesn't? Your sister will be upset, won't she?"

"Amber will go to summer school as planned. It's important for her to pull up her math marks by taking a prep course in algebra this summer."

Brad studied her for a moment. "Amber will be fifteen in a few weeks and old enough to work. What if I give her a job that will allow her to attend summer school and work part-time at Black Jack's?"

"No! Don't do that!" Lexi responded more sharply than she'd intended.

Brad dropped his arm and took a step back.

"I—I'm sorry," she stammered. "I didn't intend to sound so angry. It's just that Amber has no discipline and she's developing an attitude. If she wins the contest and earns the internship, I'll make it work somehow. But I really want her to study this summer and help me with City Seeds. Why should I pay someone to work in our business while Amber earns minimum wage working in a restaurant?"

"Because the experience would do her good," Brad replied in a strained tone that indicated he didn't agree with her. "She might discover that she doesn't care for the restaurant business."

"That's what you thought when we came to lunch." The second the words left her lips, Lexi cursed herself for saying them. "What I mean is…Amber is stubborn. She won't admit she doesn't like working at Black Jack's even if she does."

"I understand," Brad said, but it was clear that he didn't. They walked to his car in silence and he made no attempt to put his arm around her again.

CHAPTER
∽NINE∽

U nlike the preliminary round, the finals of the bake-off were held in the evening. Lexi was grateful, and she was sure the other working parents were as well.

Amber had come to Samuel Houston High School's cafeteria midafternoon to bake and decorate her torte. At this point, the chefs had sampled the desserts and decided the winner. Lexi expected Brad to make the announcement after the head of the foundation called the group in the auditorium to order.

Once again, she glanced around to see if Brad had arrived. This would be the first time she'd seen him since their disagreement last week. He might have come in through a back entrance, she decided.

A cold knot had formed in Lexi's stomach the minute she'd walked up the steps of the auditorium. She was concerned that she'd ruined her chances with Brad. No matter how many times she thought about it, Lexi felt she was right. Her sister did not need a job handed to her. If she won, that was one thing, but if she didn't, then summer school was the best place for her.

The curtains parted to reveal a spacious stage with a podium in the center. On a table stood a large silver trophy and an easel with a huge mock-up of the thousand-dollar check the winner would receive. The other side of the stage had a table with the desserts on it. Seated in the rear were the judges and several other people, including Brad and Charmayne.

Lexi tried to relax, but it was impossible. The air in the huge room seemed to be electrified as Brad was introduced and stepped up to the microphone.

Looking very handsome, he smiled at the audience. Lexi warned herself that Amber might not be the only Morrison to be disappointed today. What if Brad left without talking to her?

"I want to thank our judges for their hard work in both rounds of this Light-and-Healthy Bake-Off," Brad told the audience.

Lexi barely listened as he introduced the chefs who'd judged the contest. *Get a grip,* she told herself. Win or lose—her sister would need her. The contestants were seated in the first row with their backs to the group. Lexi could see Amber's glossy-brown hair but not her face.

"I'd like you all to meet Charmayne Collins," Brad said, "pastry chef at Black Jack's. The winner will be interning with her this summer, in addition to winning the prize money.

"My goal in sponsoring this contest is to help combat childhood obesity. I was an overweight kid myself. I know how being overweight can make you miserable, wreck your health. People need to think about what they eat."

Charmayne added, "That's where I come in as a pastry chef. Everyone loves dessert, but it isn't always good for us. That's why we've asked contestants to create healthier desserts with reduced sugar and fat."

"We have some really outstanding desserts here tonight," Brad said. "The judges told me it was difficult to pick a winner. In fact just one vote separated the first runner-up and the winner."

"Maybe we should announce the second runner-up," Charmayne cut in.

"Right," Brad conceded with a smile. "I almost got ahead of myself."

The audience laughed politely, but Lexi mentally crossed

her fingers. Please, please. Let Amber win. Despite the havoc it would cause, Lexi wanted her sister to win. She'd tried so hard, and she was truly an excellent cook.

"Second runner-up goes to Taylor Jamison for her Waldorf Cupcakes."

It took a few minutes for Taylor to come forward and accept her award, then thank everyone who'd helped her. Lexi stared at the back of Amber's head, willing her to turn around so she could smile her encouragement, but her sister remained facing forward.

"The next award is special," Brad said when Taylor had left the stage. "This entry came within one vote of giving us a tie. The first runner-up is a fabulous cook with a real future. The prize for first runner-up goes to Amber Morrison for her Diva Torte."

A wild flash of disappointment ripped through Lexi. Oh, no. Amber had lost by one vote. How terrible to come so close yet not win.

"The recipe makes excellent use of beets—you'd never guess they were beets—to achieve the red color," continued Brad. "She used grape seed oil instead of less healthy oil and agave nectar for sweetness."

Amber was approaching the podium now. She must be heartsick, Lexi thought, but she sported a smile as she accepted the small trophy.

"I encourage all of you to think about what you're

eating," she told the audience. "Go for light and healthy!" She started to step away from the microphone. "Oh, and a huge thanks to my teacher, Mrs. Geffen, and my sister, Lexi."

Lexi watched as Amber left the stage, her runner-up trophy in the crook of her arm. She kept a smile on her face as she returned to her seat. Lexi listened politely while the winner was announced. A burly youth who looked as if he'd be more at home on a football field won with his Cranberry Baklava.

One vote.

How would Amber take such a narrow defeat?

The ceremony finally concluded and Lexi rose to join her sister, but Amber left her seat and headed for the stage where the winner, Toby McCall, was talking with the chefs. Amber went right up to Toby and high-fived him. Apparently they'd become friendly during the contest.

Lexi smiled to herself. Maybe this contest was a learning experience on more levels than one.

"Sorry Amber didn't win." Brad's voice came from beside her. He'd walked up unexpectedly while she'd been watching her sister. "It was really close."

Lexi drew a deep breath and refused to reveal how thrilled she was that he'd sought her out. Maybe she hadn't lost her chance with him after all. She told herself to say something that would smooth things between them.

"Amber can be proud. She created two innovative desserts. Just because she didn't get first prize doesn't mean she isn't a winner. Still, she's going to be disappointed not to be working with Charmayne."

Amber was talking with the chefs now and they were all smiling at her and chatting as if they were old friends. Pretty amazing, Lexi decided. She would have thought Amber would have left after congratulating the winner.

"Your sister has talent," Brad said, his voice low. "Are you sure you don't want me to offer her a summer job?"

Lexi was tempted to say yes and change the dynamics of the situation. Brad could be a hero and Lexi would no longer be the spoilsport sister. She and Brad could take up where they'd left off. But she knew what was best for Amber. She boldly met his eyes. "Thanks, but Amber needs to attend summer school and help with City Seeds."

"Not even a part-time job? A couple of hours a day?" he asked, a trace of reproach in his voice.

Again, she had to resist the urge to say yes. Experience with her sister told her that Amber would find any excuse to hang around Black Jack's when she should be home in the garden or studying.

"Thanks for the offer, Brad. Maybe next summer."

"Okay," he said slowly, as if he expected her to change her mind. "Did you tell Amber that I wanted her to work for me this summer?"

"No, I didn't. I wanted her to concentrate on winning."

"But you didn't want her to win. Did you?"

"Of course I did!" Indignation rippled through her body. "I was prepared to give Joey Tran a full-time job with City Seeds so Amber could complete the internship."

Amber spotted them and dashed over, smiling. "I almost won."

"You did great," Brad said with real enthusiasm.

"I gave it my best."

"It was really close," Brad told her. "Just one vote and we would have had a tie."

"It's okay," Amber said with sincerity. "I had fun just trying."

Brad nodded his approval, but Lexi could hardly speak. Was her sister really this calm about not winning?

"I've got to run," Brad said—more to Amber than Lexi. "Saturday night is our busiest time." He turned and left without saying a word about seeing Lexi again.

"What happened?" Amber asked. "I thought you two were…you know—"

"Brad's busy. I'm swamped between work and studying for the exam. That's all." Lexi told herself this was the truth, but it wasn't the whole truth.

"Then why did Brad come over to talk to you after the contest?"

Clearly Amber was more perceptive than Lexi realized.

Her sister's voice, her expression said she knew Lexi wasn't being entirely honest.

"Brad came over to talk to me about giving you a part-time job this summer at Black Jack's."

"You're kidding! That's awesome!" Amber was practically bouncing up and down. "I can hardly wait."

"Don't get excited! You're going to summer school and work in the garden. Next summer, if your grades are still good, you can work for Brad. I'm sure he'll give you a job."

"That's not fair!" Amber practically shouted and the group nearby stopped talking to look at them. "Next summer is, like, aeons away. Brad could sell the business or something."

Just what Lexi didn't want—a scene—in front of all these parents. Over Amber's shoulder she saw Rick Fullerton and his pastry chef coming in their direction.

"Don't turn around," whispered Lexi, thankful for the diversion. "Here comes Rick Fullerton and Monsieur Broussard. I'll bet he didn't vote for you."

Tears welled in Amber's eyes. "You're right. Monsieur Broussard hasn't liked me since the first round."

Lexi shook her head. "Don't blame him. Rick Fullerton is angry that Brad now gets his produce from us." She slipped her arm around her sister. "Let's get out of here."

CHAPTER
~TEN~

A week later, Lexi arrived home and pushed through the front door. A cool wave of air indicated the ceiling fan was on low. It was a welcome relief from the heat outside.

Lexi was late—again—and she was exhausted. It was apparent the accounting firm saw the summer interns as little more than indentured servants. The work they assigned the interns always required overtime. Since they were paid a base salary, the interns didn't earn any more money for the extra hours.

"Amber, I'm home!" she called.

There was no answer. Lexi shrugged out of her jacket and hung it on the hall tree. She shouldn't be surprised

Amber wasn't around. The house was silent. Where was she?

Amber hadn't been bitter about not winning. She'd taken the loss in stride, proud of missing by just one vote. Lexi had to give her credit. The contest had matured her sister. In another week summer school would begin. With luck, Amber's transformation would carry over and she would take summer school seriously.

As she opened the refrigerator to see what she could throw together for dinner, she heard Amber blast through the front door. "Lexi, are you there?"

From her sister's upbeat tone, Lexi decided something good must have happened.

"Sit down," Amber said, her cheeks flushed.

Lexi slowly lowered herself into a chair at the kitchen table. After tossing her purse on the table in front of her, Amber took the seat opposite.

"Please, just listen. Don't say anything until I've explained." When Lexi nodded, Amber continued. "I brought up my grades, right?"

A warning bell sounded somewhere deep in Lexi's brain.

"I baked all those goodies for the contest but didn't risk triggering a diabetic episode by eating them. I had the seniors test for me. True?"

Lexi nodded. What was Amber leading up to?

Amber pulled a packet of CDs from her purse. "I want to bring up my math grade next year by studying algebra this summer. That's why I borrowed these *Learn on Your Own* CDs from Joey Tran. I can work in my spare time on the computer."

Now Lexi got it. This was Amber's way of getting out of summer school.

"I've got a job! A real job that pays way more than minimum wage!"

Great. Lexi had alienated Brad for nothing. Amber had gone out and found a job. From her glow of exhilaration, Lexi realized it would be a knock-down-drag-out fight to convince her sister to give it up.

"Aren't you going to ask where?" Amber inquired.

"Am I allowed to talk?"

"Of course!"

"Where are you planning to work?" She emphasized the word *planning* so Amber would know she wasn't agreeing to anything.

"Guess," Amber said, her blue eyes sparking fire.

Lexi knew Amber loved being in a kitchen. She might have checked local bakeries for a job, but she doubted she would have found one so quickly. The fast food places had tremendous turnover. There were always openings at them. "Bronco Bill's?"

"Nope!"

The way Amber's eyes gleamed, Lexi figured she was on the right track. "Chicken Bucket."

"No way. Yuck. Fried food."

"I give up."

Amber smiled the sly smile that said she was up to something. "Where's the last place you'd *think* I would find a job?"

Lexi crossed her arms and stared at her sister for a moment. "You didn't go to Brad, did you?"

"Of course I didn't ask your boyfriend for a job. Not when the contest winner is working there with Charmayne."

"Sorry." Lexi tried for a casual tone. "I give up. Where did you find a job?"

An expression of smug satisfaction crossed her features. "I start tomorrow morning at...Marché."

Lexi stared wordlessly at her sister. One of the premier restaurants in the city had hired Amber. How could that be? Rick Fullerton had seemed upset with Lexi since he'd met them at Black Jack's. Amber had lost the contest by one vote—Rick's vote. Or so they'd assumed.

"Say something," Amber said.

"That's...fabulous," Lexi sputtered. "I'm so thrilled for you."

"There's more."

"What do you mean?"

"I'm working in the pastry kitchen with Monsieur Broussard."

Lexi was helpless to smother her stunned gasp. "You're kidding! You said he was as friendly as a scorpion."

"I thought so at first. It's just that he doesn't speak English that well so he doesn't say much. He came here this afternoon with Rick Fullerton to pick out marionberries for a special dessert. Rick said my torte was superb and asked for the recipe."

"He did? That's—that's amazing." Lexi couldn't believe Rick would ask anyone for a recipe but Amber wouldn't make it up.

"Monsieur Brossard said he'd be 'honored' to have me work for him." Amber grinned. "Honored. That was *exactly* what he said. Rick was really impressed with me and thought I should have won. They asked if I wanted a part-time job in the pastry kitchen."

Marché hired Amber. The words repeated in her brain like a chant. Marché hired Amber. Marché hired Amber. This was just as big a tribute as winning the contest. A well-known pastry chef from Paris wanted her sister to work with him. How could Lexi say no?

"Oh my gosh! I'm so proud of you. I don't know what to say." Lexi put both arms around Amber and hugged her tight. "You're amazing."

Her sister really was special. She didn't see the world

the same way Lexi did, but she had enough confidence in herself to pursue what she wanted.

She had found a way to prepare for next year's algebra course without going to summer school. How could Lexi deny Amber this opportunity?

"Joey said he would like to work full-time at City Seeds," Amber said as she implored Lexi with pleading eyes. "I'll pay him out of what I make."

"I'm a little concerned about your health," Lexi said gently. "Being at a restaurant like Marché is going to be a major temptation."

"No, it's not. Monsieur Broussard tastes every dessert himself. He doesn't trust anyone else's opinion. He told me so."

"Okay. What about the other food? Marché is known for its cuisine."

"I swear I won't eat anything I shouldn't. I'm only there for four hours a day. That's barely time enough to do my own work."

Lexi didn't take a second to think it over. "Okay, but if you develop health issues or don't study, I'm going to insist that you quit."

Amber stood up. "I'm going to start on the CDs right after I take my blood sugar."

"Then let's eat," Lexi told her.

"I had to eat earlier," Amber said. "You were late and

I was starving." Amber kissed her cheek. It was the first time her sister had kissed her in… Lexi couldn't recall how long it had been. Seemed like a year.

Lexi waited until Amber left the room to pick up the telephone and call Brad. It was a weeknight and in the middle of the dinner hour. He would have his cell phone off, so she could leave a message without having to talk to him personally.

She didn't want Brad to hear about Amber's job and think Lexi had sent her sister to the competition. Even though Houston was a large city, the restaurant community was tight-knit.

The phone rang twice and Brad answered, taking Lexi by surprise. "Westcott."

"Brad? It's Lexi Morrison."

"*The* Lexi Morrison?" he teased.

"Yes. Sorry to call you in the middle of rush hour."

"S'okay. I'm in my office watching the lion's den. I was about to call you."

"Really?" Lexi was stunned; it was the last thing she expected.

"Have you eaten? How would you like to catch a late dinner?"

"No, I haven't eaten," she managed to mumble. "I'd like that." She could wait until they were together to tell him about Amber's job.

* * *

The waiter at the Mexican restaurant Brad had chosen strolled up to them, ready to take their order.

"I'll have a Texas Tornado," Brad told him. "What about you? Want to try the drink that won first prize in the mixology contest, or would a traditional margarita be better?"

"I'll try the Tornado," she told the waiter, and he left to fill their order.

"Was your bar—mixologist disappointed he didn't win?"

"Probably, but he was a good sport, the way Amber was."

This was her opening, Lexi realized. "Speaking of Amber, she's the reason I called you."

"Really?" His blue eyes narrowed speculatively. "Changed your mind about letting her take a summer job at Black Jack's?"

"Not exactly. She got a part-time job on her own. At Marché with Monsieur Broussard."

"You're kidding." He started to laugh. "How'd that happen?"

Thankful he had taken the news so well, Lexi smiled and explained as their drinks arrived. "I assumed Rick hadn't voted for Amber, but apparently he had."

"Good for her," Brad said with sincerity, and raised his

glass for a toast. "Next summer I'll try to hire her away from Fullerton."

Lexi clinked her glass against Brad's. "What's in this?"

"Reposado tequila, fresh lime juice and cherry liqueur. Whipped egg whites make the foam on top. Remember, I told you how popular frothy topping has become."

"Right." Lexi took a sip. "It's good, but knowing there's tequila in it makes me cautious. It's deadly."

Brad reached over and put his large, warm hand on hers. Her whole body tingled at his touch. "How've you been?"

She started to say she was fine, but decided to tell him how she really felt. "Like I told you before, I'm not enjoying working at a big firm as much as I thought I would. I just sit at a desk in a cube farm, punching numbers."

"What are you going to do about it?" Brad asked, concern underscoring each word.

"In order to become a CPA, I have to pass the exam and work under a licensed accountant for two years. I'm going to send my résumé around to some smaller firms and see what happens."

Brad leaned closer and gazed directly into her eyes. "Don't sell yourself short. Make sure your résumé includes City Seeds as well as your payroll work at the upholstery shop. You'll find another job."

His confidence was as contagious as his smile. "What

about you? How are things going at Black Jack's? How's Charmayne's apprentice doing?"

"He's great. Charmayne really likes him." Brad took another swig of his Tornado. "And the sous-chef is really working out well. Tonight Alice is in charge of the show at Black Jack's."

"Really?" Lexi was more than a little surprised. Brad had said he didn't like relinquishing his position as executive chef.

"Yes." His features became more animated. "I want to have a life that I can enjoy beyond the restaurant business. I had to figure out how to make it work for me." He slipped his arm around her. "I need to make time to see more of you."

She inhaled sharply at his words. "You do? I—I mean, I want to see more of you. I don't like spending all day punching numbers."

"When you know what you want, it's worth the risk to go after it," Brad said.

"Yes," she agreed. "Having a life you enjoy is worth the risk. Amber's going after what she wants."

"I wasn't referring to Amber's plans. I'm talking about us as a couple. I don't want to sacrifice having you in my life just to have a successful restaurant."

This man was special, Lexi realized. He meant more

to her than she had wanted to admit. Now was the time to acknowledge how she felt.

He leaned closer, halting a scant inch from her lips. "Am I part of your plans?"

"Of course. I—"

His mouth cut off her response as his lips covered hers and he pulled her flush against his chest.

Lexi could hardly believe this was happening.

Brad pulled back, whispering, "I want us to be together. You come first—before the restaurant, before everything else."

Lexi smiled. "I have no idea what it's like to come first in anyone's life, but I'm sure willing to give it a try."

* * * * *